Iceberg Slim

SHETANI'S SISTER

Iceberg Slim, also known as Robert Beck, was born in
Chicago in 1918 and was initiated into the life of the
pimp at age eighteen. He briefly attended the Tuskegee
Institute but dropped out to return to the streets of
the South Side, where he remained, pimping until he
was forty-two. After several stints in jail, he decided to
give up the life and turned to writing, crafting most
famously his autobiographical classic, *Pimp: The Story
of My Life*. He died in 1992.

ALSO BY ICEBERG SLIM

SHETANI'S SISTER

Iceberg Slim

VINTAGE CRIME/BLACK LIZARD | VINTAGE BOOKS

Penguin Random House LLC | New York

A VINTAGE CRIME/BLACK LIZARD ORIGINAL, AUGUST 2015

The Library of Congress Cataloging-in-Publication Data
Iceberg Slim, 1918–1992.
Shetani's sister / by Iceberg Slim ; foreword by Justin Gifford. —
First edition.
pages ; cm
1. African Americans—Fiction.   2. Street life—
Fiction.   3. Urban fiction.   I. Title.
PS3552.E25S54 2015   813'.54—dc23   2014037476

Vintage Books Trade Paperback ISBN: 978-1-101-87259-8
eBook ISBN: 978-1-101-87260-4

Book design by Jaclyn Whalen

www.weeklylizard.com

Printed in the United States of America
10   9   8   7   6   5   4   3   2   1

9333865

FOREWORD

Justin Gifford

In the canon of African American crime literature, there is not a more important writer than Robert Beck, better known as Iceberg Slim. The author of an autobiography, five novels, a short-story anthology, an essay collection, and a spoken-word album, Beck was the dominant black popular writer of the post–Civil Rights Era. In 1967, he released his masterwork, *Pimp: The Story of My Life*, a memoir of his twenty-five-year career as a pimp on the streets of Milwaukee, Chicago, Cleveland, and Detroit. The book was written in such specialized street vernacular that Beck's white editors insisted he include a glossary to translate terms like "bottom woman" (a pimp's main woman), "stable" (a group of prostitutes belonging to one pimp), and "circus love" (to run the gamut of sexual perversions). Even though *Pimp* was released as a mass-market paperback and was ignored by the mainstream literary establishment and the white public, it sold millions of copies at newspaper stands and black bookstores, in barbershops and liquor stores. *Pimp* became a classic on military bases, in prison libraries, and in black neighborhoods from Harlem to South Central Los Angeles. According to Beck's publisher—Holloway House Publishing Company—*Pimp*'s popularity helped make him the best-selling black American author of all time.

Beck has arguably had greater influence on contemporary black literature than any writer in the second half of the twentieth century. In the early 1970s, he inspired many black authors—including Donald Goines, Odie Hawkins, Joe Nazel, and Omar Fletcher—to write their own stories of pimps, hustlers, and ghetto revolutionaries and publish them with Holloway House. Although a third-tier press on the margins of the legitimate publishing industry, Holloway House became the center of an underground literary renaissance of black crime fiction. Over four decades, the company published hundreds of "black experience" novels by dozens of novelists who emulated Beck. In the twenty-first century, such black female novelists as Sister Souljah, Vickie Stringer, Nikki Turner, and Wahida Clark have reimagined his pimp literature for an expanding female audience, giving rise to the genre of "street fiction." Often self-published and sold online and on street-corner tables, street fiction is now one of the driving forces of the African American literary market, with hundreds—if not thousands—of titles composing the genre.

Beck has also had a tremendous impact on modern black music and popular culture. *Willie Dynamite*, *The Mack*, and many other blaxploitation films of the 1970s owe their slick style and streetwise protagonists to his literature. Comedians Dave Chappell and Chris Rock each cite *Pimp* as a cornerstone of their work. The first gangster rappers Ice-T and Ice Cube chose their monikers in honor of Iceberg Slim, and they modeled their ultra-cool personas after him. Hip-hop legends Snoop Doggy Dogg, the Notorious B.I.G., and Mos Def have all cited Beck as a key influence; Jay Z, the most successful rap mogul of all time, used to refer to himself as Iceberg Slim when he was getting his start as an artist. The Shakespeare of urban lingo, Beck gave literary expression to the secret world of pimps, streetwalkers, con artists, and players who occupied America's ghettos and prisons. For nearly fifty years, black writers and entertainers have looked to his works as the principal source of uncompromising black creativity.

Beck's life itself spanned black America's development from the Great Migration during World War I to the so-called urban crisis of the late twentieth century. He was born on August 4, 1918, in Chicago, near the time of the deadly Chicago Race Riot, and he died in Los Angeles on April 30, 1992, the second day of the Rodney King Riot. Beck's parents—migrants from Nashville, Tennessee—divorced when he was young, and his mother, Mary, married a man who owned a cleaning shop in Rockford, Illinois. Beck had a happy childhood. He was a good student and member of the Boy Scouts, and he attended church regularly. At thirteen, he encountered his first pimps, when his mother fell in love with a hustler who frequented the beauty parlor she owned. In the early 1930s, Mary moved her son to Milwaukee's Bronzeville to follow him. He eventually disappeared from their lives, but for Beck it was too late. The loss of his stable life in Rockford "street poisoned" him, as he called it. He refused to go back to school, and he started hanging out along Bronzeville's famous

Walnut Street. During the thirties, he was arrested half a dozen times for everything from larceny to immoral conduct to suspicion of rape. He attended some school, including a semester at Booker T. Washington's Tuskegee Institute, but by eighteen, he was on the pathway to pimping. His first efforts were utter failures. In the late 1930s and early 1940s, he was arrested for "advising a felony" and "carnal knowledge and abuse," and he served lengthy sentences at both the Wisconsin State Reformatory and Wisconsin State Prison. It was at these institutions that he got his first real education in the game, from cliques of older pimps and smooth-talking players. When he was released from prison in 1942, he headed to Chicago, where he hoped to make it on the "fast track."

In Chicago, Beck met Albert "Baby" Bell, a notorious Chicago pimp and enforcer for the Jones Brothers. They controlled the illegal gambling racket in the city, and they were among the richest black men in the world. From Bell, Beck painstakingly learned the "book," that informal list of rules, regulations, and rundowns that pimps used to turn out young women. Over a few years, he slowly built up a reputation as one of the South Side's rising stars. In 1944, he was arrested for white slavery, when two of his women turned him over to the police. He was sentenced to Leavenworth Federal Penitentiary, the largest prison in the United States. Beck had always been a voracious reader of fiction; during his previous prison terms, he had developed a passion for Oscar Wilde, George du Maurier, and Henry Miller. At Leavenworth, he became interested in psychoanalysis, after his psychiatrist tried to convince him that all pimps had an unconscious hatred of their mothers. He read the works of the popular psychologists Karl Menninger, Sigmund Freud, and Carl Jung, not so he could resolve his issues with his own mother or to go straight but, rather, to deepen his understanding of how to pimp more effectively. After he was released from Leavenworth in 1946, Beck spent the next dozen years pimping his way through cities across America. In 1960, he was arrested for the last time and incarcerated in a seven-by-three-foot cell in the Chicago House of Corrections, an ancient, decaying institution built in the nineteenth century. After spending nearly a year in solitary confinement, and with his mother dying in Los Angeles, Beck vowed to give up the pimp game forever.

In Los Angeles, Beck began his new life as an author. After working for a number of years as an exterminator, he wrote *Pimp: The Story of My Life* in collaboration with his wife, a white woman named Betty Shue. From 1967 to their breakup in 1978, Beck and Shue created some of the most significant crime literature of the era. With titles such as *Trick Baby* (1967), *Mama Black Widow* (1969), *The Naked Soul of Iceberg Slim* (1971), and *Airtight Willie & Me* (1979), Beck established himself as the definitive voice of black America's urban underworld. He enjoyed minor celebrity status when *Trick Baby* was made into a blaxploitation film in 1972, and he appeared on talk shows and in newspaper and magazine interviews, condemning the glorified pimp image. He famously walked six miles a day, haranguing aspiring pimps and prostitutes on the street, hoping to steer them away from the profession. After his split with Shue, Beck disappeared from public view almost altogether. In 1982, he remarried, to a woman named Diane Millman, with whom he shared the last decade of his life. He and Diane lived together for five years before he moved to a studio apartment on Crenshaw Avenue in 1985. He was visited by his daughters from his first marriage, as well as admirers such as Mike Tyson, but he wrote a lot in solitude during these final years. Despite his failing health and struggles with diabetes, he composed two final novels, *Night Train to Sugar Hill* and *Shetani's Sister*. He decided not to publish them with Holloway House. Over the years, the company had gained a reputation for not paying its authors their proper royalties, and Beck chose to hide the books away in a drawer rather than allow the company to make one more dime off of his work. In 1992, he died broke and virtually forgotten by the public.

How could an author who has sold millions of books and had such a profound effect on black literature and culture pass away in obscurity? The answers to this question are complicated. First, Beck never quite fit in with his literary contemporaries. He lived on the South Side during the Chicago Renaissance at the same time as Richard Wright, but he was not considered part of that movement. He attended Tuskegee almost at the same moment as Ralph Ellison (they missed each other by months), but Beck could not really be called a modernist. He admired both James Baldwin and Malcolm X, and he tried to imitate their works in his own writings, though his sensational criminal past kept him from becoming a member of the radical literati. As a former pimp, Beck had views on women that were out of step with the feminist writers of the 1970s, such as Toni Morrison and the newly rediscovered Zora Neale Hurston. He was a mess of contradictions; though he dismantled the glamorous image of the pimp in his works, he often did so by representing women as the victims of graphic and disturbing violence. Beck also never quite got the recognition he deserved, because he never escaped from the third-tier press Holloway House. Unlike the crime writers Dashiell Hammett, Raymond Chandler, and Chester Himes—who moved from the world of pulp magazines and paperback originals to more literary imprints—Beck remained stuck in the ghetto of cheap paperback publishing his whole life. He was probably paid only a fraction of the money he deserved, and his works were advertised as disposable pornography.

With *Shetani's Sister* we have an opportunity to appreciate Beck from a new perspective. It is in many ways his most mature fictional work, a cross between a detective novel and the pimp literature that made him famous. It provides a powerful glimpse into Los Angeles's criminal underworld, that "sidewalk parade" of "half-naked hookers, square pushovers, and sissies" who "clogged the streets and bars. Sex, crime, booze, and dope ruled the treacherous night. The melded odors of bargain colognes and steamy armpits rode the sweltering air like a sour aphrodisiac for gawking male bangers." Beck's prose in *Shetani's Sister* is as good as any of his earlier works—taut, evocative, and layered with vernacular torn straight from the street corner. At the center of the story are two antiheroes. One is Sergeant Russell Rucker, a city vice detective who struggles with alcoholism and a fierce temper, but who attempts to clean up prostitution and police corruption. There is also Shetani, a twenty-five-year veteran pimp from Harlem, who controls a stable of sixteen prostitutes with violence and daily doses of heroin. Much like the masterpiece *The Wire*, *Shetani's Sister* is a story told through the alternating perspectives of both the criminals and the cops. Each group is as courageous as they are deeply flawed, and as the novel unfolds, their competing worldviews careen toward a spectacular and devastating collision. Beck inspired a literary genre and a cultural movement with his singular vision of America's mean streets. Read his last novel and you will know precisely why.

SHETANI'S SISTER

1

It was pre-midnight in Hollywood. Sergeant Russell Rucker of LAPD Vice slowly drove his unmarked Buick down Sunset Boulevard. His big head swiveled as he eye-swept the crowded sidewalks for hookers. He saw tourists, gays, teenage chippies, and chippie chasers. He smiled satisfaction to see frustrated johns cruising the hooker-free boulevard.

Rucker stopped for a red light at Normandie Avenue and stiffened. He saw a miniskirted black hooker get out of a pickup truck parked ahead. She fast-trotted down an alley. A moment later, the elderly white driver of the truck hit the sidewalk. He waved his arms and screamed, "She robbed my money!" He stumbled on arthritic legs toward the alley. Rucker rammed the Buick through the red light and stopped at the mouth of the alley. He flashed his badge in the old man's face and pulled him into the car. Rucker hurtled the Buick down the alley. Its headlights shone on the girl as she disappeared into a side street.

"How much did she beat you for?" Rucker asked as he stomped the accelerator.

Tears flooded the victim's eyes. "Twelve hundred bucks . . . from my wallet in the back pocket." He shook his head in disbelief. "She put the wallet back and rebuttoned the pocket while she played with my prick."

Rucker nodded. "She's a stone pro, all right." He turned into the side street. He saw the girl, with shoes in hand, racing toward a silver Cadillac parked in the middle of the block. Rucker gunned the Buick past her. He braked it sharply and leapt to the street. The girl spun and ran back toward the alley. Rucker pursued and caught her at the alley. He locked his left arm around her waist and lifted her off her feet. He carried her down the sidewalk on his hip. She struggled and yelped, "Help! Help! Kidnap. Somebody, please, help me."

Alarmed faces peered from front windows. Rucker banged her butt with a heavy palm. "Shut up! You cold-blooded bitch. I'm the police, and I'm going to help you get a bit for grand theft."

Rucker noticed the silver Caddie's backup lights flash on. Its driver threw it into maniacal reverse and halted abreast of Rucker. Rucker's right hand drew a Magnum from a shoulder holster. A black Goliath, ashimmer in a white silk suit and big-brim pimp hat, jumped to the street. He rushed Rucker. He screamed, "What's going down, mothafucka? Let my woman go!"

Rucker saw the flash of a butcher knife in his right hand. "I'm the police! Freeze or I'll fire," Rucker hollered as he leveled the Magnum at the giant's chest, fifteen feet away. A mix of fear and anger wobbled Rucker's knees for an instant.

The girl cried out, "Daddy, don't fuck with him. He is the poleece!"

The giant halted and held out the blade toward Rucker. He said affably, "Officer, sir, lemme buy you a suit of clothes or somethin'." He eased forward. Rucker shouted, "Stop or I'll fire!" The giant flashed gold teeth and lunged toward Rucker. Rucker fired twice. His first impulse had been to waste him. But instead he shattered the assailant's right kneecap and drilled the second round through his left thigh. The butcher knife clattered into the gutter as he collapsed and moaned in pain. The girl bawled like an infant.

With the girl on his hip, Rucker moved to the fallen man. He was now unconscious, with his mouth agape. Rucker holstered the Magnum. He stooped and scanned his face with a flashlight to see if he knew him. The man was a stranger. But Rucker noticed that his nostril hairs were frosted with coke or H. He heard the not-so-distant squeal of sirens.

Rucker handcuffed the girl to his left wrist. He pinned his badge to his coat lapel. Then he darted his hand into the hooker's bosom stash and extracted a wad of bills. His flashlight revealed twelve new C-notes.

"So the old vic was your first and only sting," Rucker said as he dropped the evidence for booking into his coat pocket. Suddenly the scene was brilliantly lit by the headlamps of two screeching police cars. Both young uniformed officers instantly recognized Rucker. Within an hour, Pee Wee Smith, the hooker thief, was booked for grand larceny from the person. Big Cat Jackson, her notorious New York pimp, was booked for the attempted murder of a police officer. He was listed as critical in a county hospital, under police guard.

His silver pimpmobile was impounded and searched. Ten ounces of high-grade heroin was discovered stashed behind a headlamp of the machine.

Two hours after the bust and shooting, Rucker had completed his written reports. Drained, he left Hollywood Station for home, driving his personal white Lincoln Continental. He drove through the balmy May night to the far-west end of Sunset Boulevard. He turned into a quiet, tree-filled street of well-kept houses. In the middle of the block, he pulled into the driveway of the attractive cream stucco house where he had been born.

He pressed a Genie device inside the car that swung up the garage door. He pulled into the garage. He punched the gizmo to shut the garage door and got out of the car. He went to unlock the kitchen door. He stepped inside the shadow-haunted house, and loneliness assaulted him.

Rucker switched on the kitchen light. His ruddy face was drawn with fatigue. "Jesus Christ!" he thought. "I need a drink of whiskey." Instead, he got a glass of orange juice. He dropped his beefy six-four frame onto a seat in the breakfast nook. He closed his eyes in bittersweet reverie. He remembered Jim and Ellen, his dead parents. His cop father's voice and laughter had rung throughout the house like a baritone bell. Remembering his mother's tender, loving care and dulcet lullabies when he was a child misted his eyes.

He left the kitchen. He went through the dining and living rooms, still furnished with antique pieces. He ascended a red-carpeted stairway to the master bedroom. He paused in the doorway. He almost reeled in the lingering fragrance of Shalimar. Nora, his wife, had loved the perfume, before cancer snatched her from his arms forever, five years before.

He sighed and went to sit on the side of the bed. He stared at her pillow and remembered the countless a.m.'s after hair-raising shifts on the robbery detail in the deadly 77th District, in South Central L.A. He'd tiptoe into the bedroom. He'd gaze at her, asleep, and fall deeper and deeper in love with her and her angelic face, framed with silky red curls caught in a spot of moon glow.

Now he stared at a picture of his new love on a nightstand. It was the image of Opal Lenski, a striking fifty-year-old brunette. She was a New Yorker who had met Rucker the summer before, while on vacation in L.A. Leo Crane, her nephew and Rucker's close friend and a member of his Special Hooker Squad, had introduced him to the seductive widow. They had been instantly attracted to each other.

He switched his eyes to an unopened fifth of Cutty Sark on the dresser. He kept it there to prove to himself that he was strong enough to resist booze. The bottle also served as a visual reminder that his drinking problem had nearly forced the beauteous Opal to cut him loose. He had returned from a nightclub restroom to find a handsome punk hitting on Opal. The young stud ignored his command to get lost. In an alcoholic rage, he had punched out the intruder and broken his jaw. He and Opal hurriedly left the scene before the police arrived. In the car, he had ranted Opal into tears with his accusation that she had encouraged the punk's advances. He had promised her that he would stop drinking if she forgave him. He had, with difficulty, kept that promise for a year.

He felt his heart gallop at the chance he'd have to ask her to marry him when he took his upcoming vacation in New York. He went to the dresser. After the shooting, he needed a drink to guarantee restful sleep, he thought. As he picked up the bottle, he heard it gurgle like a demon's chuckle. Maybe he was strong enough to take one drink just to sleep tonight. He remembered repetitious warnings he had heard at AA meetings against sober alcoholics' taking that first drink. He slammed the bottle down on the dresser top.

Rucker showered and came back to the bedroom to do push-ups until he fell asleep on the carpet. An hour later, he was bombed awake by the telephone. He picked up to hear from the station that Big Cat Jackson was dead of shock and loss of blood. He'd be notified as to the date of the coroner's inquest, mandatory in police-related deaths. His hand shook uncontrollably as he replaced the receiver.

He got the bottle and ripped off its seal. He chugalugged a third of the whiskey before he got into bed, in the buff. He lay there, comforting himself with the fact that he had not tried to kill the madman. He rationalized that Jackson was the real killer of Jackson.

Rucker fell into a deep sleep and dreamed of his upcoming retirement. Peace of mind and sound sleep would have been impossible had he known that a psychotic black master pimp would soon arrive in Hollywood. He would work his horde of bust-proof hookers on the streets of Hollywood, with a fallout of misery and death into Rucker's life.

2

It was a carnal night on 125th Street in Harlem. The master pimp Shetani sat in his parked car. He had a rare smile on his brutish black face as he studied the sidewalk parade. Crack dealers serviced customers in cars. Half-naked hookers, square pushovers, and sissies clogged the street and bars. Sex, crime, booze, and dope ruled the treacherous night. The melded odors of bargain colognes and steamy armpits rode the sweltering air like a sour aphrodisiac for gawking male bangers.

Several black pimps in gaudy machines honked at Shetani as they cruised by. A half-dozen kids descended on him and chanted, "Mr. Shetani, how 'bout dustin' off ya 'chine, pretty and clean?"

He nodded. They ragged off imaginary dust on the spotless car from bumper to bumper. He gave the leader a twenty-dollar bill to share with the others. They split into the neon catacombs.

Immediately Shetani recoiled from the awful breath and ravaged face of a middle-aged hooker.

"Hey, sweetie, how about a lovely three-way trip with Kansas City Nettie for ten?"

His first impulse was to spit in her face. Couldn't the ugly hick bitch see that he wasn't a trick? Her almost white face and green eyes filled him with instant rage. The hag reminded him of the person he hated most.

He scowled. "You ugly bitch. Hit on me after you get a face transplant."

She reached into her bosom. He scooped up a pistol on the seat beside him. He aimed it at her forehead as she drew a switchblade. She backed away and jaywalked across the street. A moment later, he was jolted from a poisonous memory of his mother by a crunching blow to the rear of his mobile castle.

He jammed his pistol into his waistband beneath his suit coat, against his back. He sprang to the street to confront two young black men seated in an ancient Ford with Florida plates. The Ford's shattered right headlamp had apparently bashed a large dent into the pimpmobile's rear fender.

Shetani went to the driver's open window. The Floridians grinned up at him. "Are you niggers crazy?" Shetani snarled as his hand moved under his coat, toward the pistol.

"Naw, man, we ain't crazy. Why don'cha give a signal or somethin' when you pullin' out into traffic?"

Shetani felt body quakes of rage as he jerked the pistol free and held it tight against the side of his leg. He decided to kill the pair. He eye-swept the sidewalk in the immediate area and saw a cluster of people eyeballing the action. He shaped one of his hideous smiles as he backed away to his car.

He got in and keyed on the engine. The pair grinned at him as the Ford moved down the street past him. He pulled out behind them. He watched them pass a stick of grass back and forth.

Shetani tailed them to a large rooming house on a quiet street. He put his hat on the seat. Then he screwed a silencer on his pistol. He parked and left his machine. He sprinted fifty yards, to trap the Floridians in their car. He peered at them through the rear window. They were still passing the grass.

He paused behind the car for a brief moment, to catch his breath and to draw his gun. In the blue spot of a streetlamp, he was fearsome to behold. He looked like a monstrous black cat on its hind legs, dressed in pimp people finery.

He got down on his knees and crawled on grass to the front of the car. He popped up to full height and sprang to face the windshield. They couldn't see him, with their faces pointed toward the roof of the Ford in laughter. He froze, gripping the pistol with both hands at arm's length, aimed at them. He needed them to see him before he killed them. They wiped happy tears from their eyes. The driver saw him at the instant that he put lighter flame to a joint. His maroon eyes in the flare were gigantic, and his jaw hung crookedly. His companion stared at the driver for an instant before he zoomed his eyes to the doomsday vision of Shetani.

He fashioned his graveyard smile as he watched them jamming their backs against the seat in desperate escape reflex. He fired twice, at the center of their foreheads. The silencer made the shots sound like the pop of corks. The deceased slumped on the seat, with faces pressed together. He saw they were identical twins.

He put his gun away. He saw brain gore dribble from neat holes in their foreheads. He turned away and went to his car. The silent street still slept. He shot the car away, for Times Square.

On the way, the memory of his mother in the face of the hooker hag haunted him. He wished that he could have wiped out the image of the hag with the Floridians.

Times Square neon glowed like pastel flame against the skyscape. Shetani drove his gold-on-lavender Continental through the racket of traffic to his den of hookers off Times Square.

He drove to the rear of the Regal Hotel. He owned the building. Retirees occupied three floors of the building.

He drove into a brilliantly lighted garage and parked beside a huge blue van. Its presence indicated that his fifteen-girl stable had been brought home by Petra, his main woman.

Froggy, the garage guard and car polisher, a dwarfish black man with scraggly gray hair, rushed from a cot to open the driver's door of the Continental. "Hi, Cap, you goin' out anymore?" Froggy said in the croaking whisper he got after his throat was slashed in Spanish Harlem, by a food vendor who caught Froggy's hand in his pocket.

Shetani shook his long head as he slid his six-four frame out of the Lincoln. He said, "Take the car and get that dent knocked out." Froggy's eyes widened in shock as he noticed the damage. "Sure, Cap, first thing. Did you ketch the dude that done it?" Shetani smiled. "Yeah, you could say that."

Froggy, with mouth agape, eye-swept Shetani. He was adazzle in a baby-blue glove-leather suit, with a fiery network of diamonds and rubies on his throat, fingers, and wrists. Froggy exclaimed, "King Shetani, the cleanest player in the Apple!"

Shetani patted Froggy's shoulder as he moved toward a private elevator. Froggy closed the garage door and locked it. Shetani entered the elevator for the lift to the fourth floor, his domain. He stepped out onto white plush pile carpeting in the entrance hall. It was lit by a crystal chandelier that cast a pink glow. His thin, cruel lips shaped a rare smile to hear the shuck and jive of his slaves waiting for his arrival in the living room ahead.

He moved across the carpet past a floor-to-ceiling mirror. He turned back to check out his reflection. He was the product of a blue-black West Indian father and a green-eyed Irish mother.

He adjusted his baby-blue tie and palm-brushed his luxuriant mop of processed curls. He finger-stroked a widow's peak that slashed down across the ebony forehead of his ugly-handsome face. He gazed hypnotically into his strange eyes, burning like green lasers in their deep sockets. He adored his unforgettable face. He was proud of the mesmeric pull and fascination it had held for the platoons of young whores who had humped their hearts out in the street so he could afford to live like a prince for the past twenty-five years.

An orphan and escapee from a final horrible foster home, he had made his debut as a street hustler at fifteen in Harlem. He remembered why, at twenty, he dropped his real name, Albert Spires, for "Master Shetani," his moniker. One night, he had been drawn to the scene of a street emergency in Harlem by the flashing red lights of an ambulance. The attendants lifted the alcoholic victim, a middle-aged African immigrant, onto a stretcher. She suddenly opened her eyes and stared up into the apparently unearthly face of Albert Spires, awash in fire-red light. She recoiled in terror and jumped from the stretcher. She fled into the night screaming, "Shetani! Shetani!," which a fellow bystander translated as "Satan" in Swahili.

Now Shetani turned away from the mirror. He stepped through black satin drapes into a blue-lit sunken living room. His ethnically mixed stable of young junkie whores, lounging on couches and giant silk floor pillows, broke into ecstatic chanting: "Hello, Master Shetani! Hello, Master Shetani!"

He threw up a palm to silence them as he moved to seat himself in a thronelike chair of royal-purple velour.

All sixteen of the girls were bathed and naked for the delicious ritual of the spike. His compelling eyes fixed on the face of each girl with deep, probing intensity. He did this to reinforce their conviction that he could read their minds.

He nodded to Petra, his main woman and stable straw boss, seated beside him on a pillow. The ravishing blonde Amazon said softly, "Master, love, no one requires punishment and everybody's money is respectable. May I rise?" He nodded. She went to a corner of the spacious room and wheeled a blond wood serving cart back to Shetani. He shuffled through sixteen envelopes, with stable names and cash amounts noted in ink on each.

All eyes watched raptly as he put premeasured amounts of distilled water and China-white heroin into a miniature brass pot atop a tiny butane stove. He turned it on and watched blue flame lick at the pot bottom for a minute or so before he turned off the stove.

He took a syringe marked "P." for "Petra" in ink on a strip

of masking tape, from among fifteen other syringes individually marked on the cart top. He wrapped a bit of filter cotton around the needle point. Then he drew the syringe full from the pot.

Petra positioned herself on hands and knees with her buttocks between Shetani's legs. He shot the dope into a vein between her vulva and high inner thigh. Petra kissed her master's feet and seated herself on the floor beside him. She watched as the others received their good-night dope. She hugged each of them.

Petra and Shetani were finally alone. "Master, later I'll show you a surprise package I brought you. May I sit on your lap so you can hold me?" she said in a child's voice, with her dope-dreamy eyes upturned.

He flung his arms open. "Get up here, sweet bitch, close to my heart, where you belong," he said in his silky baritone that vibrated in the blue-lit stillness like muted thunder.

She rose from the floor pillow and nested her naked curves on his lap. He held her very close. He rocked her gently as he made an erotic crooning sound deep in his throat that shivered her with excitement.

"Oh, Daddy darling, I'm going to start missing you terribly the minute I get on the plane to L.A.," she whispered.

His white teeth fanged into the side of her throat, and she gasped in pain.

He said brutally, "Miss me? You negative motherfucking bitch, how can you miss me when you know I'm always with you, awake or asleep, tricking or crapping? You know the power of my spirit will always be beside you, watching you, guarding you. Miss me? Petra, don't ever again hurt and insult your sweet master like that."

She said softly, "Forgive me. You know I'm your slave until I cash in. Master, I meant I'll miss your arms and your delicious candy dick. I wish I had a supply of your nectar in a jar so I couldn't starve for it while I'm taking care of all that business in L.A."

He finger-stroked her face. "Petra, your L.A. business is not that complicated. You scout Hollywood and the rest of L.A. for the chance that our family can get down there and make lots of bread. Off your reports, I'll decide to move or stay here. But I hope you find Hollywood fine and dandy. If so, I'll wire you the bread to lease a monster house. Shit, we all deserve to live and hustle in the sunshine for a change, like rich suckers, in a fucking mansion in the hills."

They laughed. Petra whispered in his ear, "Sweet Master, can I have some bye-bye candy?" He bit her earlobe and sucked scarlet skin berries on her throat.

"Sic your candy, you one-track-minded freak-dog bitch," he commanded as she unzipped his fly and his wombstroker leapt free in the blue haze.

As she performed state-of-the-art fellatio, he tattooed crimson stripes on her alabaster ass with a coat-hanger whip. He leaned to feather-stroke her clit. Shortly she made a shrill sound through her teeth. They both climaxed, and then Petra stood. She took his hand and led him to her bedroom, to present the surprise. She paused at the bedroom door to whisper, "Master, I stole her around nine in that coffee shop with the pink front in Times Square. She's seventeen, obviously gorgeous, and fast! She's holding five bills. I told her to personally give you her first money."

She opened the door, and they stepped inside the gold-and-white lair. They stood at bedside, looking down at the cream-colored sexpot. She was nude and supine in the junkie limbo between heavy intoxication and sleep. Green fire flared from her slitted eyes.

Shetani, a fanatical reincarnation buff, barely suppressed a gasp. He trembled and sat down on the bed beside his new slave. He leaned to scan every plane of the girl's face. His whole body vibrated with excitement and joy. He was certain the girl was his dead baby sister, returned to life. She was Tuta Spires!

Anxiety jolted him. He had to find a way to get her off the street without blowing his career and rep as king of pimps. Awful rage twisted his face for an instant. He vowed to himself that he would find the man or woman who had turned her out in her second life and kill the guilty one.

He felt the girl's pulse. Petra said softly, "Master, she's all right. The Harlem jive ass that turned her out in the street and on stuff was copping three-percent garbage. I gave her a very light hit of stuff when we got home."

Shetani scowled. "What his name?"

The tone of his voice caused Petra to give him a look. "Ronald somebody. He's just a piece-of-shit horn blower from Pittsburgh. We saw him on our way home, looking for her in the Square."

He flashed his black-leopard grin. "I'll find him to hip him that his girl has chosen me . . . and maybe he's got a few of her things she wants to cop. Introduce us."

Petra covered the girl with a robe. She said, "She has eyes like yours." She gently shook the girl's shoulder. Her radiant green eyes fully opened to gaze into the hypnotic eyes of Shetani.

Petra said, "Master Shetani, meet Maxine."

The girl smiled and extended her hand. "It's really neat to meet you, Master Shetani. You're famous!" she said in a sweet voice, coarsened by the China white.

Maxine's hand hung in air for a long moment in the tense silence, before she lowered it.

Shetani crooned, "Girl, we can't touch yet. But I'm happy to meet a fine and lucky ho like yourself—lucky 'cause you've joined a family of love and success."

Petra said, "Give Master your lines."

Maxine took the money from beneath a pillow and put it into Shetani's palm. He shoved it into his shirt pocket. He said, "Touch me," as he leaned the side of his face close to hers.

She kissed his cheek. He held her head against his for a moment. He stood. "Everybody will call you Tuta, my sweet pet name for you . . . We'll have a heart-to-heart rap before you get down in the street tomorrow night."

He turned and left the room, followed by Petra.

"Say, Master, that was a cute touch, laying your baby sister's name on the package. She looks like a Tuta. Does she resemble your sis?"

They paused at his bedroom door. "Not at all, except for her eyes," he lied as he opened his door.

She tiptoed to kiss his lips. "Goodbye, sweet Master. I'll call you tomorrow from L.A." She turned and walked away.

He stepped into his mirrored ho-trap. He sat down on the side of his emperor-sized bed, still shaken and thrilled by Tuta's return from death. She was the first and only female he had ever loved. He said, "Come in," to a light knock on the door.

Brute-faced Eli and Cazo Brooks, street guards for the

stable, entered the room. Shetani nodded toward a couch. The blue-black twins dropped down their fearsome six hundred pounds of muscle. They chorused in pipsqueak voices, "Cap, we got the cocksucker!"

"You mean the one that mugged Petra last week?" Shetani said as he gave them a vial of coke and a snorting spoon.

"Yeah, a dude named Joe Springer. His nephew, Judas Jimmy, got sick and fingered him for a shot of our China white," Eli said as he dipped the spoon into the vial.

Cazo giggled. "Cap, he fainted after we lugged him up a alley. We busted his elbows and both kneecaps with a hammer. He ain't never gonna mug nobody again, 'less he do it from a fuckin' wheelchair."

Shetani peeled off two hundred dollars from the Maxine money. "Here's a bill apiece, bonus," he said as he leaned to put it into Eli's hand.

"Thanks, Cap," Eli said as he passed the coke spoon to Cazo.

Shetani said, "Pet is flying to L.A. tonight to scout it. If her report is good, we'll all move out there. You two will go in the next ten days."

Eli frowned. "But, Cap, we can't split before the girls. Who's gonna look out for 'em in these mean streets?"

Shetani said, "Railhead and his cousin Cool Walker. Remember them from our grammar-school days in Harlem?"

Cazo nodded. "Sure do, Cap. They sho' can look out for the stable."

Eli chimed in, "Shit, they was and is the baddest niggers in Harlem 'cept for me and Eli."

Shetani stood. "There's no reason to worry about moving until I hear Pet's report."

The twins stood. Cazo handed Shetani the coke vial and spoon. The twins turned and moved toward the door. Eli wheeled around. "Hey, Cap, I know you seen the new girl Petra stole in the Square. It sho' was spooky when we first seen her. She's the spittin' image of Tuta. Ain't she?"

Shetani nodded and moved close to them. He half whispered, "I'm counting on both of you to keep it a stone secret between us that she looks like Tuta. In the meantime, we and everybody else will call her Tuta."

The twins waggled their bull heads in puzzlement as they grinned and left the room.

Shetani went to stand at a picture window. He stared out north, toward Harlem, where he had picked up his heavy baggage of inner pain and hatred of women. He grimaced, remembering Tuta when she was four and he was eight. His drunken mother, Inez, had been a cruel, foulmouthed monster who abused and beat him and Tuta daily. He glanced at the cigarette-burn scars on his hands and wrists. He remembered how Inez would violently shove him and Tuta away with curses whenever they tried to climb into her lap or even touch her. The final brutal scene with the three of them, the last day of Inez's life, rolled like videotape inside his head.

He and Tuta were playing tag in their fourth-floor slum apartment. Inez was drinking whiskey and playing solitaire on a card table. Tuta bumped the table and overturned a water glass of whiskey. Inez knocked Tuta down with her fist and straddled her. "You stupid motherfucking bitch! I'll kill you for that!" she shouted, as her hands were choking Tuta.

He snatched up an empty whiskey bottle and struck her on the top of her head. While Inez lay stunned, he took Tuta to a hiding place in the basement of a tenement down the street. At twilight, he went back to the fourth floor of his building to find a chance to steal some food from his apartment. He waited in the shadows at the far end of the hallway until the last of Inez's drunken girlfriends and five-dollar johns departed.

He sneaked into the apartment, expecting to find Inez snoring in a drunken stupor as usual. Instead, she was leaning through an open front window, watching a street fight down the block.

Festering hatred ruled him. He eased up behind her and pushed. She landed skull-first on a spike of a dilapidated wrought-iron fence. Her split head burst forth brain matter.

Her death would be officially determined as an accidental fall by a notorious drunk and mental patient. He remembered that his loving and sensitive father, Oscar, had been driven to blow out his brains nearly a year to the day before Inez's death by her craziness and relentless bitchery.

Shetani thought about the succession of loveless, even hateful foster homes he suffered in. For six years, every day, he missed Tuta and ached to be reunited with her. At fourteen, he joined an army of Harlem street kids. He teamed up with the teenage mugger Big Cat to get a bankroll. He haunted every grammar school in several boroughs until he found Tuta, right in Harlem. She was in her recess period. She immediately left the school grounds with him and never returned to her foster home.

Shetani remembered how joyfully they lived together in a Harlem kitchenette until she died the next year of leukemia. He'd gone totally berserk with grief and rage against all the doctors and nurses in the county hospital for failing to save Tuta. He grinned, remembering the bloody chaos of broken

jaws, noses and lacerated faces before seven cops finally sub-
dued him. He thought about his seemingly endless confinement in a state mental hospital, until he was released at the
age of eighteen.

Now Shetani felt suddenly very tired. He turned away
from the window and went to the bathroom for a shower.
After that, multiple images of himself animated on the walls
and ceiling of the mirrored white-and-gold room as he put on
gold satin pajamas. He got into bed. The only light was from
an amber lamp on the carpet behind the bed.

He took a dope kit from beneath a satin pillow. He prepared and injected a shot of China white into an arm. He lay
back, admiring the gorgeous image of himself in the ceiling
mirror. The horse kicked him into dreamy ecstasy.

3

Several days after Big Cat's death, Rucker pulled his Lincoln into his space on the parking lot of the two-story brick police building. He entered and greeted a half-dozen police and civilian employee acquaintances. He was told at the sign-in desk that the lieutenant wanted to see him.

He went to Lieutenant Bleeson's office, at the rear of the building. Rucker's massive, hard-faced boss smiled and greeted him with his booming voice. "Hello, Russell. Sit down for good news."

Rucker said, "Thanks, Lieutenant," as he seated himself in front of Bleeson's cluttered desk.

Bleeson, in shirtsleeves, leaned back in his chair and studied Rucker for a moment. "Russell, I've cleared your vacation, and I'm glad for you, because you look frayed."

Rucker grinned. "Six weeks of twelve-to-sixteen-hour shifts on that fast track out there would drag the ass of an iron man. I will be happy to take a vacation."

Bleeson stood with his hand extended. "Russell, you and your guys won the war and set an example of grit and accomplishment for every vice cop in the department. Take three weeks, whenever you wish."

Rucker shook hands. "I appreciate that, and thanks so much, Lieutenant."

Rucker turned away and walked to the door. He stopped and faced Bleeson, seated behind the desk. "Lieutenant, someone in our squad will have to fill my spot while I'm away. I'd like to recommend Leo Crane."

Bleeson smiled and nodded his head. "That's a very good choice, Russell."

Rucker opened the door. "Thanks again, Lieutenant," he said as he pulled the door shut behind him. He walked toward the front of the building. He paused beside lanky, fortyish Leo Crane at the sign-in desk. Crane's sleepy gray eyes widened for an instant when Rucker banged a palm against his shoulder as he turned away from the desk.

"Hey, Russ, what the hell are you so happy about?" Crane said as he studied Rucker's grinning face.

"I'm taking three weeks off from the fucking sewer, and guess who is covering my spot?" Rucker said as they walked toward a briefing room a few yards away.

"Shit, that's easy. It's gonna be me, the cop that makes the pimps and whores piss on themselves before they flee into the wind."

They laughed as they entered the medium-sized room where Rucker would brief the first shift. The four members of the special team were seated at a rectangular table, joking and shooting the breeze. The squad worked two five-man shifts, from 3:00 to 11 p.m. and 11 p.m. to 7 a.m.

The room became silent as Crane seated himself, followed by Rucker, who took his seat at the head of the table. The group's ages were between twenty-eight and forty-three, with Rucker, at fifty-two, the oldest member.

Rucker glanced at his wristwatch. "Men, it's late, so I'll be brief with my remarks. I've got myself a three-week vacation, and Leo will be in charge in my absence. You guys are gonna be all right so long as you don't rest on your laurels and let the bad guys and broads get another foothold. True, there are a lot of Hollywood hookers doing bits at Sybil Brand. But there is an army of them working sections of L.A. and Vegas and Albuquerque. That army is waiting to get the message that the heat is off in Hollywood, hooker heaven. You guys are the best cops there are, and I'm confident they will never get that message from you. I know you're gonna keep the streets of Hollywood clean for decent people. They deserve it."

Rucker got to his feet as the group applauded. He turned and moved into the hallway, followed by the others.

Two days after Rucker's meeting with his squad, he arrived at New York's Kennedy Airport. Opal Lenski and her mother, Rebecca, met Rucker. He was surprised to see how closely they resembled each other. Like Opal, Rebecca was a statuesque, shapely woman with magnetic dark eyes and a mane of blue-black hair slightly streaked with gray.

They rushed him with hugs and kisses before he claimed his luggage. They went to the Lenskis' vintage Packard. Rucker insisted that he would do the driving to their home in distant Brooklyn. He opened doors for them and got under the wheel, beside Opal.

"Russell, when you leave the airport, I'll give you directions for the shortest way home," Rebecca said from the back seat.

Rucker said thanks as he half turned toward her. He froze for an instant before he keyed on the engine and moved the Packard. Rebecca was holding a *Christian Science Monitor* publication! His prejudice against and opposition to the cult were white-hot and soul-deep. He thought of Ray, his lovable and late older brother. He had been a Christian Scientist when he got pneumonia. Rucker had begged him, even tried to force him to get medical attention. Ray refused it and died. Now Rucker was tense with the possibility that his life was in danger of being touched again by the unrealistic cult.

Fifteen minutes after getting directions from Rebecca, he glanced at her through the rearview mirror. She was intently reading the *Monitor*. Was that a whispered "amen" he heard from the back seat? He dared not think the unthinkable, that Opal was a member of the cult. No, that couldn't be. She would have mentioned it long ago on the telephone.

Rucker's palms were damp when he pulled the Packard in front of the Lenskis' well-kept two-story brownstone. Jesus Christ! He needed a drink.

Shortly, he was settled into a guest bedroom on the second floor of the grand old Lenski house. He took a belt of 100-proof vodka from a fifth before he unpacked his luggage. He couldn't risk the odor of his favorite Cutty Sark with Opal around.

He felt better, but his peace of mind was threatened by the possibility that Opal was a Christian Scientist.

He went into a bathroom adjoining the bright blue-and-white bedroom to gargle a mouthwash and take a shower. He heard Opal purr sweetly, "May I join you, Ruck?"

He boomed out, "Yes, you may! Yes, you may!" with a fair Gordon MacRae imitation. She stepped in and pressed herself against him. They kissed passionately beneath the jet stream. She stooped and lifted his glistening sex works in her palm. "Gorgeous, I've missed you so," she cooed as she smooched his penis.

After their shower, Rucker carried her to his bed. He felt the giddy excitement of his amorous youth as she straddled him with her fragrant heat. She volleyed his face with suckling kisses. He embraced her and wondered again if she was a Christian Scientist. He loved her, but he couldn't ask her to marry him if she was. What if she got sick after they married? He couldn't face losing her for lack of medical attention.

"Oh, Ruck, I'm so totally hot!" she whispered. She rubbed his crotch with her bulging bush. He decided to postpone the big question and make love. They did, passionately. Afterward, he lay caressing her back. Finally, he said tenderly, "Dear, let's talk for a moment about something very important to us. Okay?"

"Sure, Ruck," she whispered. She lay within the circle of his left arm.

"Well, I'm going to be direct. Are you a Christian Science member?" he asked softly.

"Yes. I've been a member for about a month. Why?" she said as she scooted free of his arm to lie on her side, facing him.

Their eyes locked together. He dry-swallowed. Christ! Her dark-brown eyes were so beautiful. "I am aware that everyone has the right of religious choice," he said raggedly. He sighed deeply. "Opal, your answer disturbs me more than you can imagine."

She frowned. "Disturbs you? Ruck, I can't understand that."

He reached to stroke her hair. She moved her head away. He said stoutly, "I know firsthand about your religion's rejection of medical help for sick members, for even the sick babies of members." His jaw set in a hard line as she studied him in a long silence. He continued in an edgy voice. "Opal, I will never understand your religion's reliance on a so-called lay practitioner for sick people who require professional medical attention. It's unreasonable. It's almost crim—"

In the manner of a mother stifling the protest of a child, she pressed a palm against his mouth. "Darling, please, let's don't quarrel. We are having dinner downstairs this evening with Brother Jenkins, a practitioner. Perhaps through him you will become more informed, and then you might have a change of attitude. Fair enough?" She stood beside the side of the bed, studying him with radiant eyes. He shrugged and smiled. "We will see." She leaned and kissed him before she went to her bedroom, on the other side of the bathroom.

Rucker immediately started to hit the vodka to relieve his tension. At eight-fifteen, he went to the dinner table, loaded and fifteen minutes late. Opal frowned and introduced him to Ralph Jenkins, the practitioner, and his tiny wife. Rucker grunted and sat down next to the burly healer-through-divine-power.

Rucker picked at his roast duck while the Lenskis and the Jenkinses carried on a spirited conversation about documented miracles experienced through faith. Rucker instantly disliked Jenkins's naked skull, blunt ugly face, piggish eyes, and sanctimonious voice.

"Well, Sergeant Rucker, what do you think about our discussion of God's miracles?" Jenkins softly inquired.

Rucker stared at him through slitted eyes for a long moment. "Mr. Jenkins, since I'm not on duty with the LAPD, call me Mr. Rucker . . . Miracles are great, but how many sick people have died that medical doctors might have saved, Mr. Jenkins?"

The women were visibly shocked. Jenkins replied, "Oh, you poor man. Doctors! You mention earthly doctors? God is the quintessential doctor on whom we rely. We know—"

Rucker cut him off. "Come on, now, Jenkins. I lost a Christian Scientist brother who wouldn't seek medical attention. What about the sick people you lose?"

Jenkins smiled, "Mr. Rucker, I can't 'lose' anybody. I am just a humble conduit of God's healing power. God, in his divine and perfect wisdom, saw fit to take your brother and others who believe in him to everlasting bliss. It's impossible to be lost with faith in him."

Jenkins's wife and Opal's mother snickered. Opal just glared at Rucker, who was enraged at the trap he had set for himself.

Rucker pushed his chair back and got to his feet. He exploded, "I think it's criminal for you and your religion to let people die for lack of medical care."

Jenkins sprang to his feet and seized Rucker's coat sleeve. "You retarded son of Satan! I demand an apology for that remark," Jenkins commanded as he jerked the coat sleeve.

Rucker spun and punched Jenkins hard on the jaw. He fell heavily and lay moaning on the carpet. Rucker turned and went up the stairway to his bedroom. Opal joined him several minutes later.

"Ruck, are you insane? How dare you strike a guest in this house!" she said angrily.

He looked up at her from the side of the bed. "I'm not insane or sorry."

Opal's eyes softened. She sat down beside him and stroked his back. "You're drinking again . . ."

He jerked himself to his feet and paced the floor. He stopped in front of her and looked into her eyes. "Yeah, my drinking is as much a part of my life as your lousy religion is to yours. So what?"

She got to her feet. "So I'm sorry about us, Ruck," she said softly as she turned to leave.

"Tell Rebecca I'm going to check into a hotel in the morning," he said to her back. She nodded and went through the bathroom to her bedroom. He got a bottle from his bag and sat in a leather chair near a picture window. He stared out at the lights of Brooklyn's streets and blotted out his pain and unhappiness with vodka.

Leo Crane, Rucker's longtime friend and protégé, awakened in North Hollywood after a fitful night of Seconal sleep. He winced and closed his eyes against a spear of late-morning sunlight coming through an opening in heavy blue drapes. He heard the drone of a vacuum cleaner issuing from the living room. He bolted upright on the bed. What if Millie, his wife, got to the mail first and found a notice from the bank, warning that their house note was two months overdue? He looked at ten-thirty on his wristwatch. He sighed relief. The mailman wasn't due for an hour or so.

He let himself down on the pillows and lit a cigarette. Bleak wings of depression flapped inside his head. He glared at his nearly emaciated face, reflected in the dresser mirror like a death mask, starkly pale in the near-darkness of the room.

Tension and misery fluttered his heartbeat. Suddenly a recurring panic seized him. He again jerked upright in the bed. His heart drummed wildly, and he felt drenched in sweat. His hand shook like that of a palsy victim as he put his cigarette on an ashtray. He was transfixed, staring at his bulging eyes reflected in the dresser mirror. He was convinced that he was close to death. He shook in terror for two minutes before he collapsed to a prone position, free of the attack. Finally, he got up and staggered to the closet. He took a packet from the toe of a shoe at the back of the closet. He went to the bathroom and stripped off his pajamas. He unwrapped the brown paper packet. He shook cocaine from a nearly empty glassine bag into water in a bent spoon. He stirred the mix with a long fingernail before he filtered the liquid into a syringe through a bit of cotton.

He raised his left arm and put his palm against the wall above the washbowl mirror. His armpit was shaved clean. He eased the spike into an armpit vein. He vomited into the bowl as he shot the dope. He backed up and sat on the toilet seat to defecate. A moment later, he frowned at the only fair quality of the coke, and there was his suspicion that it had been cut heavily with mannitol, a baby laxative. He sat there, hating his dependence on the drug. He smiled bitterly as he remembered how he had started using the treacherous powder a year ago. He had busted a small-time narcotics suspect dealing out of a poolroom john. His curiosity about the drug of the stars and the affluent had led him to retain one of the twenty-odd retail bags of coke when he booked the evidence and the suspect into Hollywood Division.

After relieving himself, Crane got under the shower and made a mental memo that he just wouldn't spend $130 per gram for low-quality coke.

He shot his coke bag empty before he left the bathroom to dress. The coke hadn't lifted him to the ideal height of ecstasy, but he whistled as he dressed, without depression.

Finished, he studied himself in the full-length mirror on the closet door. The dark-gray business suit didn't fit perfectly anymore. He promised himself that he would eat more starches—more food, period—to gain weight.

He moved closer to the mirror and frowned as he noticed a new sprouting of gray hairs in his full auburn mop. He sighed and turned quickly away, toward the door. He nearly bumped into Millie entering the bedroom.

"Good morning, handsome. Breakfast is ready," she cooed as she embraced his waist and tiptoed, with her lips pursed for a kiss.

"Hi, Mil," he said as he kissed and hugged her.

She stepped back, with a proud look on her cute round face. "Leo, I weighed myself this morning and I've dropped two more pounds. Look at this!" She spun around, her back facing him. She pulled her tentlike nightgown tight across her ample waist and heavy buttocks. "See, I'm getting a waistline again, and my rear end is going to be the way you like it, round and pretty again. Isn't it wonderful?"

Crane embraced her and nuzzled the back of her neck through her long black hair. "Sure, Mil, you're doing great.

Stay with it, sweet girl," he said as he released her. He took her hand and led her down the hallway toward the kitchen.

She sat at the table with him while he had oatmeal and rye toast. He was rising from the table when he saw the mailman leave the front porch. Millie was putting dishes into the dishwasher.

She followed him to the front door. "Darling, I hope you get the chance to come home early one night soon . . . I've been saving a bunch of sugar," she said, with her large brown eyes and sultry voice dripping starved passion.

"Baby, I hope so, too. But we may be out of luck until Rucker gets back from vacation," he said softly as he swung open the door. He kissed her forehead and stepped onto the porch.

"I'll see if there's mail," he said as he went to the box, out of her sight. He riffled through several pieces and removed a Bank of America envelope, which he put into his coat pocket.

He gave the other mail to Millie, went to the garage, and backed his three-year-old Ford LTD station wagon into the quiet street.

He drove directly to a record shop on Hollywood Boulevard. He got a parking space a short distance from the shocking-pink-façaded mecca for punk and hard-rock fanatics.

Ralph Rosen, his cousin and football pal from high school, was the owner. Rosen had copped the cocaine for Crane that had him fullbacking through startled pedestrians in his rush to relieve himself.

Crane trotted into the garish interior of the shop, where Rosen was spinning a deafening record for a group of androgynous rock freaks.

Crane dashed behind the counter. He gave gigantic Rosen

the heel of his hand to a shoulder as he galloped to the john behind a curtain at the rear of the joint.

Rosen was alone when Crane emerged. Rosen's bearded face was concerned. "Hey, buddy, you sick?" Rosen asked in his pipsqueak voice.

"You're goddamn right I am. That alleged coke you copped has me crapping every hour. Do me a favor, Ralph, and—"

Crane was cut off by one of several horse players who entered the shop in succession to lay bets.

At the last departure, Crane said, "As I was saying, do me a favor and cop from another dealer. I can score fucking laxative myself over the counter."

Rosen nervously shuffled his feet under Crane's hard gray eyes. "I'm sorry, Leo, I'll find another dealer. It may take a few days to score for high-grade stuff."

Crane leaned into Rosen's face. "I'll appreciate it . . . How is your book doing?"

Rosen's tongue flashed across his red lips. "Pretty good, but it's been better. You in trouble?"

Crane smiled. "Yeah, old buddy. I need eight bills for a couple of months, to keep the bank from stealing my house."

Rosen went behind the curtain and returned, palming a wad of bills. They shook hands.

"Thanks, Ralph. See ya," Crane said as he turned away for the street. He drove east on Hollywood Boulevard, looking for hookers who might be working early in the day. As Rucker's replacement, he drove himself to work longer hours than his boss to keep Hollywood free of street hookers. If he got fatigued, he'd go to one of the cots in the squad's briefing room to catnap.

He thought of Millie. He remembered that, five years before, he had developed a passion for young hookers. His sex life with straitlaced Millie had waned and soured.

Hollywood Boulevard was hooker-free. He worked in his own vehicle, with a department gas allowance. He believed that driving a station wagon would enhance his trick image for hookers.

He stopped at his bank to pay the overdue house notes. He cruised sun-splashed Sunset Boulevard. He hawkeyed the crowded sidewalks. He stomped his brake pedal. He'd come within inches of rear-ending a vehicle ahead of him. His eyes had been the captive of a snow blonde. Petra!

At first stare, he didn't make her as a hooker. She had a starlet's image in her short but chic ice-blue dress and off-white bag, with baby-doll heels. But after his trance, he saw her spin and dart too quickly into a drugstore with just a subtle hooker's look of apprehension on her patrician face.

He glanced at his rearview mirror. He saw a black-and-white squad car several cars behind him to confirm his suspicion. She was the sexiest, most gorgeous hooker he'd ever seen. She was any magazine's candidate for centerfold, he thought.

He turned into a side street. He came back to park diagonally across the street from the drugstore.

Petra came out of the store. Within seconds, he saw her get into a vintage Lincoln. It was driven by an elderly white man.

Crane shook his head and wondered how such a creature could become a hooker. He knew the odds were she wouldn't turn the old john in his car in bright daylight. He couldn't U-turn in the heavy traffic to follow and bust her in the act if she was that reckless. He'd wait to pick her up and bust her later.

He drove two blocks away from the drugstore and parked. He scooted over to the passenger side of the front seat. He put binoculars on the sidewalk in front of the drugstore. If she showed again, he'd pull into the store's red-zone curb, as the john had done, to take a shot at her.

After forty-five minutes, he gave up and combed Sunset to spot her.

After 3:00 p.m., he nodded in passing to members of his squad's first shift. He also dipped his head to several decoy policewomen, starting their shift, to bust johns who offered them money for sex.

He had busted two young white hookers before twilight arrived. At this point, he usually snorted coke or went to the briefing room to let down or to catnap.

He was out of coke and yet felt no fatigue. He was energized by his search for Petra. It was after 8:00 p.m., near Crescent Heights and Sunset, when he found her. Her waist-long mane was like white flame on the backdrop of night. Her short black dress squeezed her curves. Rhinestones on her red shoes showered sparkle like shooting stars as her exquisite gams balleted her down the boulevard.

She surveyed car traffic with her peripheral vision and an almost imperceptible turn of her head.

Crane, following her, was timing his moves so that they would arrive at the next street corner together. They did. He smiled and stared at her, john fashion. He turned past her into the side street to park. If she decided he looked like a customer, she would come to his car to size him up at close range.

His pulse hammered when he saw her coming toward him. He told himself the lie that he was always this excited when he was about to spring a trap on his quarry. He leaned toward the open window on the passenger side.

Satan's slave stuck her radiant head into the wagon and electrified its interior with sex appeal. He was speechless for a moment. She filled the vacuum. "Oh, I'm sorry, I thought you were someone I know that would give me a lift," she said as she started to withdraw.

He found his voice, Israeli-accented. "Say, wait! My name is Chaim. I'd be delighted to drop off such a beautiful lady like yourself."

She studied him for a long moment. He smiled inside. He thought that using the accent and giving the Hebrew form of "Herman" as his trick name to hookers helped to throw them off.

It worked a bit. She smiled and got in. She was still not sure his pedigree was trick. She said in her soft contralto, "I'm Skye. Thank you so much, Chaim." She noticed his Adam's apple wobble when his eyes were snared by her sculpted thighs, exposed to a mere two inches from the bush that bulged her panties.

He felt his penis stir and thicken. "Skye, I hope you won't mind if I say a few words before I drop you off," he said with a hot quaver.

Instantly he regretted his loss of control, because he knew of the hooker paranoia about johns who got emotional up front. He thought of Rucker, his strong mentor, and regretted his weakness even more. He vowed to himself that if he trapped this heavenly body he'd bust her. He wouldn't fuck her, as he had done in the past with girls who had wow appeal.

He softened his gray eyes as she studied his face with a slight frown. He thought, would she decide he was an over-acting cop or a high-risk rapist, a killer type?

Primarily, Petra read voices rather than faces, which most street hookers were prone to do. She heard the heat in his voice as real. This, coupled with the Jewish image, relaxed her somewhat.

"Say away, Chaim," she said sweetly, with her New York accent.

He almost whispered, "I've got a lovely wife at home, and I can't complain about her as a lover . . . This is crazy!" He closed his eyes and pressed fingertips against his temples before he continued. "I saw you walking down that sidewalk like a Viking princess. Never have I been so excited. I guess, as the rabbi would say, my desire to go to bed with you over-whelmed my sense of morality. I'm not a rich man. But, Skye, I'm willing to reward you to the limit of my purse for a few minutes in bed with you."

He felt in control. He remembered that his pitch had conned dozens of hookers into Sybil Brand jail. He knew it was entrapment. So what? he had thought. His conviction rate was very high. Now he felt that his pitch, and her likely Big Apple contempt for hick West Coast cops, would block out her caution. It was a fact that the shark vice cops in the Apple had not busted Petra in more than two years.

"Chaim, I may be too expensive," she said as she leaned to finger-stroke one of his nipples through his shirt.

"How much, Skye?" he asked, with his head cocked to the side like a child.

"A C-note for a short-time half-and-half, Chaim," she sang as her fingers stroked his rising enemy through his trousers.

He slapped away her hand, and she recoiled with mouth agape. She was doubly shocked to see triumph transform his face. She jerked her head toward the door beside her as he clicked it locked from his door.

"You're under arrest for violation of Code 647b," he said in his normal voice. He keyed on the engine. He looked into the rearview mirror for the chance to pull the wagon into the flow of traffic.

Petra stared at him. She was stunned, and then she was desperate to free herself. It wasn't the bail. She had more than enough for that in her bosom. It was the spirit of her master, Shetani, that seemed to invade the wagon and her head that prodded her to beat the bust.

Crane eased the wagon into traffic. She remembered her master's compliments for her long street roll with no arrests. And he had thrilled her soul and nourished her hooker heart when he trusted her to scout L.A. No, she told herself, she couldn't let this cop, who she felt strongly was just a trick with a badge, bust her. And, she reminded herself, she was main bitch in a sixteen-girl stable. She wouldn't hold still for this bust, like some rookie hooker from Podunk Nowhere.

She could cry angry tears at will when she thought about her socialite mother, dead for a decade. She wept and drew herself into a fetal ball, with her dress hiked up to her waist. Her alabaster ass, scarcely covered by red bikini panties, shone for Crane.

He eyeballed it at a red light. His enemy throbbed and hardened on the green. "You goddamn cunt! Stop that crying!" he shouted as he violently jerked her dress down to cover the oval seducer. He shot the wagon away toward the station.

"This is unfair! . . . I'm not really a whore. I've never tried this before. Please, let me go!" she blubbered.

He laughed. "You mean I'm the first man you've propositioned?" She nodded. "You're a damn liar. I saw an old guy pick you up in front of the drugstore on Sunset."

She half turned her face toward him. "Forgive me. I honestly forgot him . . . He was broke. If you knew why I'm out here, you would let me go."

He snickered. "You're out here to keep your pimp's foot out of your ass."

She sat up and blotted tears with tissues from her purse. She shook her head vigorously as her mind raced to structure sure-shot con. He had driven to within five blocks of the station. "Please, don't take me to the station. Please, pull over to hear how I was forced into the street," she begged, her soulful eyes beaming into his for a moment.

He turned his head and stared straight ahead. His face was hard as he pressed down on the accelerator. "I don't want to hear your crap."

She moved across the seat to press herself against him. "Please! Give me just a couple of minutes."

"Don't touch me, bitch!" he said coldly as he jabbed an elbow into her side.

She moved away and spewed tears again. He jerked the steering wheel toward the curb and parked, with the wagon's engine running. His fingertips drummed the steering wheel. "Spill it fast."

She cleared her throat. "I've got a kid brother on dialysis back in Syracuse, my hometown. He's in line for a donor kidney and transplant. I'm sure you know how expensive that can—"

He flung an arm through the air near her face to cut her off. "Shut up! You think I'm a fucking idiot? You're twice as beautiful as any model I've ever seen. Syracuse is like the backyard of the Apple, the capital of the model agencies. You expect me to believe that you're such a dummy that you would choose the mean streets of Hollywood instead to raise the bread you need?"

She said firmly, "Please, don't use up my time. Listen to the truth. My figure is too full for modeling. I was tricked into coming west by a small-time con man with a stolen Mercedes and fake diamonds. He promised to get a large loan on one of the valuable properties he owned in Vegas to solve my money problem." She paused to heave a dramatic sigh. "All he really owned was several thou and a sucker system he was certain could beat the roulette wheel at the Sands. He busted out. He went to jail when he tried to sell the Mercedes with a phony pink slip to an undercover cop. I came to L.A. this morning."

In a long silence, he scrutinized every plane of her face for a lie tic. Her eyes were wide and unblinking. Compulsively, he thought about Rucker even as he decided he couldn't bust her.

She thought, This bastard's dick rules him like any other trick. "Sweetie, you're not going to book me?" she said softly.

"No, I'm gonna fuck you into a coma . . . Bitch, don't ever call me sweetie again," he replied in a voice hoarse with heat.

He moved the wagon into traffic. Her junkie gut quivered and knotted to remind her that she needed a fix.

Within fifteen minutes, Crane parked and they entered a motel room. She said, "I have to use the bathroom."

He sat on the side of the bed. "All right. We'll take a shower together when you finish," he said, as he craned his neck to see that the bathroom window appeared to be too narrow for her escape. He fidgeted. Maybe that window is wide enough.

Inside the bathroom, she took a cellophane packet from her bosom. It contained a small glassine bag of cocaine and another, nearly empty bag of heroin. She quickly snorted the H and dropped the empty bag behind the radiator. An instant later, Crane's cop instinct had brought his eye to peer at her through the keyhole.

She removed her shoes and stuffed the cocaine into the toe of a shoe. He watched her sit down on the stool to pee before he went back to sit on the bed.

He searched her purse and found a Skye Olsen ID. He was certain that she was a drug user. He'd find out what drug was in the shoe toe. He had absolutely no desire for H addicts, no matter how beautiful. If he found her H dirty, he'd bust her for prostitution and possession of the skag. He could conveniently revise the true scenario with her in court.

Shortly, she left the bathroom, carrying her shoes. She smiled as she came to sit beside him on the bed. She placed the shoes on the carpet between them. He placed a hand on her thigh and fixed his eyes on her face. "Are you wanted in the U.S. of A. for any capital crime or crimes?" he asked.

She moved away from his hand. "Shit, no, cop!"

"Are you a heroin addict?" he said as he leaned to push up the sleeves of her dress past her elbows.

"No! Fuck this inquisition, man! If you don't want to have some fun, bust me," she loudmouthed as she sprang to her feet.

He stood and pushed her back onto the bed. He glanced at her shoes. He saw alarm in her eyes. He sat down beside her and picked up the shoes. "These are jazzy. Are they lizard?" She nodded. He put an index finger into the stash shoe and pulled out the bag of coke. He opened it to smell the contents. He dumped a line of it onto the back of his hand. He greedily snorted it away. He closed his eyes for a long moment and swayed. "Sweetheart, you've just made a friend. This shit is almost pure!" he uttered in an ecstatic whisper.

She stood, with contempt on her face. "You corrupt bastard! Let's take that shower so I can get the hell out of here."

He watched, with his enemy rigid, as she took off her dress, gartered stockings, and panties. She glided to the bathroom.

He tore off his clothes and joined her in the shower. After that, he carried her to bed. His rage against himself for his weakness and his violation of Rucker's trust in him increased after the coke. So he marauded her tender flesh with rough hands and his teeth. Finally, she, the long-term masochist, screamed and leapt from the bed.

"I'm not taking any more of your animal shit. I'm leaving," she shouted angrily.

The swollen head of his enemy thumped his thigh when he jumped from the bed. "C'mon, get back in bed," he begged, with his arms flung wide open.

She gazed at his giant enemy and remembered the crack about fucking her into a coma. She pointed a finger and said in a little girl's voice, "I won't get in bed unless I can suck that gorgeous thing first. Okay?"

He nodded his head and they went to bed. She immediately attacked their enemy with ferocious fellatio. Within twenty minutes, she exploded him twice. Then she moaned, "I'm so hot for your dick."

He mounted her and tried to stuff his burned-out rod inside her.

"Come on, fuck me into a coma," she taunted, as he rolled off her to lie panting on his back.

She moved to sit on the bedside. She used a rolled bill to snort up almost all of the coke. She watched him snort up the rest as she dressed.

He watched her, with his mind in riot. He thought about how desperately he needed access to the purest cocaine he'd ever had. He felt the staccato of his heartbeat in the witchery of her presence. And his crotch, still atingle from her incomparable head, was the convincer that he would need her again and again. He knew the slickest hooker there ever was couldn't work the streets of Hollywood for long without getting busted repetitively by the super-clever cops on his special squad. She was certain to disappear after it hit her that Hollywood was too hot to work.

She sat on the bed to put on her shoes. She stood and moved toward the door. "I guess I'll be forced to see you around," she said over her shoulder.

"Give me a moment to dress and I'll drop you off wherever," he said gently.

She paused, with her hand on the door knob. "Thanks, but I'd rather take a cab from the stand across the street." She opened the door. He glanced at his watch. It was after midnight, and the sharpest cops on the squad had gone on-shift. The door was closing behind her.

"Skye!" he said loudly.

She stepped back into the room with raised eyebrows.

"Are you going back to work?" he asked.

"Why would I do that after a zero night in the fucking sack with a cop?" she said icily.

He propped himself up against pillows. "I wouldn't bet that your kid-brother story was true. But I'd lay a sawbuck to a nickel that you will take a fall if you work Hollywood tonight."

She drew herself erect like a midnight soldier. "I can take care of myself."

He shrugged. "Maybe you can, in ordinary heat . . . Why don't you knock off now? Let's have lunch together tomorrow. You had to see the turf had almost no hookers. I can help you with info to protect you." He jiggled his hands helplessly in air. "But I need time to think out certain things . . . to come to a decision."

She opened the door. "Say, man, I don't have time to unravel your riddles. I'm not a heist broad. I've got the bust bread for hooking. If the turf gets too hot, I'll just get in the wind. Bye-bye."

She turned to go out the door. He sprang from the bed and seized her around the waist.

"Let me go, you crazy sonuvabitch!" she hollered.

He kicked the door shut and pulled her back to the bed. He pulled her down to sit beside him on the bed. His hands vised her wrists as he moved his face close to hers. "Listen, you uninformed bitch. I'm acting leader of the special squad that cleaned up Hollywood. We're famous."

She shrugged. "Congratulations. So what does that mean for me?"

He said, "I hope I haven't decided to help a dummy. You need license-plate numbers and descriptions of the cops driving the undercover cars to work Hollywood." He released her wrists. She smiled and reached into her purse to extract notebook and pen.

"I'm ready, baby. Lay it on me," she cooed as she scooted close to him.

"Your ass I will, just like that. I want two things from you. Cut me into your coke connection. I won't bust anybody. I just want to cop."

She moved away from him. Her pale face reddened for an instant. "No. You insulting creep. You think hookers don't have principles?"

He grinned. "All right, then, cop for me."

She nodded. "It will cost you a hundred and forty a gram. What else do you want?"

He eye-swept her body. "You! I want your ass in bed with me at least once a week. Agreed?"

She smiled and nodded.

He went on. "I'll meet you nightly, between nine-thirty and ten p.m., in the parking lot of that drugstore on Sunset where I first saw you. At those times, I will give you any changes of license plates and descriptions of new cops. I could get angry enough to kill you if you share the info with anyone. Understand?"

She leaned to stroke the nape of his neck. "Of course I do . . . What should I call you?"

He removed her hand from his neck to kiss the back of it. "Call me Jerry. Now, take down this info carefully," he said, as he moved to prop himself up in the bed with his hands clasped behind his head.

4

It was 3:00 a.m. in the Apple. Shetani's phone awakened him. He picked up to the voice of Pee Wee Smith. She was known from coast to coast as one of the best thieving hookers ever to hit the track. Pee Wee's voice broke as she told him about Big Cat's death.

Shetani pounded his bed with his fists. The Cat, his best friend since they were teenage hustlers in Harlem, had been iced by a pig in L.A.!

She went on tearfully with details. The shock, for a moment, blocked out his pimp lust to cop a hooker with such superstar credentials. What? She was calling from a Times Square restaurant? He'd send his car for her. He'd blot out her grief with the best dope in New York. He was so kind to care, she blubbered.

He hung up and pushed a button on a panel on the bed's headboard. Within two minutes, Eli stormed into the bedroom.

"Pee Wee just called to tell me a pig wasted the Cat in L.A.," Shetani said sadly. "Eli, take my ride and pick up Pee Wee at the Thompson Restaurant in Times Square," Shetani ordered.

Eli spun and left the room. Shetani immediately went into action to set the copping stage for Pee Wee. He took his blazing arsenal of jewelry from the nightstand and arranged it on his person. He flipped on a spotlight above the bed's headboard. It illuminated a giant portrait of just his green cat eyes aglow against a background of pitch-blackness. The spotlight would also set his rubies and diamonds afire. His coat of arms, a hypodermic spike crossed by a wire coat-hanger whip, was painted in flame red at the bottom of the portrait.

He gazed at it for a moment and remembered that the Cat had cracked that he used the whip on Pee Wee and her stablemates when they broke his rules. Had Pee Wee begun to like the fiery sting of the whip? If not, he knew how to teach any ho to adore it. He knew his insensate hatred of women would drive him to insanity, to murder, if he didn't relieve his deadly tension through the whip.

He felt the horse kick him into dull rapture. He needed to be sharp upstairs to play his best game. He took his dope kit to the bathroom. He shut the door behind him as he checked his watch. Pee Wee should be arriving at any moment. He put down the toilet top and sat down. He injected a powerful shot of top-quality cocaine to clear his head of the heroin's dreamy cobwebs.

Shortly, he heard Eli's bass voice, and he knew the prize had arrived. He'd wait and let her absorb the splendor of his bedroom. Perhaps she'd feel her hooker heart rock when his mystical orbs in the portrait trapped her eyes. He had detected an emergency tone of junkie need in her voice. She had probably come directly to Times Square from the airport to cop her medicine. The federal and city narcs had combined to sweep up a dozen pushers and to terrorize the others off the street the week before. He felt that Pee Wee couldn't risk buying the dope in Harlem, which was now being cut with everything from quinine to strychnine.

Shetani smiled. Pee Wee had run into a dope panic. She knew he kept dope for his girls. So she had looked up Albert Spires's phone number and called him, he reasoned.

Eli had seated Pee Wee in the chair at the foot of the bed. The jazzy bedroom and the hypnotic eyes in the portrait had indeed caught her attention. But now she got to her feet and went to the mantel above the fireplace. She studied the fifteen Polaroid shots of girls: white, black, and a pair of Asians. In the center of the pack was a larger picture of Petra.

Pee Wee frowned at the radiance of the Caucasian beauty. She was very pretty in her own Afro way. But she had an unconscious hatred of her blackness, and she was strongly opposed to black players' having a white main or bottom woman.

She felt a tremor in her legs as she turned and went back to seat herself in the chair. She stared at the portrait's cold but, for her, alluring eyes. She was uncomfortable in her position of extreme vulnerability. After all, she was street cream, a superstar. But here she was, in the bedroom of a player famed as master of the fast cop. She didn't want to be anybody's slave again for a while. She certainly couldn't see herself in a sixteen-girl stable with a white sexpot as the bottom woman.

She got to her feet. She'd leave and try to cop her medicine in Greenwich Village. She fell heavily back into the chair. She remembered that she'd been told in Times Square that the Village was suffering a dope panic of its own.

She sighed deeply. She comforted herself a little with the thought that the sad news of Cat's death had been at least flimsy cover for her raging need for a fix.

Shetani opened the bathroom door and stepped into the bedroom with disarming cool. He extended his arms. "Hi, lil sting queen!" he sang in a voice just above a whisper.

She said, "Hi, Shetani."

His face hardened almost imperceptibly when she stiffened and hesitated for an instant before coming into his arms for a hug. He disengaged and flung a palm out toward the side of the bed. She sat down.

He arranged himself against the bed's headboard so that the portrait's spotlight could ignite the fireworks of his jewels. He felt her ambivalence. He decided to talk shit and let her monkey kick her ass before he gave her a fix.

"I've been thinking you could sue the L.A. police for the wrongful death of the Cat," he said in a whispery voice that forced her to lean toward him to hear.

She placed a palm across a yawn. She shook her curly head. "No chance. White square asses on both sides of the street saw Cat charge the pig with a butcher knife. Besides, I jumped grand-theft bail."

He gnawed his bottom lip. "How much was the bond?"

Her fingers nervously toyed with a gold chain around her throat. "Ten G's."

He grinned. "Who got fucked?"

She said impatiently, "A square nigger barber. He put up his house. The week before, I was waiting for Cat in an after-hours joint when he cut into me with his card and a hard-on." She shrugged and lit a cigarette from her lizard purse.

He took a crystal ashtray off the nightstand and placed it on the bed between them. He shook his head when she extended the pack of Camels. "Shit, girl, cigarettes are bad for your health." They laughed flatly together.

"What happened to Cat's bankroll?"

She moistened her sensuous lips with a sharply pointed tongue. "It disappeared along the line. The police, ambulance dudes, or somebody at the hospital could have beat him."

During a long silence, he played his Mona Lisa bit.

"What you smiling about?" she asked.

He floated a bejeweled hand in the air. "I remembered some shucking and jiving I did with the Cat a few months ago."

She wiped sudden springlets of perspiration off her brow with the back of her hand. "Like what?" she said in a feeble voice.

"I cracked that I wanted to buy you. He cracked back that he wouldn't take all the bread I could raise and all the ho's I had for you. Then he cracked seriously: 'Pal, if anything happens to me, I'll rest happy in hell if the two of you hook up. You're the only player there is who could take care of her good as me.'"

She dabbed a powder puff at her feverish brow. "Daddy Cat had a lot of respect for you, all right. He told me stories about capers in Harlem that went down when you two were kids . . . about how you and him heisted drug dealers. By the way, baby, didn't you mention on the phone about some China white you had?"

He waved her to him. "I sure did. Put your bare ass up here between my legs. I'll do you where I hit all my ho's."

Again, she hesitated at a crucial point. His fierce eyes burned through her. "Bitch, you having some kind of problem with our new friendship?" he said harshly.

She waggled her head and crawled across the bed. She got into position. She hiked up her red silk skirt. He pulled down her black lace panties to bare her round ass.

"Please, don't hurt me," she moaned, with her face buried in the bedspread.

With a spike, a match, and a spoon from his dope kit, he prepared a medium fix of the potent dope. As always, he shot the dope into a spot between her vulva and high inner thigh. He felt her quiver between his legs when the dope slammed her.

Within twenty seconds, she collapsed to lie on her right side. "Ooee! Baby, your shit is so goood!" she cried out ecstatically. Her enormous honey-colored eyes were dope-clouded slits gazing at her reflection in the ceiling mirror. His snowy teeth shone in a wolfish smile as he studied her.

"Naturally, you motherfucking bitch. This is a sacred happening. You just received your first blessing from Master Shetani, the ho's god."

She switched her slits to his fearsome face. He said solemnly, "I forgot to mention that I promised the Cat that I would take care of you if he died. Bitch, I intend to keep that promise to the dearest friend I ever had."

She shook her head. "I can't be your woman just like that. I gotta have time . . . Besides, I don't dig players with a silk bottom woman."

He threw his head back and belly-laughed. Then he said quietly, "Can you keep a secret?"

She lit a cigarette. "Sure can."

He braided his fingers together over his heart. "Petra is on the way out. I'm gonna fire her in a few months, when the statute of limitations runs out on a trip to Pennsylvania. It was supposed to be just a pleasure trip for her and several other girls. I drove them across a state line and made the mistake of working them in Pennsylvania. You gonna be my secret bottom woman for a short time."

She licked her lips. "I'll still need a little time." Then, foolishly, she plotted a con to cop a supply of the quality skag. She finger-stroked his lavender-painted toes. "Beautiful god, will you please lay a quarter-ounce on me while I make up my mind about us?" She fumbled a roll of bills from her bosom. She propped herself up on an elbow to fan out the bills on the bedspread. "See, before I split L.A., I stung the square-ass barber for a stash of thirty-six hundred. I'll pay whatever you charge for a quarter-ounce."

He leaned and banged a heavy palm against the side of her face, which knocked her on her back. "You dare to insult me? You dizzy bitch, I ain't no motherfucking dope dealer!" he shouted as he scooped up the bills from the bed.

She scooted off the bed with an angry face. She sat in the chair and glared at him. "So the great Shetani has to gorilla a ho out of her bread? Right?"

He leapt from the bed and went to stand between her legs. He vised her tiny face between giant palms. He tilted her face up, forcing her to look into his eyes. "Gorilla you, my ass. You played on me for my stuff. If you're my woman, the bread I took is your claiming bread to get me. You've got a two-hundred-grand bankroll behind your thieving ass. Kill a trick, bitch! I can raise you! If you're my woman, you got my personal guarantee that you will always have the best medicine there is." He paused and gritted his teeth. "If you ain't my woman, I'm gonna charge you the thirty-six hundred for wasting my time and forcing me to break my promise to Cat to take care of you. Well?"

They stared into each other's eyes until she averted her eyes in surrender. "Were you leveling about firing Petra?" she asked in a child's voice.

"My word is like a gold bond, you secret lil bottom bitch, you," he crooned as he lifted her into his arms. He carried her to the bed and lay down beside her. "Tell me you're my woman and you're gonna obey all my rules!" he said in a low but commanding voice.

She burst into a torrent of tears and blubbered, "I'm your woman and I'll obey all of your rules."

He took her drained body into his arms and winked at his reflection in the ceiling mirror.

5

Several days after the Crane encounter, Petra excitedly raced the horses of a Hertz chariot toward L.A. International Airport. Her master was flying in from the Apple with a supply of medicine. She was hoping he'd sex her as a reward for the Crane coup.

She arrived and left the airport parking facility to seat herself in a corner booth of the uncrowded restaurant in the sky. She gave a waitress an order for two glasses of pineapple juice.

Ten minutes later, she didn't recognize Shetani until he limped to within six feet of her on a cane. He was disguised as a minister in black suit, white collar, and a black hat atop a "natural" wig. He was carrying a satchel, which he put on the floor between them as he sat down.

Petra moved to embrace and kiss him. His eyes, through the plain glass of heavy spectacles, and then his voice warned her away.

"Nix, bitch! You're just having a chat with a black preach," he whispered harshly.

"Oh, Master. You're so fucking cute in that getup. But why?"

He looked at his watch. "Listen and don't speak. I got a kilo of boy and one of girl in that bag. Safekeep it, except for what you need. There's also the bread to lease a monster house in an isolated spot. Rent some furniture—modern, flashy shit. Tomorrow I'm gonna start sending our family out here in groups of five. We've got to . . ."

To cut him off, she held her hand up like little kids do to catch the teacher's attention.

He frowned.

"May I ask a question, Daddy?"

He nodded.

She went on. "Jerry, the cop, he's a coke freak, like I told you on the phone . . . Well, suppose he fucks up. I mean, what if he gets bounced off the squad and we've all moved out here with our big nut to crack and Hollywood gets too hot to work?"

He chuckled. "If the sucker stands up for just a couple months, we'll take off a bundle. Besides, I'm sick of New York's winters, and there are several niggers I'm gonna waste if I stay there. Shit, I just need a base on the coast. You ho's can work Albuquerque, maybe Vegas, and Seattle for sure."

Her face became serious. "Daddy, Jerry said he'd kill me if I shared his inside info with anyone . . . Isn't he a cinch to know I've tipped our girls when his squad can't bust them?"

Shetani grinned. "Sure, he'll wake up, down the line. But he ain't gonna ice a ten-plus bitch that supplies him with ninety-percent-pure coke. Sit in his face and sport his sucker dick with lots of head. When he wakes up, I'll bet your million-dollar life against a pile of dog shit he'll opt for a shakedown to get his medicine bread."

He took a sip of juice before he went on. "I'm gonna be out here with you to guide you with him." He leaned toward her, with his strange green eyes aglitter. "I'll protect you from harm, Star Baby. If necessary, I'll chop off his motherfucking head with that hatchet I carry in my ride."

Her blue eyes were dreamy with passion as she gazed at him. "Master, I'm not afraid of anything, with you in my corner." She wiggled the tip of her tongue at him. "I want some candy so much my cunt and throat ache. Let's go to my motel . . . someplace. Please!"

He shook his head and looked at his watch. "My flight back leaves in less than a half-hour. Besides, my dick is fasting."

She moaned. "Then sweet-rap me off."

He smiled. "All right, you stone-to-the-bone freak. Do your clit."

She darted a hand under cover of the tabletop into her crotch. "I'm so wet already," she exclaimed.

His hand left the tabletop to pinch her savagely on the side of a buttock. "Feel me drilling into your hot throat with my choice dickhead. Close your eyes and see it, doggy."

She closed her eyes and trembled for a long moment. "Ooeee! I can see it, Daddy," she screamed in a whisper.

"Now I'm fucking your cunt up to your navel with those circular hard strokes that hurt so good and make you cry. See it, freak!"

"I see and feel it, Daddy. I'm almost there!"

He pinched her again. "I'm stroking your tonsils again. See it and feel it. Come!"

Suddenly her orgasm bucked her body with great spasms of release. A startled waitress passing by paused for a moment. She went about her business when she saw Petra regain composure.

"Thank you, sweet Master," Petra said softly.

"Star Baby, it was a thrill to get you off like that," he said as he reached into his coat pocket. He brought out a slip of paper and pushed it toward her on the tabletop. "Here's the twins' phone number and the address of their two-bedroom house in the Wilshire district. They are waiting for you to move into one of the bedrooms. They will protect the kilos and cash until we all move into the big house. Any questions?"

She shook her head and put the paper into her purse.

He stood. "Phone me every night at the usual time . . . See you again soon."

She lifted the satchel to the seat beside her. "I'll miss you very much until . . ."

He said, "By the way, I copped Pee Wee Smith the night you left the Apple. I'm sending her to the Midwest to do her thing." He turned and limped away on his prop cane.

Eight days after Shetani visited L.A., Crane cruised Hollywood. He stopped the station wagon at Vine and Sunset at a red light. A new white Eldorado passed in front of him. It was driven by a sleek black dude with a snow blonde cuddled close to him. Crane was certain the stunner was Petra, and the red satin ascot around the dude's throat screamed pimp.

Rage claimed him. He bombed the wagon into Vine Street traffic against the red light amid an uproar of noisy horns and strident brakes. He tailed the Caddie down Melrose Avenue. He hoped the driver would turn off the crowded street. He'd pull him over on some pretext and beat up the dude if he gave any lip whatsoever.

Finally, the driver pulled into a gasoline station on the western end of Melrose. With his palms dripping sweat, Crane pulled into the station. An attendant was pumping gas into the target car.

Crane eased the wagon abreast of it on the other side of the pumps. The girl wasn't Petra!

He was drained, and he felt a panic attack coming on. He drove to a far end of the station's lot. He parked near a bank of telephones. This time was unlike most of the attacks, when he feared imminent death.

Now he lay in a knot on the front seat. His palms squeezed his head, which vibrated violently in terror that he was going crazy. He lay there shaking for several minutes before the attack ended. He sat up and mopped sweat from his brow with a coat sleeve. He told himself what an absolute fool he was to let a hooker blow his common sense. He vowed to himself that he'd cut her loose before she destroyed him and his career. He promised himself he'd do without her body and high-grade coke. And he wouldn't tip her to any changes of squad licenses or personnel.

He drove the wagon to the street and resumed his shift. Yes, he'd also reduce his coke usage until he booted the habit, he assured himself. His jawline hardened. He was going to straighten out his life and get some peace of mind. He would become the solid rock that his wife, Millie, Rucker, and his cop associates believed him to be.

A week later, at 10:00 p.m., Crane sat in the station wagon on the parking lot of the Sunset drugstore, waiting for Petra. He had decided to take her last coke delivery. Earlier, he had noticed two new girls working up and down the boulevard. He had tried to snare a couple of them, but they ignored him.

At ten-thirty, he became angry with himself when he realized he had thought about Petra for most of his shift and couldn't stop thinking about her and missing her on the street. Now he wondered if he could cut her loose just like that. And his nerve ends shrieked for coke.

He drove from the lot into Sunset traffic. He stopped for a red light and glanced down Normandie Avenue. He saw the silhouettes of several scantily clad female figures alight from a large dark van that U-turned and disappeared. On the green, he drove across the intersection and parked.

Through his rearview mirror he saw the interracial quartet of strange young hookers come to the intersection and split up. Tuta and her black stablemate came down the sidewalk toward him. They eyeballed the heavy traffic for tricks.

Crane leaned across the seat and smiled at them through the open window as they passed.

Tuta came to him. He saw the other girl move away to glance at the wagon's rear license plate.

He said, with the Israeli accent, "Hello, pretty lady. May I give you and your friend a lift?"

Tuta frowned at the accent. She glanced back at her buddy, and turned back to face him. She said, "I think no. I'll have to ask my sister Mamie."

Mamie walked up to join Tuta and said, "What's happening, Pat?"

Tuta winked. "This guy wants to give us a lift. What do you think?"

Mamie shook her head and said, "He looks like the Boston Strangler to me." She then grabbed Tuta's arm and steered her into a nearby coffee shop.

He tried to pick up seven other new hookers that passed him. They ignored him. Petra had crossed him! He sat, whitened with anger, for a moment. He screeched the wagon into traffic to search for Petra. At midnight, he parked at an intersection on the other end of Sunset. He spotted Petra passing and then getting out of an elderly white trick's car on a side street.

He moved the wagon into the side street as soon as the trick pulled away. Petra spotted him. She walked toward him as he parked and doused his headlights in the middle of the block.

He removed his gun from its shoulder holster and put it behind his back on the seat. His head felt like a red-hot balloon ready to pop. He watched her approach in his rearview mirror and gritted his teeth. He'd take her to an isolated spot and wrench the truth from her one way or the other. No fucking hooker was going to make a sucker out of him.

He opened the passenger door. A moment later, he constructed a smile when she got in. She scooted her blue-silk-clad curves against him. She finger-stroked his thigh.

"Jerry, I'm sorry I couldn't meet you, I've been so busy."

His impulse was to smash his fist down on her hand. Instead, he gently removed it. "Don't be sorry. You bring the package?" he managed to say sweetly.

"I sure did, sweet dick, and it's heavenly," she said as she fumbled in her bosom. She dipped a tiny coke spoon into a glassine bag. She extended it and the bag. "There's more than the gram you ordered in this bag."

His right hand took her wrist and guided the spoon to his nose. "I'll pay you for the coke before we split," he said as he hungrily snorted the spoon empty. She nodded.

The quality dope enhanced his rage and impaired his judgment. He took the bag and shoved it into a coat pocket. "Thanks, I needed a lift, with all the new girls running my ass ragged."

She gave him a look. He knew the crack was stupid. He'd have to control himself until he could have his way with her.

He took Cahuenga Boulevard on his way into a section of the Hollywood Hills. He knew a spot that was ideal for a mind-blowing inquisition. Ten minutes later, he was well into the hills.

"Hey, honey, where we going? Don't forget, I'm a working girl," she said in a strained voice.

"No way, sugar, can I forget that. In a few minutes, we're going to have some class-A privacy together." He bared his teeth in an awful smile as he finally drove through the open wrought-iron gates of a once-opulent estate.

The concrete foundations of the razed mansion and secondary buildings gleamed white on an incline in the moonlight.

He took a side road into a densely forested area and parked. His right hand took her left hand and studied it in the dash light. His left hand darted into his jacket pocket and removed handcuffs.

He vised her left wrist and handcuffed it to the steering wheel. She screamed. He cut her off with a violent launch of his right elbow to her belly button. She vomited on the floor mat. He seized her long white mane and jerked up her sagging head. He stared coldly into her glazed eyes.

"Jerry, why are you doing this?" she mumbled piteously.

He backhanded his right fist into her rib cage. She groaned in pain. His left hand got the revolver from behind his back. He started to unload the gun beneath her bulging eyes. "You conning cocksucking bitch! Let's play an old game. I'm going to spill your brains if you don't spill your fucking guts," he warned as he finished removing all but one of the bullets before her terror-bright eyes.

He dropped the bullets into his shirt pocket. He lifted the gun from the seat between them. As he did, he removed the remaining bullet and palmed it in his left hand. He spun the chamber and rammed the muzzle of the gun against her left temple. He pulled the trigger.

In a violent spasm of fright, her buttocks bucked a foot off the seat at the sound of the metallic click of the gun.

"That was for me, the friend you double-crossed. Why did you tip that gang of girls to my Israeli accent and the plate numbers?" he stage-whispered, with his gray eyes afire.

"I just wanted to help them because they're working girls, too."

He pulled the trigger. She broke into wild weeping and

pounding of her thigh with her right fist. "Please, don't do that again. Those girls are my friends, my stablemates," she blubbered.

"Where is your pimp, and where are you and the others from?"

"He's visiting in Chicago. We came from the Apple."

"What's your boss's true name?"

She shook her head vigorously. "Please don't ask me to do that to my man . . ."

He pulled the trigger. She shivered uncontrollably and released a fresh flood of tears.

"Give me his name, stupid bitch. I'm pulling the trigger, and this may be the end for you. Well?"

She blurted, "Master Shetani."

"I said I wanted his true name, not a moniker."

"Oh Jesus! Please, believe me, that's the only name he's known by."

Crane reloaded the gun and pondered his position and what to do about Petra. He could cut her loose in the raw. That would be without an ongoing deal to supply undercover plate numbers for her and the others. She or her pimp could drop a coin on him to Internal Affairs that would kick off an investigation that would destroy him.

He surveyed Petra's curves. He decided that, as lush and gratifying as she was sexually, his personal risk and the pressure of their deal with no money payoff would have to be terminated. He could squeeze a payoff out of her pimp, but that would only be insurance against the dropping of a dime to Internal Affairs. It was the return of his mentor, Rucker, with his sixth sense that concerned Crane most. He'd played himself into a trap. He decided reluctantly that he would have to kill her to escape.

She stared into his grim face as he again placed the gun's muzzle against her temple. "You don't have to kill me. Let me go back to New York," she pleaded with desperate eyes.

His finger pulled lightly against the trigger as he stared into her enormous eyes, fiery with fear. His trigger finger pulled harder. The cylinder started to roll. He felt drenched in sweat. He jerked the gun from her temple and rammed it into its holster. She collapsed forward. She cried, with her face against her knees. He slit-eyed her.

"Does anybody besides you and your boss know about how you got tipped to the plate numbers?"

She shook her head.

"How old is your boss?"

She blubbered, "Around forty. I don't really know."

He grabbed a fistful of her hair. "Sit up and look at me," he commanded as he yanked her erect on the seat.

She took tissues from her purse to blot her eyes before she faced him.

"I want eleven hundred bucks a week for the plate numbers. You've got until the day after tomorrow to lay it on me. That's when new cars and plates hit the track. Understand?"

She nodded. He shouted, "Goddamn you! Say it."

She said softly, "I'll bring the bread when I come to work tomorrow."

He turned on the engine and lights. He backed out of the estate and headed down the hill for Sunset Boulevard. She lit a stick of grass to relieve the mad uproar of her nerve ends. She held the burning match and stared hypnotically at her reflection in the windshield. Aging angles of shadow and light in the flare of the match made her the mirror image of the one person on earth she truly hated. Helga Lindstrom, her mother.

The flame of the match scorched her fingertips. She flung it into the dash ashtray. She thought of Carl, her sweet father. She remembered mean-spirited Helga, the neurotic social climber. She was responsible for Carl's suicide in prison when Petra was turning sixteen. He had been the treasurer of a New York firm owned by a group of his close friends. He embezzled sums of money over a period of years to satisfy Helga's ferocious drive to outdo the extravagant Joneses of Long Island, New York.

Petra's fingernails stabbed into her palms as she remembered Kristina, her younger sister, and the other reason she hated Helga with soul-deep venom. Kristina, the angelic, the adorably good apple of Helga's heart, could make no mistakes and do no wrong whatsoever. If she did, that was always bad Petra's fault for not preventing it.

Petra remembered the countless times that she had heard Helga praise Kristina for being wonderful and good. She shuddered now at a vision of herself, recoiling from Helga's index finger, slashing at her like a stiletto as she condemned Petra as the baddest girl there ever was.

Petra shaped a bitter smile as she thought about the midnight when she fled the family mansion. She was only seventeen, but she was determined to show Helga what bad really was. She'd go to the capital of bad, the Big Apple, and become a gun moll or even a whore. That would give self-righteous Helga a kick in the gut, all right.

Now the station wagon lurched Petra from her painful

reverie, when Crane jerked the steering wheel to avoid a gaping pothole on Vine Street.

"Say, man, you owe me for the coke," Petra said as Crane pulled into Sunset and stopped in a red zone.

Crane reached across her to open the passenger door. "Consider the hundred and forty bucks as a penalty for your double-cross." He stroked the back of his hand across her bosom. "Don't plan anything for tomorrow around two p.m. We've got a fuck date at the usual motel."

She slid out to the street and stomped away. Minutes later, she was driving her rented car toward the isolated house in the hills that Shetani and the rest of the family now occupied.

Four days before the end of Rucker's vacation, a phenomenon occurred in Hollywood. Like lice on a bum, black, white, brown, and Asian hookers reinfested the streets, especially Sunset Boulevard. They had apparently gotten the underworld hot wire that the intense heat was off in Hollywood. For Crane, this was a break and a hardship. The break was that the swarm of hookers camouflaged the action of the Shetani girls, who had embarrassed and frustrated the cops on Crane's special squad. The hardship for Crane was that Lieutenant Bleeson rode him hard, because Bleeson became the target of the rekindled outrage of civic and business groups.

Crane and his squad members busted a hundred hookers in a twenty-four-hour period. But still the gaudy flesh tide flooded Hollywood.

With three days of Rucker's vacation left, Bleeson decided to call him back to L.A. Bleeson repeatedly called Rucker at his hotel without connecting. The reason was that Rucker and Opal had reconciled, to a degree. They were attending a Broadway show, and after that having a late supper at a fashionable restaurant.

At 3:00 a.m. Apple time, Bleeson called again. Rucker was performing acrobatics between Opal's voluptuous thighs when his phone rang. He remained inside her and picked up.

"Rucker here," he said breathlessly.

"Hi, Russ, this is Bleeson. You don't sound right. You okay?"

Rucker leaned away from Opal. "I'm fine, Lieutenant. I was involved, let's put it, with a lady."

Bleeson cleared his throat. "I'm sorry I disturbed you, Russ, but we have a condition red out here. The goddamn hookers have all but taken over. It's unbelievable! I want you back here no later than tomorrow night."

Rucker rolled from between Opal's thighs. "Will do, Lieutenant. See you."

They hung up. Rucker opened his arms. Opal topped him and eased him back inside her.

6

It was noon in the Apple. Shetani lay beside Pee Wee, staring at her while she slept. He'd never owned a thief. He'd always wanted to have one. That and Pee Wee's hatred of white women had driven him to con her that Petra would be dumped. He decided to send her on a stealing tour of several Midwestern states to get her off-scene. Then, too, he thought, the tour would test her and up his income.

He lip-brushed her eyelashes until she opened her eyes. "Good morning, Wee," he said softly as he watched her eyes sweep the room for a moment to realize where she was.

"Mornin', She— . . . uh, Daddy," she mumbled. She covered a dope-fiend yawn of need with wizard fingers that had burgled pockets from coast to coast.

He looked at his watch. "Wee, let's get right," he said as he took his dope kit from beneath a pillow.

"I'll cheer for that, Master," she said as she swung her feet to the carpet.

He punched a button on the console of his headboard. Fingers of sunlight sneaked through the half-opened drapes to caress her coffee curves as she went to the bathroom.

He banged a speedball and saved enough in the large syringe for her. She came out of the bathroom and noticed her luggage from airport lockers in a corner of the room.

"Eli picked up your bags this morning," Shetani said as he watched her go to take a black satin gown from a bag. She slipped into it before she returned to bed.

He said, "Sugar Wee, it's against my rules to make shit tracks on arms or any spot that's easy to see. Now, take that mirror off that table, and hit yourself in the fold between your cunt and the low inner side of your ass."

She rested her knees on her chest. She held the mirror to the side below her buttocks. She tried several times with the spike before the syringe registered a red hit. She emptied it into the line. She lay back on his arm with her eyes closed.

"Master, it sure is a sweet thrill to be your woman . . . At the git, I backed up, 'cause you're so fuckin' fast . . . and with Big Cat jus' buried, you know? But, shit, I'm the kinda star bitch that needs a star man . . . Thank you, Master, for coppin' me strong and fast."

He squeezed her close to him for a moment. She moaned as he raked her face from forehead to chin with the edges of his teeth. After they had a breakfast of pastries imported from Paris, he pushed a console button that delivered music. He nearly recoiled when she caressed his penis. But he remembered the thirty-six hundred claiming dollars he had taken from her. He relaxed while she fellated him with uncommon artistry.

"Please, Master, put it inside me," she implored, with sable eyes dreamy with skag.

He shook his head. "Wee, it's too soon to hook up my dick with your cunt. Suck on, sweet bitch. I'll do you off."

He strummed her clit with an airy finger to the rock beat of Prince's "Purple Rain." Shortly, she climaxed with a squeal.

He remembered that Petra had robbed his semen bank just hours before. He lifted Pee Wee's bobbing head and took her into his arms. She pouted.

"Oh, Master, I wanted to get you off."

His face hardened for an instant as he got a vision of his slaves sucking him into a coffin. He smiled and touched his head. "Wee, sometimes for me the thrill is bigger here when I don't come."

She sighed and snuggled close. "Master, am I gonna work the Apple?" she whispered against his throat.

"No, you're going to work Iowa, Indiana, and Wisconsin. If you fall, you call Feinstein the bondsman, collect, around the clock. He'll wire the bail, and you jump it to the next city on the list I'll give you."

She said softly, "How about my medicine?"

He rubbed her shoulders. "You'll get it in a wrapped leather hat box on general delivery at the post office. The return name and address on the package will naturally be phony, like Mary Johnson. Remember that, and claim the packages with the phony ID's I'll lay on you before you leave today. By the way, send my money in a hat box special delivery. Is everything clear?"

She said, "Sure, Master. I love it! I'm gonna feel so strong and brave, stinging the suckers."

In the late afternoon, Pee Wee took a flight to Ohio. Later, in the early evening, Shetani received a pair of dapper visitors.

"Joey! Angelo!" he exclaimed when Eli brought them into the bedroom.

They nodded and managed pleasant smiles on their cold, dark Sicilian faces. Their silk-suited bottoms hissed against the leather couch when they sat down facing Shetani, seated on the bedside. Eli hovered over them until Shetani waved him from the room.

Angelo, the older, taller of the two Mafiosi, opened his briefcase. He leaned to place two plastic-wrapped kilos of heroin on Shetani's lap. Shetani jabbed a diamond stick pin into each package to taste the contents on a fingertip.

Joey's potbelly jiggled in mirthless laughter. "Al, it's really great to feel trusted after ten years of doing business together."

Shetani pointed to the dope on the bed. "Man, don't get upset because I checked the merchandise. I'd check it if you were the fucking Pope."

Joey grunted and lit a cigarette. Peacemaker Angelo grinned at Shetani and hunched his shoulders.

Shetani took two bundles of large bills from his robe pockets. He placed the cash in Angelo's hands and said, "Count it square, and sixty grand will be there."

After the pair did a fast count, Angelo peeled off bills before he put the purchase money into the briefcase.

"Here's a ten-grand rebate from the boss . . . He wants your twins to take care of some business for him." He extended the money in his palm.

Shetani frowned and ignored the money. "What kind of business?"

Angelo smiled and dropped the money on the bed. "Same business like a coupla years ago."

Shetani's eyes narrowed. "Are we talking about another VIP white man for a chickenshit ten grand?"

Joey piped up, "Jesus, Al, you're touchy today. The target is a big black dude called Tree. He's been heisting our retailers in Harlem."

Angelo laughed, "Yeah, the boss wants him chopped down on Friday. It's his birthday. Eh?"

Shetani picked up the cash. The pair stood. Joey took a slip of paper from his suit-coat pocket. "Here's Tree's address, hangouts, and other stuff on him."

Shetani took the paper and glanced at it. They studied him for a moment with hooded eyes before they turned away. He walked them to the door and shook hands with them. He stood and watched them move down the hallway. They muttered in Sicilian to each other. Angelo turned and walked back to him. He stood close to Shetani. His long neck stretched to push his bright cobra eyes very close to Shetani's wary face.

"The boss has been good to you, selling you almost pure stuff at discount prices, eh?"

Shetani nodded. "Sure, and I appreciate it." He paused to throw his head back toward the bedroom. "I can stomp on that shit three, four times and still keep my ho's well and happy with the best medicine out there."

Angelo patted Shetani's shoulder. "You're a wise man to appreciate your friends . . . The boss will be disturbed if your twins fail to complete your end of our deal tomorrow before midnight."

Shetani stepped back and said harshly, "Say, Angelo,

you're rapping to maybe the baddest motherfucker in New York, if not the world. I'm a stone responsible man. I don't need no fucking pressure to keep an agreement. Eh?"

Angelo's eyes glinted murder for an instant before he smiled stingily and turned away to join Joey.

Shetani went into his bedroom and slammed the door behind him. He collapsed across the bed, dripping sweat. His macho performance for the Mafia soldiers had been desperate bravado to cover his soul-deep terror. He was aware of the Mafia's contempt for the lack of balls in most black and even powerful white men to demand respect. He hated the organization to the full degree of his fear.

He sat up on the bedside and stared at himself in the dresser mirror. He hurt inside and shook with rage at the realization that he, the whoremaster, was himself just a Mafia whore. He was a slave to their dope, and he was trapped into murder for them.

To stop his raging head from exploding, he quickly shot a heavy load of skag. He fell back on the bed in a rapturous trance. He smiled, ecstatic that a dope panic had driven Pee Wee into his stable. He remembered how, five years before, a dope panic had driven Petra to him. He had spotted the teenage beauty leaving an apartment building on Park Avenue that housed a colony of call girls. He had tailed her to Times Square, where she copped H from a black dealer he knew with a costume-jewelry storefront. He found out from the dealer that Petra had a heavy habit, and a white gigolo boyfriend she wanted to dump.

In the next three weeks, in his spare time, he stalked her as she made the bars and restaurants where she recruited her call tricks. A week before the dope panic came that he had expected, he saw Petra's drunk boyfriend beating her in a gangway between two buildings. He double-parked and rushed to the fray. He punched out the punk and carried her to his car.

Shetani remembered her torn clothes, and how she thanked him again and again when he drove her home to Park Avenue. She gave him her phone number, but she was too upset for him to make a copping play.

The second day into the panic, he tailed her while she tried to score. He noticed how feeble and haggard she was when she got out of a cab at her apartment building. He waited for a half-hour before he called her. He told her he was in the neighborhood and hoped she was well. He also confessed that he was a user and had just copped some pure China white. Would she like a taste?

"What a beautiful coincidence, and what an angel you are to call. I am a user, too, and against the wall of a current panic." She paused to laugh nervously. "I'll expect you quickly, Albert."

An hour after he fixed her, he copped her. Within the hour after that, the twins had moved her belongings into his domain on the top floor of his Regal Hotel.

Now, several days after he had ordered the twins to hit Tree for the Mafia, Shetani stepped out of the shower. He toweled off and donned peach satin pajamas. He was snorting coke on the side of the bed when he said, "Come in," to a knock on the door.

The grinning twins burst into the room. Eli threw a local Harlem paper onto Shetani's lap. He studied a photograph of the dapper Tree on the front page. He smiled as he read the account of how Tree had been shot to death while apparently watering his marijuana garden in his backyard.

Shetani gave the twins a five-bill bonus each.

"Thanks, Cap!" they chorused as they left the room.

Shetani stared at a row of books on reincarnation in a bookcase across the room. He thought of Tuta, his sister. He shook his head at the miracle of her reunion with him as the newly recruited Maxine. His face was mean as he thought about the young pimp who was spotted in Times Square, apparently searching for Maxine.

Shetani furiously rifled through his mind for a plan to punish and get him off the scene quickly. In a moment, he grinned. He pushed the headboard button that brought the Brooks twins into his bedroom within several minutes. They seated themselves on the sofa and watched him exercise, in a long silence broken only by the squeak of pulleys on the platform on which he lay.

Shetani paused and lay panting for a long moment. Twilight sparkled the beads of sweat on his chest and brow as he cat-leapt to his feet. He sat on the bedside, facing the twins, as he towel-blotted himself dry. He dipped his head toward the window, flooded with deep-purple light.

"It's almost time for you to take the girls to the street . . . but don't put Tuta down. Ride her around the Square until she points out that chump she ran away from."

Eli opened his mouth to speak. Shetani's deadly monotone cut him off.

"Then put Tuta out and kidnap the motherfucker. Hold him and call me. Got it?"

The twins nodded and got to their feet. Eli said, as he

followed Cazo from the room, "Cap, we'll bag the bastard if he's out there."

Shetani lay back on the bed to do a hundred leg raises. As he did, he pondered the most complicated problem he had ever faced in his entire pimp career. How could he, the acclaimed King of Pimps, rescue Tuta from the danger and ruin of the street life without destroying his rep and losing Petra, and even the rest of the stable? He shuddered at the prospect of kicking his monstrous dope habit and having to work to eat. He lay rigidly and stared at the gold-leafed ceiling.

He could cut her loose, drop her from his life and sight, he thought. But he winced at that thought, for he knew she'd simply go on selling her ass somewhere else, for some new slave-master. He couldn't bear that. He loved her. He had to protect her. He sat up and groaned as he massaged his throbbing temples.

Two hours later, Cazo phoned to tell him that Tuta's ex-boss was bagged. Shetani slipped on a pink satin robe over matching pajamas and raced to rendezvous with the huge blue van.

It was parked in a deserted lot behind a fire-gutted tenement in Harlem. He eased his gold-on-lavender Continental to a stop beside the van. He slid from the car to the trash-littered lot. Eerie shadows haunted the ghostly carcasses of deceased jalopies strewn about the lot. In the starglow, Shetani's strange eyes fired bright-jade murder.

The piercing squeal of a bitch rat scampering across his instep startled him. An instant later, he spotted her suitor in hot pursuit and shattered the spine of the rodent Romeo with a savage stomp of his boot heel.

The twins opened the side door of the van and flung the bound and gagged victim to Shetani's feet, on his knees. His straight blond hair was matted with terror sweat. He piteously walled his blue eyes up at Shetani.

"This cocksucker is a peckerwood!" Shetani exclaimed harshly.

The victim frantically shook his head and tried to speak through the gag. Shetani drew a Luger from his robe pocket and squatted down close to the trembling figure.

"I'm gonna let you rap, bitch face. If you scream, I'll spill your brains. Don't say shit until I say you can. Got it?"

The youngster nodded. Eli removed the gag.

"Go back to the Square and look out for the girls," Shetani ordered the twins. They got in the van and drove away.

Shetani said, "Now you can con me for your life."

The kid burst into a torrent of words. "I ain't white! I'm a nigger, a Creole. I ain't white! You got the wrong guy. I don't even know you! I ain't done nothin' to you. Please don't kill me, mister. Please. You're making a mis—"

Shetani ripped open a bloody rill on the side of his head with the barrel of the Luger.

"Shut up, chili pimp asshole. You turned out Maxine, my baby sister. You deny that?"

The kid's mouth gaped open. He wailed, "Her brother . . . She told me she had no one except her old man, doing a double dime in Sing Sing . . . I didn't really turn her out. She was turning tricks when we hooked up. Take me to her and she'll tell you I ain't lyin'."

Shetani whipped out his organ, fully erected by his kill lust. He said icily, "She left you because you kept your foot in her ass and took her trick money."

The kid recoiled from Shetani's swollen penis with wild eyes spewing tears. "Please, mister, don't make me suck your dick. I can't do that, mister," he blubbered.

Shetani shoved himself closer to the piteous face. "Do it, cunt, and split the city, and I'll let you live," Shetani whispered hoarsely.

The kid lightly touched the bluish hammerhead with his lips and vomited violently. Shetani shoved the snout of the Luger against his temple to blow out his brains. But even as he squeezed the trigger, some childlike quality in the kid's upturned face, so ethereal and angelic in the starlight, forced him to thunder the shot into the earth.

Shetani stared down at the kid as he collapsed and lay still. He kneeled beside the kid to find his pulse and listen for his heartbeat. He neither felt nor heard anything. He straddled the lifeless form and tried the CPR he had seen paramedics do on the streets of Harlem countless times. He rhythmically pressed his palms against the kid's chest and gave him mouth-to-mouth air until he was drenched with sweat. Finally, he gave up and got to his feet. He staggered into his car and drove like a demon toward Times Square.

7

It was 6:00 p.m. in L.A. when Rucker's flight from New York sliced through balmy August air and landed at International Airport.

Crane embraced Rucker on the sidewalk outside the terminal. "It's great to see you, Russ!" he exclaimed. "Welcome home."

Rucker grunted and turned away to help a skycap load bags into the rear of Crane's station wagon. Crane helped to load the rest of the bags before he got under the wheel of the wagon. Rucker's generous tip pasted a toothy grin on the skycap's mug. Rucker got in beside Crane. Crane moved the wagon into traffic.

"Leo, I can't understand how that hooker problem could escalate to the max so fast. What the hell happened?"

Crane stopped the wagon at a red light. His lean face in a spot of streetlamp was tight as he stared through the windshield. "At first, it wasn't like an escalation. A mob of strange hookers just descended suddenly."

Crane drew a deep breath as he pulled the wagon away on the green. "Like the other guys on the squad will tell you, the first wave of hookers none of us could bust. The big second wave of hookers we've been busting by the dozens. We should have everything under control in a few weeks."

Rucker said, "That first wave is why the second came in. New waves will keep coming as long as that first wave is immune to arrest. It's odd that none of them has taken a fall to any of our undercover guys. Any ideas as to why not?"

Crane shook his long head. "None. Now, I look like a sodbuster instead of a cop, so I gotta look like a trick to a hooker. Right? Well, I pulled to the curb for a dozen of them the first night they showed. None gave me a proposition on Sunset, from Normandie to Havenhurst. All of them came to the car and either ignored me or cracked BS like 'Oh, I'm sorry, I thought you were a friend of mine,' before they split. We've rotated our vehicles from the permanent-impound lot, switched in local and out-of-state plates. We've even used our personal cars. Maybe one of our guys . . ."

"Stop it, Leo. You know better than that," Rucker said sharply as he loosened his tie and wearily combed his fingers through his silver-streaked blond hair. He dropped his head back on the seat and closed his eyes. He pondered the possibility that someone had staked out the task force at its staging point and shot its members with a telescopic camera. Perhaps he or she had peddled or given the close-up shots to the new hookers' pimps. Rucker silently vowed to get to the bottom of the problem and run all the new whores out of Hollywood on a rail.

Shortly, the muted roar of the wagon and the silky whispering of its tires on the freeway eased Rucker into a catnap. Crane drove to Western Avenue and Sunset Boulevard before he broke the long silence. "Hey, Russ, we're in freak city."

Rucker opened his eyes and straightened up on the seat. The wagon inched westward on Sunset in bumper-to-bumper traffic. Rucker's jaw muscles knotted as he stared at the busy sidewalk arena of mean-faced black and brown snatchers, slashers, and stompers, slit-eyeing the tourist sheep. Gargoylish homosexual queens—blond, bewigged, and decked out in outrageous drag—jiggled bony behinds stuck out and melon-red tongues to snare the kinkiest tricks walking and riding.

Rucker murmured, "As always, the criminal scum floats back with dogass hookers."

Crane nodded agreement. "Yeah, robbery and assault beefs have shot up since you left."

The traffic thinned a few blocks farther west on Sunset. The detectives spotted two black and two white young working girls dressed in colorful halters and short shorts. They were lounging against the retaining wall of a parking lot, hawkeyeing traffic. Crane pulled into a parking space twenty-five yards away and cut off the wagon's engine and lights. He recognized them as part of the Shetani stable.

Almost immediately, a pickup truck pulled up in front of the foursome. Rucker said, "That's Reggie Stone, on our squad."

The four hookers ignored the truck. The cop driver pulled it into traffic. Within five minutes, three of the girls left in trick cars.

Ten minutes later, a flashy Buick Regal double-parked in front of the remaining girl, a high-yellow beauty.

Crane said, "That's Phil Wexler in the Buick, one of our guys."

The cops watched the girl ignore him. The undercover car gunned away.

Rucker said, "You got any Excedrin?"

Crane touched the ignition key. "Not a one, but there's a liquor store in the next block."

Rucker waved a hand forward. "Let's go."

Crane turned on the engine and lights. He started to turn the front wheels toward traffic.

"Shut off the lights and engine!" Rucker ordered. He dipped his head. They stared as a mammoth black dude in an out-of-style gabardine suit with rust shoes and accessories alit from a battered gold '73 Eldorado parked at the curb in front of the bantam hooker. He walked up close to her and crooned, "I'm Lovely Leon. We've been seeing each other around, pretty mama. I'm hip you got eyes for me. 'Scuse me for waitin' so long to cut in. You sho' a lucky ho, 'cause this mornin' I'm adoptin' you for my own, right here and now. Let's ride and put our wonderful shit together."

She said, "I got a man. Now, let me work." She turned her head and ignored him. He seized her wrists and slammed her into his chest. He leaned down and bit her earlobe. She struggled and screamed, "Help!" A crowd appeared.

Rucker said, "I know that joker from the Seventy-seventh."

Crane and Rucker burst from the wagon and trotted toward the pair. Crane drew a pistol from a shoulder holster.

Leon glanced down the sidewalk at the officers and released the girl. She split through the crowd and disappeared. He flashed gold teeth and flung out his upturned palms toward the officers as they reached him.

Crane holstered his gun and quickly frisked him. Leon whined, "Officers, ain't nothin' wrong went down here . . . just a little hassle with my lady."

Rucker moved in close to give Leon a shot in the shoulder with the heel of a hand. Leon stared at Rucker for a long moment before he exclaimed, "Well, ain't this a bitch! It's my man, Sergeant Rucker."

"Leon Scott, let's go talk," Rucker said as he grabbed Leon's arm and walked him down the sidewalk toward the wagon. Crane dispersed the crowd and followed closely behind.

Crane and Rucker seated Leon Scott between them on the front seat of the wagon. Rucker gave him a second, more detailed frisk. He discovered a small glassine bag of grass inside the lining of Leon's tie. He found six fake Cartier wristwatches on Leon's right forearm.

Rucker said, "Let's go, Leo." Crane turned on the engine and lights. Leon's flat, broad face reflected severe alarm.

"Sergeant, that ain't even a ounce of grass. And them watches ain't real, just some slum for the suckers. Gimme a break!" Leon said with a quaver.

Crane cut the wagon into traffic. Rucker said coldly, "Leon, that wasn't your girl that we saw you assault . . . or try to kidnap. You lied to me, so I'm arresting you for disturbing the peace, for possession of the grass, and for possession of counterfeit, or maybe stolen merchandise for sale."

Leon groaned, "C'mon Sergeant, you know them pieces ain't real. Please don't bust me . . . I'm on paper!" Leon dropped his head on his knees and moaned.

Rucker winked at Crane and jerked his head toward the upcoming corner. Crane made a right and parked on the side street. Crane lit a cigarette and went to sit on the stoop of a vacant house adjacent to the wagon.

Rucker said softly, "All right, Leon, straighten up, and let's talk." Leon sat erect and stared ahead. Rucker said, "How long have you been out of the joint?"

Leon dropped his massive hands to his lap and popped his knuckles. "Six months or so. I did eight years in Q on twenty."

"I remember the case. You firebombed a whorehouse to get even with a hooker that dumped you for another guy. You almost killed three people . . . How's Sadie?"

Leon half whispered, "Mama's fine. I saw her yesterday."

"Where are you living?"

"In my ride, temporarily."

"Leon, you're really pitiful. You never had the knack to mack even when you were young. Now you're past forty, out on parole, and I see you try to muscle that hooker into working for you."

Rucker paused to pat Leon's shoulder. "You're a master carpenter. Do something worthwhile with your life. Do it for you, do it for Sadie."

Leon lifted his chin haughtily. "Shit, I can mack good as any of these chumps out here. I just been gettin' bad breaks."

Rucker shook his head. "I see you dying in the street or in the joint, sucker. But it's your ass . . . Let's wind up our business."

Leon turned his head and stared at Rucker with saucer eyes. "Business, Sergeant? I ain't gonna have no bread till I down the ticks."

Rucker leaned into Leon's face and ground his fist into his rib cage. "You jive bastard! You or any other cocksucker have never known me to take a bribe. All I want from you is info. If you're dry, then I'll bust you, and you can finish your bit in Q."

Leon moved away from Rucker. "'Scuse me, Sergeant, ast me and I'll tell it if I know it."

"About two weeks ago, a gang of hookers, probably in one stable, hit Hollywood. Shortly, they were followed by a larger gang of unconnected hookers."

Leon nodded. Rucker said, "Tell me what you know about the first gang."

Leon loosened his tie. "I heard they all from the Apple and alla them belong to one black dude."

"What's his name or street moniker?"

"I don't know, ain't nobody seen him, and don't nobody know him."

"Find out who he is and where he lives and anything else you can get on the girls. Call in your info in early afternoon."

Rucker scribbled a number on a piece of notebook paper and shoved it into Leon's shirt pocket. Rucker scooped the grass and watches off the dashboard ledge and stuffed them into Leon's suit pocket. "You're free to go, Leon."

Leon stalled and fidgeted on the seat. "'Scuse me, Sergeant, but I, ah . . . wonder if you could loan me the bucks to cop a hotel pad till I down this slum . . . Livin' in my ride keeps me sleepy and tired. I ain't gonna be sharp enough to follow the ho's and the action on the fast track late at night. Will ya, huh, Sergeant?"

Rucker took his wallet from his jacket pocket. He extracted a twenty and waved it like a club before Leon's face. "Leon, don't try to pimp on me for this twenty. I'll hurt you bad, boy, if you don't pay it back soon or deliver the info I need."

Leon took the bill to his trouser pocket. "Thanks, Sergeant. I ain't goin' to fuck you around. I ain't crazy."

"Get out of my face, Leon, and take care of business."

Leon slid across the seat and exited the wagon. Crane rose from his seat on the stoop of the vacant house and hurried to enter the wagon. Rucker stretched and yawned. "Go slowly through the rest of the sewer before you take me home."

Crane U-turned back to Sunset. Rucker eye-swept both sides of the boulevard as he made a rough count of new hookers. He also scrutinized the drivers and license plates of a number of Rolls and wildly customized Lincolns and Cadillacs.

Rucker said, "The snitch told me that the new girls belong to one unknown pimp from the Apple. We, the whole squad, must make it a priority to stop and check every strange black male who fits the pimp profile. I mean, whether he walks or rides the boulevard in a pimpmobile."

Crane shook his head. "Russ, if it's true, the guy's a wizard. He's controlling fifteen to twenty girls. I'm in constant high risk of my old lady controlling me."

Rucker smiled. "Yes, the fact that our undercover guys have been buffaloed indicates a master pimp in charge." Rucker sighed. "Leo, we're in large trouble."

The wagon cruised past a cluster of new girls at Havenhurst, posed languidly, like slick magazine models, in rhinestoned near-bikinis.

"Russ, those brazen bitches are an insult to all vice cops. I'm going to celebrate when we drive them out."

"I'll join you, Leo, and let's hope it's soon," Rucker said as he swiveled his head to stare at a handsome black dude driving a jazzed-up orchid Continental. "You see that, Leo?"

"Yeah. The next time I see him, I'll stop him."

A block away, Crane left-turned off Sunset into Rucker's street. In the middle of the block, Crane pulled the wagon into the driveway of Rucker's home.

After the luggage had been unloaded, Rucker and Crane drank beer in the den. They watched a few minutes of the late news on TV. The segment focusing on the Sunset hookers working the car tricks came on, to open with the question: "Where are the police?"

Rucker snorted and lunged from his chair to turn off the set. Crane rose from the couch. "Well, Russ, I guess I'll get back to hooker land." Rucker followed him to the front door. "Good night, Russ."

"Good night. See you," Rucker said as Crane opened the door and stepped into the quiet darkness. Rucker closed the door and chained it. He went across the living room, with its ancient mahogany furniture, to the staircase. He slowly ascended it. He smiled, remembering how he used to race up it when he was growing up in the old house. He reached the top of the stairs. He stood in the blue moonglow beaming through a stained-glass window in the hallway. The windows' snowy lace curtains reminded him of his mother. He remembered following in her crisply starched, fragrant wake as a little kid. He sniffed the air for a scent of his father's pipe that had lingered for two decades in the hallway. He felt a sense of excruciating loss, and a pang of loneliness, as he moved down the hallway to his bedroom.

He stepped into his bedroom and sat on the side of the wide brass bed. He removed his jacket and hung it on a bedpost. He took off his shoes and lay down across the blue-quilted bed. Finally, he drifted into ragged sleep, tormented by a grinning pimp and the rhinestoned hellions on Sunset Boulevard.

Less than a mile away, on Sunset, Lovely Leon sipped a shake beneath a colorful umbrella at an outdoor table. Leon eye-swept the circular counter of the open-air sandwich joint through dark glasses. It was crowded with tourist squares, gays, several hookers, and a few johns comparison-shopping the hookers.

A middle-aged white man in a rumpled seersucker suit ambled toward Leon's lair near the sidewalk. "Psst!" Leon hissed as the target came abreast. The mark halted on the busy sidewalk and gazed down at the explosion of phony fire on the zircon-encrusted dial of the watch in Leon's palm.

"Everybody's business ain't nobody's business, Mr. Brother Man. So ease outta traffic and sit down, and look at a bargain you ain't never gonna see again if you live to be a hundred."

The mark hesitated. Leon leaned and pulled him down beside him by his coat sleeve. A police car approached slowly. "Now, be cool and act natural, mister, like we salt-and-pepper buddies, 'cause this piece ain't hot in L.A."

The cop car cruised by them. The mark took the watch to examine it. He sighed. "It's a pretty thing, all right, but I'm afraid I can't afford it." The mark put it against his wrist and stared at the fireworks ignited by the bright lights. "How much?"

Leon patted the mark's wrist. "Gimme two bills, and you know jus' the gold is probably worth that."

"I'm sure I don't have more than a hundred or so in cash. Guess I'll have to let it go."

Leon snatched the watch off the mark's wrist and shoved it into his shirt pocket. "Gimme the C-note! Hurry up, before I change my mind!"

The mark took the watch from his shirt pocket to scrutinize it again, especially the 24-karat stamping on the back. He counted out the hundred in tens, fives, and singles. He shook hands with Leon to close the deal and happily faded into the sidewalk traffic.

Tuta, watching and carrying a Coke, paused to glance down at the pile of bills in Leon's palm before seating herself at a table next to his. She was sexy in candy-striped short shorts. She leaned her nearly nude bosom toward him. "Say, Babio, how about having some fun?" she said with her New York accent.

Leon shoved the bills into his pocket and grinned. "How much, Miss Black America?"

She frowned. "My name is Tuta, and what do you wanta do?"

Leon finger-stroked his crotch. "I'll go for some cap if it's righteous."

"For a short time, it's fifty for the best in Hollywood."

Leon stood up. "Let's take care of business in my car, in back of the joint."

They went to the small parking lot and entered Leon's old Cadillac. He stared at an odd tattoo—"Shetani"—defacing the inner surface of one of Tuta's thighs.

He pointed. "What's that on that fine thigh, girl?"

She frowned. "Shetani—that's my boss. Now, let's take care of business." She extended a hand.

He counted the fee into her palm, which she shoved into a boot top. He noticed the bulges of other fees in her boot as he unzipped to free his blood-bloated organ. Within several minutes, he bellowed and bucked in climax.

"Don't forget where you got it, Babio," the hooker said as she opened the car door.

Leon seized her left arm. He twisted it up near her shoulder blade. He slammed her face down on the seat to muffle her scream. "Bitch, I'll break your motherfucking arm if you make a sound," he snarled as his left hand ripped off the cache of bills in her boot.

He pitched her through the open door onto the ground. She slid on her hipbone and lay stunned for a moment. Leon bombed the Caddie into the adjacent alley as the hooker struggled to her feet. She staggered to the alley and saw the Caddie turn into a side street and disappear. Her dollish face was grim as she went to a bank of telephones.

High in the Hollywood Hills, swimsuited Shetani sipped champagne in rainbow light at poolside. His rented white stone mansion gleamed like an alabaster palace in the moonlight.

The Brooks twins, on short street break, frolicked in the pool like pygmy whales. Tuta's call jingled the phone near Petra, seated across the table from Shetani. She picked up the receiver and purred "Hello," thinking it was a trick calling.

"Calm yourself, Tuta. Here he is," she said as she gave Shetani the receiver. His perpetual poker face became fearsome with rage as he listened.

"Tut, lay there until the twins get there to help you look for the mother." He threw the receiver across the tabletop. Petra cradled it. He screamed at the twins.

"Get over here!"

They swam to him, with their cruel, hooded eyes upturned.

"Tut's been heisted and roughed up. She's waiting for you at that foot-long-hot-dog joint on Sunset. Find him!"

They got out of the pool and stood beside him. "How do you want him handled if we catch him?" Eli asked.

"Ice him!" Shetani exclaimed. The twins turned and walked away.

Petra was surprised and upset to see him so emotional in the face of such a common street happening. After all, she thought, Tuta wasn't dead, just bruised a bit.

She said, "Wait a moment," to the twins' backs as she placed a hand on Shetani's wrist. "Say, Daddy, I like Tuta a lot, and I've got a hooker's empathy for her . . . but don't you think that killing some mugger jerk is maybe too extreme? I mean, Master, is he worth the heat?"

The twins walked back to the table. The strange look on Petra's face tipped Shetani that he had overreacted. He said, "I get so fucking mad when somebody fucks over any one of my ho's I want to bury the bastard. But just beat the bloody shit out of this one and engrave his face with a knife if you find him. He's black, with a beat-up gold Cadillac. Cruise the South Central ghetto after you comb Hollywood."

The twins nodded and hurried away. Petra stood. "Master, may I take a little nap before I hit the streets?"

He dipped his head. She walked away.

He felt suddenly chilled. He covered his shoulders with a terry robe and remembered that look on Petra's face when the Tuta call had blown his cool. His head ached. He massaged his temples. He had felt off-base all day. He took a dope kit from his robe pocket and shot a load of skag. He stiffened at the distant sound of an ambulance siren.

Shetani glanced at his watch. Today was August 20! He closed his eyes. He remembered how, on this date thirty years before, he had taken a running start and shoved his slut mother through an open window.

His eyes popped open. He looked nervously behind him. He wished that she wouldn't show, to bug him, as she had every year since her death. He cocked his head. Was that her whiskey voice croaking obscenities?

"Albert, only a piece of shit like you would kill his mama. You're gonna pay, asshole."

It was her voice, clear and hateful. He spun around in every direction to see her. He stared into the pool. He recoiled when her crushed head, oozing blood and brain, popped to the surface only eight feet away. Its hellish eyes glared through the gore. Its purple tongue whipped out at him.

He screamed in an adolescent voice, "Mama, get out of my face! Go away, Mama!"

The terrible head bobbed in the water and tilted back in maniacal laughter. Shetani scrambled to his feet, shaking like a Parkinson's victim. He ran for the house, glancing fearfully over his shoulder.

8

The Brooks twins and Tuta, in a black van, searched West and East Hollywood for Leon and his gold Cadillac. Finally, driver Eli said, "He ain't in Hollywood."

Cazo mumbled, "Naw, I guess not. Let's try the ghetto."

Eli grunted, abruptly pulled the van to the curb, and parked on North Western Avenue.

"Say, man, why you stop here?" Cazo exclaimed.

Eli said, "'Cause you gonna drive some." He slid from the van to the street. Cazo moved over to take the wheel. He pulled away when Eli got in and sandwiched Tuta between them. Cazo drove south on Western toward South Central L.A. At Western and Sunset, several of Tuta's stablemates gave a finger-to-the-chin signal to the troubleshooting twins that they were okay.

Several blocks south, Tuta shouted, "There's his ride!" She excitedly pointed at Leon's car, parked in a grocery-market lot. Cazo turned into it and parked next to Leon's Caddie.

Tuta pointed toward a group of telephone booths. "There he is, using the phone."

Eli took a blackjack and a wide roll of masking tape from beneath the seat as Tuta scrambled over the seat to conceal herself.

"Bro, you need my help with that nigger?" Cazo asked.

Eli smiled and shook his head. "Unlock the hood." He got out and quickly masked the van's license numbers with tape before he raised the hood.

Inside the phone booth, Leon was concluding a long conversation with his mother, Sadie. He had stopped at the market to buy her a C-note money order. He did this to relieve his guilt for his neglect of Sadie, and for the long-term misery his recent prison bit had caused her.

Cazo stuck his head under the hood of the van when he saw Leon leave the booth. He let Leon pass him and open the Caddie's door. He sprang and smashed the blackjack down on the top of Leon's skull. Leon collapsed silently to the concrete between the two vehicles.

Eli knelt beside him and cleaned out his pockets of all cash and slum jewelry. He ripped off Leon's pants and underwear. Leon stirred as Eli, with a switchblade, carved a gaping bloody "X" on his forehead. Eli stood and systematically kicked the prostrate form from head to ankles. He then went to slam the van's hood down as gawkers gathered at the scene.

Cazo shot the van away to a nearby alley, and parked. Eli peeled off two hundred from Leon's roll and gave it to Tuta. "Here's yours, Toot, and you can split back to work. Look out for the green van, 'cause we gonna switch this one out for a while."

Tuta shoved the bills very deep into her boot. She kissed the twins' cheeks and left the van. She stripped the tape from the plates. The van roared away as she turned and walked toward the boulevard.

It was a week to the day after Leon received his awful lumps for the Tuta caper that Rucker sat in his kitchen, sipping his morning coffee. His smooth forehead was ridged as he finished reading a scathing article in the *L.A. Times.* The paper editorialized that a hooker horde had apparently defeated the police in the war on Sunset Boulevard.

Rucker felt a flash of hot pain in his gut that popped out sweat on his palms and brow. He held his breath for a long moment and hoped it wasn't a flare-up of an old ulcer condition. It had nearly killed him when he was up against robbers and killers in the super-stressful 77th Division in South Central L.A.

He leaned back and closed his eyes against the splash of dazzling sun on the breakfast-nook tabletop. He thought, what a rotten turn of fate's cards that, within a few weeks, he and his task force had fallen from heroes to horses' asses, in the media and public opinion. He remembered that he was fifty-two, with retirement in mind at the end of the year. He gritted his teeth. He couldn't retire until he won the war on Sunset. He told himself he would die before he left the scene dishonorably. He had minutely inspected undercover vehicles and had not solved the riddle of how the wave of new hookers made his undercover guys.

Frustration and anger ached his head. He got to his feet, stooped and feeling ancient. He realized it instantly and straightened his spine. He went briskly to his bedroom to dress for the street.

A pang of Opal need raced his heart for an instant. He was removing his pajamas when the phone rang. It was Leon's mother, Sadie. She said that Leon was fresh out of County Hospital. He had massive injuries and was recuperating at her place in South Central L.A. Would Rucker come to get some very important information?

Within an hour, Rucker parked in front of Sadie's modest wood-frame house on Martin Luther King Boulevard. He saw a flutter of lace curtain as he walked to the front door. It was swung open before he could push the doorbell button. White-haired, heavily wrinkled Sadie greeted Rucker with a wide smile and a hug.

"Mr. Rucker, it's sure good to see you again, lookin' so well. Praise the Lord!"

Rucker kissed her cheek. "Bless you, Sadie, and I'm happy to see you again."

Sadie led him through the well-kept living room to a hallway. "Leon's room is on the right. He's waiting for you."

Rucker walked to the rear bedroom, which had been Leon's since boyhood. Rucker lightly rapped his knuckles on the half-opened door.

"Come in, Sergeant," Leon said weakly.

Rucker entered the small room, its walls decorated with plaques and trophies awarded for Leon's excellence in athletics.

"Hi, man," Leon said as he dipped his bandaged head toward a chair at the foot of the bed.

Rucker sat down and stared at Leon. His broken right arm and hand and his right leg were in casts.

"You have a rumble with the Crips?" Rucker said as he shook his head.

Leon laughed. "No. A robber did this."

Rucker pressed. "That's tough . . . Any tie-in with the info Sadie told me you had for me?"

Leon swallowed hard. "I don't believe so . . . but I know the dude's moniker that owns all them untouchable new ho's in Hollywood." Pain deformed Leon's face as he shifted in the bed.

"Well, Leon, lay the moniker on me, and anything else you know about him and the girls."

Leon leaned and half whispered, "The dude's moniker is 'Shetani.' That's 'S-h-e-t-a-n-i.' I'm cinch sure, 'cause I over-heard two of his bitches rappin' about him."

Rucker's face twisted in disgust. "Leon, are you saying the girls spelled out that name for you, an eavesdropper? Leon, you're either full of shit or brain-damaged."

Leon shifted his eyes to the ceiling. "Well, I was, uh, kind of ashamed to tell you how I really caught the dude's moni-ker."

Rucker leaned and patted Leon's leg cast. "You can trust me with the truth. Tell it!"

Leon licked his chops. "Well, about a week ago, I woke up with a hard-on a cat couldn't scratch without rippin' out his claws. Shit, I had to chill on Miss Five Fingers and buy some sure-enough pussy for the first time in my life, and that ain't no lie. I went to . . ."

Rucker's booming laughter cut him off. "You're funny, you jive-ass would-be pimp. Go on."

Leon winced as he scooted up on his pillows. "I laid a Big Apple ho in my ride, finer than Prince's Apollonia. I dug the

Shetani tattoo on her thigh. She cracked that it was the name of her boss. My jones fell soft after I paid her and stayed that way. I guess 'cause I knew I was violatin' the pimp code. She got up to split when I wouldn't come up with more bread for her time. So I just snatched my bread outta her boot and split."

Rucker said, "I'll buy the general outline of that story, but your robber tale stinks. You must be six five and two fifty. I find it hard to believe there's a robber in L.A. with the balls and muscle to heist you and bust you up like this. C'mon, now, how many jumped you, and why? I suspect your beating is connected to that hooker you refunded on. Well?"

Leon raised his good arm and waggled his palm in the air. "Sergeant, I swear it was just one motherfucker. I never saw his face, 'cause he had it stuck under the hood of a black van. He KO'd me with a sap or piece of pipe. He cleaned me out and did this number on me. And all of that ain't no lie."

Rucker said, "What else do you know about Shetani and his girls?"

Leon sneezed into a tissue. "A slum hustler like me from New York told me the dude and all his girls is dope fiends . . . He's got a lavender-and-gold ride, and he . . ."

A bullet of red-hot pain spasmed Rucker's gut. Rucker's suddenly reddened face and harsh expression stalled Leon's voice.

"Hey, Sergeant, why you lookin' so evil?"

Rucker despised all breeds of pimps. But the breed that hooked young girls on heroin to enslave them, Rucker hated with an all-consuming passion.

Rucker regained his composure. "I've got a bit of a stomach problem, Leon. Do you know anything else?"

Leon lit a cigarette. "Nothing, except I was gonna say he's a tall blue-black dude with green cat eyes."

Rucker stood. "Thanks, Leon. And I wish you a fast recovery and the best in every other way." They shook hands.

As Rucker left the room, Leon said, "I'll be up and out on them streets on crutches in a few days. I'll hip you to any info I get on Shetani and his ho's."

Over his shoulder Rucker said, "Leon, I'll appreciate that." He was at the end of the hallway when he barely heard Leon say, "Come here, Sergeant, I just remembered somethin' else."

Rucker came back to stand in the bedroom's open doorway.

"Sergeant, that slum hustler from the Apple pointed out a stallion snow-blonde who is Shetani's bottom bitch. Her name is Petra, and she's a stone fox."

The Petra info brightened Rucker's deep-blue eyes. "She's a fox in more than the obvious sense. I and half a dozen of my cops have tried to bust her. Can you recall anything else, Leon?"

Leon rolled his eyes toward the ceiling and drummed the fingers of his able hand against the leg cast for a long moment. "That's all I heard, Sergeant," he said with a sigh.

"Thanks again, son. I hope to see you on the boulevard soon," Rucker said as he turned and strolled away.

When Rucker reached Hollywood Station, he was both relieved and furious after getting Leon's finger on Shetani. Rucker regarded Shetani as the enemy of his reputation, pride, and self-respect as the leader of the now maligned Special Hooker Squad.

Rucker immediately called a friend in NYPD Vice to get Shetani's real name and rap record. Rucker also got the details of Albert Spires's commitment to the facility for the criminally insane, when, in grief and rage, he had inflicted multiple mayhem upon members of the staff of the hospital where Tuta died of leukemia.

Rucker took the data into Lieutenant Edwin Bleeson's office, the commander of detectives.

"Sit down, Russell, and share the good news with me," Bleeson boomed, with a toothy smile on his caveman's face.

Rucker placed the Shetani data on the desk as he sat down on a chair beside Bleeson's desk.

"Lieutenant, the good news is that I've ID'd the boss of that stable of seemingly arrest-immune hookers who've been giving us all an ass ache. The bad news is that he's a junkie and certified crazy. He'll froth at the mouth when we come down on him—six arrests on suspicion of Murder One . . . went to bat after three of them . . . got acquitted. It's all there, Lieutenant."

Bleeson shook his head as he scanned the pages of the arrest record for other crimes, including burglary, robbery, extortion, attempted murder, assault, pandering, and arson of an inhabited building.

Bleeson shoved the pages toward Rucker. "Russell, he's a volatile cookie, for sure. I don't have to tell you to take every precaution when you bear down on Albert Spires. I'll cajole and con to get you any extra personnel needed to stop him and his operation."

Rucker stood and took the data back from the desktop. "Thanks, Lieutenant. I needed that," Rucker said as they shook hands.

"Keep me updated on this investigation, Russell," Bleeson said as he stood and banged Rucker's shoulder with a beefy paw.

Rucker turned away and left the room.

A moment after leaving Bleeson's office, Rucker left the building and nearly collided with Leo Crane on his way in. Rucker grabbed Crane's coat sleeve as he waved at Crane's wife, driving away in Crane's station wagon. Had he really seen a bluish bruise on Millie's cheek, just below the rim of dark sunglasses? No, Rucker thought, it had merely been an illusion of afternoon sun and shadow.

"Say, buddy, I'm glad I bumped into you. Let's go to the Chinaman's."

Crane smiled stingily and stepped back. "Thanks, Russ, but I just ate at home, and I've got to pick up an arrest report I left in the briefing room . . . Maybe we can make the China-man's together later in the week."

Rucker's twinkling eyes, and the rare expression of seren-ity on his otherwise uptight face since the Shetani invasion, surprised and threatened Crane.

"Leo, I have big news, so get the report and at least have tea at the Chinaman's."

Crane seized Rucker's hand and shook it. "You sonuva-gun! You and Opal are going to get married after all."

Rucker shook his head. "No, Leo. Nothing close to that dream with your aunt yet. We have to talk about this news. I'll wait for you in the car."

Crane nodded and went into the building. Rucker went to his Lincoln, parked nearby.

On the way to the restaurant, Rucker told Crane about Leon's beating and his visit to his home. Within five minutes,

Rucker and Crane sat down in a red leather booth at the rear of the restaurant on Hollywood Boulevard. A black couple were the only other patrons in the dimly lit stillness.

A sweet-faced Chinese waitress took Rucker's order for his three-times-a-week favorite, egg foo yung. Crane ordered tea and fidgeted.

"An hour ago, I ID'd the ass kicker who controls our problem hookers. Of course, after Leon supplied his moniker."

Crane managed to smile. "That's great, Russ. Who is he?"

Rucker leaned forward. "His moniker is Shetani. That's Swahili for 'Satan.' He has lived up to that tag in New York since his early teens as Albert Spires. He did a stint in the nuthouse, and his arrest record includes Murder One and arson. We've got to hit this bad sonuvabitch and his whores soon and hard."

Crane fought to control the muscles of his face from twitching with Rucker's face so close. "Any idea as to our point of attack, Russ? Maybe he's got outstanding warrants at the New York State or federal level."

Rucker shook his head. "I checked. He's clean . . . Point of attack? Any pimp with a stable that big is bound to have a sour defectee on the turn down the road. Maybe she'll help us make a pandering case against him. He and his stable are all junkies. After we find out where he lives, et cetera, perhaps we can nail him on heroin possession. This guy's setup is vulnerable to a number of points of attack."

Rucker took a sip of water. "I also found out the identity of Shetani's bottom whore. Guess who?"

There was a long silence as Crane closed his eyes to conceal his shock. Crane opened his eyes and said, "Is she a blonde?"

"Yeah," Rucker said. "That's Petra, that statuesque snow-blonde with the aristocratic bearing who none of us can bust."

Crane stiffened and felt a familiar nausea in his belly pit. He knew that always signaled a panic attack. He knew he'd feel terror that death was imminent or that he would lose control of his mind and become a raving lunatic. His head roared so loudly he had to half read Rucker's lips as he went on.

"The lieutenant will give us the extra personnel to kick off a comprehensive investigation. For now, Leo, we have to discover our best point of attack."

Crane's face glowed like a phosphorescent mask in the gloom as he stood up. "Yeah, Russ, it looks good for us for a change. Excuse me," Crane said before he moved away for the restroom, past the waitress coming with their orders.

Crane went into a toilet stall and locked the door. He collapsed to his knees, his heart galloping madly from the terror of dying. He rested his head on the toilet seat and vomited until his guts dry-locked. He clung to the toilet-bowl base for the three minutes the attack lasted. He struggled to his feet. He went to rinse his face with cold water. He snorted coke and squared his shoulders. He inhaled and exhaled deeply several times before he stepped out into the cozy murk of the restaurant. He went to the table and sat down. He managed somehow to calmly sip his tea, chitchat, and watch Rucker devour his favorite food.

Rucker dropped Crane back at the station in time to begin his newly assigned 3:00-to-11:00-p.m. shift. He drove from the station lot toward the downtown criminal-courts building. He remembered the night he arrested Pee Wee Smith, the thieving hooker. He thought about the insane eyes of her slain New York pimp, Big Cat Jackson.

Rucker parked his car and entered the criminal-courts building. He went into a courtroom where the coroner's inquest into Big Cat's death was to be held. The hearing officer made brief orientation remarks about the case to four women and three men drawn from the county jury pool to hear witnesses.

Rucker and several neighbors who had seen the entire scenario gave brief testimony. The hearing officer declared the death of Jackson as justifiable homicide.

Rucker left the courtroom with a vision of the Jackson shooting haunting him all the way back to Hollywood. He was then bothered by the high degree of discord in Crane's normally harmonious and fluid body lingo in the restaurant. And there was the possibility that the bruise on the cheek of Crane's wife, Millie, was real, rather than a trick of light and shadow. Then he thought the unthinkable. Was Crane in such a tensioned state that he would beat up Millie?

Rucker drove the Lincoln down the street where the Cranes resided. A block away from their house, he spotted Millie, in a bright-red halter dress, watering the lawn.

He parked in front of the house. Millie glanced at him through dark glasses, over her shoulder, as he left the car. He approached her.

"Hi, Russ," she said, too cheerfully, and moved away.

He pursued her as he said, "How are you, Millie?" He faced her and saw she had a blackened left eye socket and a lumpy bruise on her left cheek.

"I'm all right, Russ," she mumbled, and averted her eyes. "How about a glass of lemonade," she said in a breaking voice as she dropped the hose and moved quickly toward the front door.

Rucker followed. He paused to turn off the water hose at the front of the house before he entered the living room.

He sat on the sofa for a moment before she brought two glasses of lemonade on a tray. She placed the tray on a coffee table before them, and sat beside him. They took a sip of lemonade.

"Millie, you've always been able to talk to me. What's wrong?" he said gently.

She threw her plump but tiny hands into the air. "Everything!" she cried out, and burst into tears.

Rucker took her into his arms. "Easy, now. Control yourself. Tell me about everything. You'll feel better."

Sobbing racked her for a long moment before she blubbered, "Leo hates me because I'm fat and ugly. He ignores me and screams at me for the smallest things. He's fooling around with someone."

Rucker rubbed her back. "Oh, Millie, please, don't let your imagination run wild. You and Leo are strong Catholics. He loves you, Millie. You're wrong. Leo is just job-stressed and off-center. All cops get frazzled occasionally. I'm sure this unhappiness is temporary."

She stubbornly shook her head. "I tell you he's involved with another woman and my misery is permanent," she uttered, in a voice so full of despair that Rucker was jolted.

"How can you be sure about another woman?" he asked softly.

She leapt to her feet and wrung her hands. "Now, look, your precious Leo is guilty, whether you can accept it or not. I found lipstick stains on his clothes." She ripped off her sunglasses, pointed to her bruises, and exclaimed, "He did this because he's guilty and I told him so."

Rucker stood. "Millie, Leo has physical contact with women suspects all the time. On occasion, he struggles with them before making arrests."

She heehawed hysterically and clapped her hands. "Very good! You'd say anything to defend your friend."

Rucker moved toward the open front door. "Millie, you're too upset today to reason with. I'll call you later in the week," he said firmly.

He went down the walkway to enter his car. She followed and stuck her head inside. "I didn't say exactly where the filthy slut he's got left those lipstick stains."

Rucker said wearily, "Where, Millie?"

She spat it out. "On the fly of his trousers and on his underwear."

Rucker leaned in to pat her wrists. "Please, Millie, stop tearing yourself apart. I'm on your side."

She burst into fresh tears and half whispered, "I will . . . but Leo is on an express train to hell, Russ. I'll show you. I'll be right back." She turned and hurried into the house.

In a moment, she returned. She held out a plastic syringe and a glassine bag in her palm. Rucker took it and stuck an index finger into the nearly empty glassine bag. He touched his tongue to his finger. He said, "It's coke. Where did you find this?"

She said, "I was cleaning out the closet. It was in the toe of one of Leo's shoes."

Rucker said, "He's been shooting coke . . . Let's keep my visit with you today just between us, okay?"

She nodded.

He said, "Put this back in the shoe, and don't say anything about it."

She took it and said, "I won't," and turned away.

. . .

Rucker pulled the Lincoln down the street. His face was a hard mask of determination as he drove toward Hollywood Station.

He would turn the Crane case over to Bleeson and the department Division of Internal Affairs. He pulled his car into the station lot and keyed off the engine. He sat watching young uniformed cops and detectives entering and exiting the building. He felt a pang of sympathy for Crane and Millie. He remembered the brilliant summer day, twelve years before, when the rookie detective Leo Crane was assigned to the 77th Division in South Central L.A. He had liked Crane immediately. A month later, the green youngster became his partner. He had admired his courage, intelligence, and absolute honesty. He was sure it was a friendship that would last forever when both of them were transferred to Hollywood Division.

Rucker rolled up the car's windows, got out, and locked it. Like his father, he had faithfully followed the department's rules and procedures from the start of his career.

Now he moved into the building and walked toward Bleeson's office. He told himself that he couldn't let his affection for Crane interfere with his duty and responsibility as an honest, by-the-book cop.

He halted ten feet from Bleeson's office at a water cooler. He stood there trembling, staring at Bleeson's name stenciled on his office door. "Leo, you dumb sonuvabitch!" he screamed in a whisper. Suddenly he remembered his raging love for Opal Lenski, Crane's aunt. He knew there was a fifty-fifty chance they would marry one day. He couldn't throw Crane to the wolves of Internal Affairs.

Rucker almost visibly recoiled when the gargantuan Bleeson popped out of his office.

"Good afternoon, Russell. Did you want to see me?" he said as he paused in front of Rucker.

"No, Lieutenant, I'm getting a refill," Rucker said lightly as he bent over to drink from the fountain.

Bleeson smiled and went down the corridor. Rucker immediately left the station. He drove to an agency whose rental cars were mostly in the older-but-roadworthy category. He left his Lincoln on the lot and drove away in a '76 dark-blue Buick sedan. He parked it in his garage.

He put on his house slippers and sat down in shirtsleeves in his living-room recliner. At twilight, he had decided how he would address himself to the explosive Crane turn of events. He would surveil Crane himself. Hopefully, he thought as he remembered Crane's almost empty coke bag, he would catch him dead-bang dirty after he scored. Then he could force him, under an assumed name, to kick his coke addiction on an outpatient basis at one of the rehab centers.

Rucker heaved a sigh. Bypassing Bleeson and Internal Affairs would be risky to the extreme. He realized that, if detected in his role, he would face disgrace and the destruction of his career and reputation. He also realized that coke banger Crane would be unpredictable and difficult to protect, and to free from his coke trap.

He went upstairs to shower and dress for the street. He covered his silvery mop with one of his father's old golf caps. He drove down Sunset, determined to help his friend no matter what the risk.

9

It was a balmy summer night in Milwaukee, Wisconsin. Disgusted, Pee Wee Smith had not taken off a good score since her arrival. She was trick poison in a skintight red mini-dress and matching high heels. Her huge sable eyes flashed in her cute face as they sought connection with drivers of cars moving past her. She had turned a few white tricks, working the perimeter of the black ghetto. But she was a superstar of pocket larceny and didn't like to screw for her money.

She stopped for coffee in a café, deserted except for a waitress, to rest her aching feet. She was on her second cup when she heard the door open behind her. She sensed a presence near her back. She started to turn her head. She was startled and then surprised by a high-yellow trick trapper.

"Guess who?" the girl said in a reedy voice as she placed her palms over Pee Wee's eyes.

"Oh, shoot, Bianca, who else but you with that rapper," Pee Wee said as she slapped her hands away.

Bianca laughed and sat down beside Pee Wee at the counter. The waitress took her order for coffee.

"Girl, how long have you been in this lousy boondock?" Pee Wee asked as she eye-swept Bianca's curves, sausaged in white blouse and short shorts.

"Two weeks too long. I'm splitting back to the city and Daddy this week."

Pee Wee leaned toward her to say something, but she didn't until the approaching waitress delivered Bianca's coffee and departed.

"I haven't stung for any respectable bread since I came here three days ago. How about you?"

Bianca darted a glance at a pair of black teenagers who stopped to ogle the girls through the café's plate glass.

"One fair sting is all I took off," Bianca replied as the boys moved on.

They sipped coffee and smoked cigarettes in a long silence before Bianca looked at her watch. She put coins on the counter and stood.

"Wee, it's nice to run into you. I got to split to turn what's gotta be the only C-note trick on this side of town. Be careful, Wee."

"It was good to see you, Bianca. Good luck," Pee Wee said as Bianca turned and went to the sidewalk.

Pee Wee placed a dollar on the counter. She freshened her makeup in a compact mirror. She left the café and walked toward the trick run at a busy intersection down the street.

"Hey, Wee, wait!"

Pee Wee stopped and turned to see Bianca hurrying down the sidewalk toward her.

"Wee, that C-note trick of mine carries heavy bread. I

can't take it off alone—he keeps his wallet pocket locked with safety pins. It hit me after I split that you could creep on him while he sucks my pussy. You in?"

"What kinda dude is he, and what kinda bread is he luggin'?" Pee Wee said, with eyes asparkle.

He's a sixtyish German ex-con thug and stickup man who owns a plumbing business. I admit cracking his pants safe ain't to be considered a piece of cake. He keeps a dagger on his leg. But, shit, he's gotta have six to eight grand in that leather. Wee, let's try the motherfucker. Fifty-fifty."

Pee Wee took her arm. "Let's go," she said, and she and Bianca hurried down the street.

They entered a sparsely furnished kitchenette off an alley a block away. Bianca glanced at her watch. "We've got a few minutes before he shows."

Pee Wee looked about the room. "Where does he put his pants?"

Bianca tossed her head toward a battered couch near the foot of the four-poster brass bed. They sat on the side of the bed.

"Is that closet crowded?" Pee Wee asked as she stared at the closet door to the left of the couch.

"It's empty. This is just a trick crib. I live in a hotel. Girl, I'm sorry about Big Cat . . . Is Shetani treating you right?"

A frown flicked across Pee Wee's face. "Yeah, sure." She paused to laugh. "I've been sending him long bread. So, naturally, he sweet-talks on the phone and keeps my medicine comin' on time." She went on, "I'm gonna be his bottom woman. That's gotta be any day. He's gonna fire that white bitch Petra, if he ain't already. He copped me on that promise."

Bianca said, "That's great, Wee."

Pee Wee got up and went into the bathroom. She looked at an open window above the commode. She would be able to slide through it to the alley in a flash, she thought.

"Nice big split window for us, ain't it, Wee?" Bianca said.

Pee Wee placed a hand on the teenager's shoulder. "Bianca, I ain't tryin' to be hipper than you or nothin', but I'm twenty-eight and been on the fast track since I was fifteen. Keep your body and voice loose when I creep on the sucker. Otherwise, he could wake up . . ."

She reached into her bosom and took out a tiny .22-caliber automatic. Pee Wee went on, "I don't give up no sting bread, and I don't wanna shoot no white man in Wisconsin. So, baby, please be cool and loose. I'll know his head is between your legs when you moan. By the way, you can split out the door after me if he goes to the bathroom. I'll meet you at Third and Vine to lay your end of the score on you."

Bianca said, "Don't worry, Wee. I'll play it right."

Pee Wee concealed herself in the closet.

Shortly, the elderly trick arrived, with suck lust aglitter in his blue eyes.

"Sweetie Franz, I got so hot waiting for you, I can fry an egg on my pussy," Bianca crooned as she extended her palm.

He placed a C-note bill in it and dropped his massive frame onto the couch.

"Yah, I'm very hot myself. How is your mudder?"

She bent to kiss the top of his graying blond head. "She was fine when I stopped by after I finished cleaning for one of my ladies in Whitefish Bay."

She sat on the foot of the bed, facing him, and slipped off her short shorts. She jackknifed her legs to display her pouted vulva, nesting in a curly jungle of auburn bush.

Excitement daubed his pale cheeks crimson as he ripped off his shoes and hooked his eyes to her lure. He tore off his shirt and pants. He threw them on the couch. He uttered a guttural cry and crawled on his hands and knees to bury his head between her thighs.

She seized the back of his head and held it tightly against her. She fucked his face and moaned.

Pee Wee eased from the closet on her belly. She wiggled her way to the back of the couch. She got to her knees and hand-swept the couch for his pants. She located them. She peeped over the top of the couch for an instant to see precisely how they lay before she took them.

Her fingers worked rapidly to unfasten the four safety pins that secured the flap of the payoff pocket. She took a bundle of C-notes from the wallet. She rolled the bills into a fat suppository. She used spit to lube it before she shoved it up her vaginal stash.

She replaced the wallet's cash with a wad of Kleenex before she replaced it and refastened the safety pins.

She returned the pants to their original spot and position on the couch. She moved toward the bathroom in a crouch below the level of the couch.

Bianca's moaning stopped. Pee Wee froze in Bianca's plain view. The trick had lifted his head to catch his breath.

"Oh, shit, Franz, don't stop now!" Bianca said as she looked into the trick's upturned face.

Still frozen like a statue, Pee Wee spewed sweat. Her heart was beating crazily. She couldn't stand there another moment. She crept like a cat toward the half-opened bath-room door.

The trick started to lower his head between Bianca's yellow thighs. At that instant, the trick caught Pee Wee's movement reflected in a brass bedpost.

He spun around on his knees and drew a hunting knife from a scabbard strapped to his leg. He cocked his head as he stared at the bathroom door.

Bianca managed to say calmly, "Sweetie, why you actin' like this? Come on and finish doin' your baby."

He leapt to his feet and bulled into the bathroom. He whirled back into the bedroom. Bianca was snatching up her shorts and shoes. She streaked for the door.

"You goddamn bitch!" he hollered as he lunged to block the door. He grabbed her wrist and hurled her across the room, onto the couch. He sat on her while he discovered his looted wallet.

"You and your lousy pimp set me up. Right? Take me to him now or I'll kill you," he screamed into her terrified face.

"All right. You'll get your money back. Don't kill me. I'll take you to him," she said in a fear-choked whisper.

He raised his bulk to free her body. He pressed the knife point against her throat as he tried to slip on his pants. "Don't you move!" he warned as he pulled up his pants with both hands.

In that instant, she leapt over the back of the couch and scrambled for the bathroom. He kicked over the couch and chased her with knife in hand. He tripped and fell heavily near the bathroom door. He stabbed her deeply into the flesh behind her kneecap as she darted inside and locked the door.

Crippled, she vainly tried to step up on the commode and escape through the window. The trick started to kick in the door. She stood in a widening pool of blood and screamed up at the open window.

"Wee! Wee! Help me!"

Pee Wee was just exiting the far end of the alley when she heard Bianca screaming. She stopped and stood still for a long moment, to make a very difficult decision.

Suddenly she kicked off her shoes. She took her gun from her bosom and raced to help Bianca.

The trick smashed in the door. In a frenzy of rage, he hacked and stabbed Bianca, who cowered in shock in a corner.

Pee Wee burst into the bedroom. The blood-spattered trick staggered into the room. Exhausted, he panted as he halted to stare balefully at Pee Wee.

"Bianca! Say something!" Pee Wee shouted.

"You're da fucking nigger dat took my money. Right?"

Pee Wee gritted her teeth and leveled the automatic on him. "Right, motherfucker! Now, drop that blade and get away from that door so I can check out my friend."

He grinned obscenely. "She's had it. Fuck your pea-shooter." He lunged for Pee Wee. The automatic spat sparklets of blue fire as she emptied it into his head and chest.

He crashed on his face a mere foot away from her. She went into the bathroom. She threw herself down on the bathroom floor beside Bianca's limp form. She opened her eyes. "Wee, call an ambulance and get in the wind. Send my mama my end of the score."

Pee Wee rushed to a telephone at the corner. She called the ambulance and went to her pad to pack her things. She had left the city within an hour.

At that moment, in Hollywood, Rucker watched Crane through binoculars. Crane nervously paced the drugstore parking lot where he frequently rendezvoused with Petra. He looked at his watch for the dozenth time. It was 10:15 p.m. She was fifteen minutes late with his bag of coke and his weekly payoff. After he soothed his nerves with coke, he would also need her body tonight, he thought.

Paranoid because of his restaurant ordeal with Rucker earlier in the day, he eye-swept passing vehicles and people on Sunset.

Rucker was parked on the crowded lot of a fast-food place across the street. He tensed inside his undercover Buick when Petra, adazzle in a gold minidress, entered the drugstore lot. She and Crane got into the squad's red Toyota. They went west on Sunset, followed by Rucker.

Crane made a right turn off Sunset onto the freeway on-ramp. He proceeded to a quiet motel in North Hollywood.

Rucker parked across the street. He watched Crane register before he took Petra into a ground-floor unit. Rucker sat immobile for several minutes. Anger and the shock of the situation maimed his cop's common sense. He was certain a coke banger like Crane wouldn't take Petra to a motel unless he or she was coke-dirty. He was also 90 percent sure that Crane was responsible for the Shetani stable's immunity to arrest by his squad.

He swung out of the Buick and actually crossed the street. He took two steps into the motel lot before common sense jolted him. He turned and hurried back to sit in the car.

Anger and the humid night made him feel red-hot. He mopped perspiration from his brow with a sleeve of his seersucker suit coat. He realized that he could have busted them with a ton of cocaine, and the possession charge couldn't stand past the preliminary hearing. He couldn't prove probable cause for an invasion of the room. Also, without a search warrant, illegal search and seizure would be a likely ruling.

No, he decided, he would have to alter his strategy with the Crane problem. Ninety-percent certainty that Crane was a squad traitor wasn't enough. He would devise a trap for Crane to prove him 100 percent guilty or innocent.

He pulled away for the station to brief the 11:00-p.m.-to-8:00-a.m. shift on Shetani.

Inside the motel room, shirtless Crane finished shooting coke into a vein. Petra sat fully clothed on the bed beside him.

"Don't you want me to hit you with a light one?" he said as he stroked the bluish veins on her forearm.

She jerked her arm away. She, the stone H-junkie, enjoyed an interior chuckle. "Hell, no! I just snort a little. I don't want to be a fuckin' dope fiend."

He said, "You forgot to give me something."

She took a five-hundred-dollar roll of bills from her bosom and held it in her fist. He held out his palm.

"I didn't really forget. Listen, baby, your candy account is almost four grand in the red. I've got orders from the boss to start deducting a grand a week from the payoff until it's paid."

He glared at her as he took the money. He shrugged his shoulders. "Massa's word is de law."

Her face flushed scarlet. "That's nasty cute, you racist prick," she hissed.

His fingers crawled up her inner thigh toward her sex nest.

"Leo, what is the important matter that you wanted to talk about?" she said as she clamped her thighs together.

He got to his feet and strolled the carpet for a moment.

"Well, uh, we're going to have to tighten up the security of our relationship . . . I, uh . . ."

His hesitancy made her paranoid. She crossed her legs and leaned back on her elbows before she cut him off.

"Say what! Why? What's going down, Leo?"

He stood in the blue heat of her eyes for several heartbeats. "Doll, nothing went down. I just think we should be more careful. Believe me, everything is super-normal."

She grimaced. "Hey, copper, what the fuck is super-normal?"

He forced a grin and sat down beside her. "All right. Here it is. I heard a rumor—I repeat, a rumor—that a citizens' group has hired a firm of private investigators to look into the vice situation in Hollywood." He paused to try for a light-hearted laugh that bombed her ears.

"So how do we deal with that shit, Leo?"

He went on. "We stop meeting every night. I'll tape any new squad license numbers and other info under the middle phone ledge inside the drugstore. I'll meet you every Saturday night, around eleven, at different motels to get my coke and payoff. What motel or any other item will be with the squad info. The main thing is to be always alerted for a tail anytime you're in the street. Got it?"

She studied him. She was certain he wasn't leveling with her. "Yeah. I got it," she said softly.

He leaned to suck her earlobe. "Take off your clothes, doll," he whispered.

She moved her head away. "Leo, I don't want to fuck tonight. How about settling for a blow job?"

He unzipped his pants and lay back on the bed. She knelt and attacked his organ with oral ferocity until he ejaculated.

Fearful and distrustful of Crane, Petra called Shetani to get permission to bring the stable home at 1:00 a.m. This was several hours earlier than usual. All the girls had been given bedtime shots of skag by 2:00 a.m. Shetani and Petra sat on a sofa in the redwood den of the mansion. She had just finished a detailed rundown of her motel tryst with Crane. She nervously watched purple-robed Shetani's face harden as she waited for his response.

Finally, he fractured the silence with a rumble of his basso-profundo voice. "Girl, it was a mistake to let you play me into pulling the girls off the track early. I see at least a couple grand blown away by bullshit."

He rumbled on, with his nightmare eyes mesmerizing her. "Bitch, you sounded so motherfucking shaky on the phone, I knew we had a legit problem. But, shit, it turns out you reacted like a dumb turnout with some cunt vibes off that sucker pig. If all you ho's get busted, I got the bankroll to raise everybody."

He leaned his brutish face close to hers. "You're supposed to be the toughest and strongest ho in the family. Don't you know, bitch, that they ain't gonna have no more guts than you got. When you shit your pants, they shit with you. We got a three-way hook in that pig's ass. Don't waste your time trying to read his mind, bitch. Read the license-plate numbers he gives you. I'll know you're hot when you get busted."

He stood up. He took a length of chain and a padlock off the fireplace ledge. He slapped the chain against his thigh. "Follow me. I'm gonna lock you up until noon tomorrow."

She fell to her knees and clasped her arms around his legs. She shrieked, "Oh, please, Master! Whip my ass, anything. I can't stand that tight place and that darkness! Please!"

He stooped and jerked her to her feet. "Follow me or I'll lock you up for the rest of the week."

Sobbing, she followed him down a hallway to a mahogany door. He swung it open. He flipped a light switch. They descended a stairway to the musky basement. A small cell with silver-and-red-painted bars shone eerily in the pale light. It had been constructed by a prior occupant of the mansion with a passion for bondage-and-discipline sex play.

"Please, Master, don't put me in there!" she wailed as he hooked an arm around her waist to half carry her into the cell.

He stepped out and slammed the door. He locked it with the chain and padlock. He stood staring at her. She moved close to the cell door. Her eyes were dry now, and her voice was clear and calm. "Master, I'm taking this from you. But I know this is unfair and you'll know when you think about it. I don't deserve this, after all I've endured for you. Think about it, Master."

He turned away and went up the staircase. She squatted to pee into a hole in the floor. Then she went to sit down on her bed, a slab of thick steel jutting from the concrete wall.

When Shetani reached the top of the stairs, he heard the ringing of the den phone. He hurried and picked up, to Pee Wee's troubled voice.

"Daddy, I'm in Chicago, at the airport. I took a nice order from a customer, but got a big hassle behind it . . ."

He cut in. "Say, girl, run it down. You—"

She cut him off: "I can't run it down on the phone. Daddy, I'm on the way to L.A. Bye!"

He stood in the middle of the floor, glaring at the receiver in his fist.

"Master, can I come in?" a sugary voice purred behind him.

He whirled around to tongue-lash the intruder. It was Tuta in the doorway, gazing at him with dreamy eyes. She wore see-through pink bikini panties and top.

He constructed a smile. "Hi, sugar, come in and listen to some music."

She smiled wickedly and came to him. He cradled the phone and hugged her. He froze as her fingertips stroked across his ass and then his testicles. He disengaged.

She gave him a look before she went to an old Seeburg jukebox. She pushed in the coin slot and punched on "You'll Never Find" by Lou Rawls. She sat down beside him and dropped her head into his lap. He squirmed, for he was naked beneath the robe. He could feel the pressure of her head against his scrotum. Her green eyes sparkled with guile and hot mischief as she looked up into his tense face.

"Master, do you think I'm sexy?" she said in a contralto whisper.

He nodded.

"Master, you won't get salty if I ask you something personal?"

"No," he croaked.

"Have you got a dick?"

He frowned. "Don't ask silly questions."

She rose out of his lap to press her shoulder against him. She giggled. "I'm serious. I touched your balls. I mean, I'm a curious bitch. I want to know whether my man's dick is sweet or sour, long or short, fat or skinny, ugly or pretty, or whatever. Is that unreasonable?"

His left cheek twitched. "Shut up, girl. You can't see or have my dick yet."

She moved away, her cute mouth petulant. "I'll work after the other girls come home. Please, let me suck it for just a couple of minutes," she begged.

He shook his head. "No, Tuta, not tonight."

She sprang to her feet. Her high-yellow cheeks were rosy with angry frustration. "If I had the right paint job, like Petra, I'm sure I could get it."

He stared at her until she averted her eyes. In a painful silence, he, the wizard rapper, discovered for the first time that he couldn't rap himself into control.

He fought against confiding in her the secret fact that she was his blood baby sister, returned to life—she'd think he was crazy, he thought.

He stood and kissed her forehead. "We're gonna have lots of fun together, Tuta. Now, go to bed and wake up sweet."

She brushed her lips against his mouth and giggled as she turned to leave.

He grabbed her arm and pulled her close. "What's so funny, girl?" he asked sternly.

She smiled. "You won't get salty?" He shook his head as they locked eyes. "I was thinkin', if you don't get me off soon, I'll find a nice street mailbox. I'll drop my bread in it and rub my pussy 'ginst it till I get off. Master, ain't that funny?"

He dropped his arms from around her waist. She wasn't smiling when she broke away and left the room.

10

Rucker dressed for work several mornings after he discovered Crane's intimate connection to Petra. He hadn't taken a drink since he left New York and had resumed attending AA meetings. He hadn't yet thought of a way to trap Crane. His difficulty in devising a plan of entrapment was due to his reluctance to use other cops in a plan. However, he was certain that very soon he would solve the problem, since his mind addressed it for most of his waking hours.

He left the house and drove down Sunset. He frowned to see a parade of half-naked hookers. They strutted beneath the bright early-September sun like vulgar birds with painted faces.

At a stoplight, he heard a familiar voice.

"Hi, Sergeant."

He turned his head toward Leon, under the wheel of his gold Caddie, stopped adjacent to his Lincoln. He was irritated that Leon had spoken to him with a passenger in his car. Unsmilingly, Rucker nodded at Leon as the light turned green.

Inside the Caddie, Leon turned off Sunset onto Western Avenue. "Rainbow, that was Sergeant Rucker, the only good cop I've ever knowed. He's the boss of the special ho squad in Hollywood," Leon said to his dwarfish companion.

"Well, bro, I guess you must know the only good cop alive," Rainbow said as he hunched bony shoulders inside his shocking-pink sports coat.

Leon pulled into a supermarket parking lot. Rainbow flashed his gold choppers in his flat black face as he tipped his sky-blue hat to an Arab woman pushing a grocery cart. She gave him a venomous look.

Leon parked. They got out and split up. They had fake Cartier wristwatches and phony diamond rings. They hustled the grocery shoppers for nearly a hundred bucks apiece net, in less than an hour. They got in the Caddie and emptied a pint bottle of 100-proof vodka.

As Leon drove down Sunset, Rainbow said, "Bro, downin' slum is great, but I ain't goin' to stop tryin' to cop a ho and pimp my ass off before I die."

A half-block away, Leon parked near a cluster of hookers. They sat there, watching and wishing for a chance or cue to take a shot.

At that moment, high in his Hollywood Hills mansion, Shetani was refusing a Pee Wee Smith request.

"Girl, I'm still hurtin', too, about the cruel way that customer hurt Bianca. I can understand why you want to send a piece of the sting to her mama for the plastic-surgery nut . . ."

He wasn't a square-ass sucker who would send even a buck to the Apple, he thought. He paused to snort coke from a diamond-encrusted spoon. She lay in his arms and shook her head when he moved the spoon toward her nose. She sighed.

"But I feel so shitty about keepin' the whole six grand after what she went through. Daddy, please let's send at least a grand. I'm so—"

He cut her off as he stared at a reflection of their nude bodies in a ceiling mirror.

"Now, listen, Baby Wee, don't forget what was said about the case in the *Milwaukee Journal* that Eli copped from the out-of-town newsstand. Remember, the Beer Town police are looking for a girl that split the scene who fits your description like a glove. They got a eyewitness, Wee, waiting to finger you. The beer pigs have run a FBI make on Bianca's prints. Then they'll wire up the Apple pigs to find out if the bitch that split was also in Sugar Red's stable."

He paused to take a sip of wine. He continued: "Suppose it hits the street grapevine that Bianca's mama got some pay-off bread from the West Coast. Why, shit, a slew of mother-fuckers—my enemies, and the Apple police—would figure the bread was sent by the little black fox with a doll face who blew that peckerwood away. If the heat don't pick up your trail, Red will be out here to shake us down. Then we'll pay off. Wee, don't crack nothin' else about that score and mur-der. We got to worry about keepin' you, the livin', out of the joint."

She moved out of his arms. They lay in thunderous silence. She bombed it with a harsh whisper: "When you gonna fire Petra, like you promised?"

He glared at her. "You motherfuckin' bitch. Don't pressure me. You ain't in a position to demand nothin'. You jumped

Iceberg Slim

bond in L.A., bitch. Brucker, the pig that killed Big Cat, is achin' to bust you."

She spat out, "It's Rucker, not Brucker."

"Shut up. You so hot you couldn't be the bottom woman. So get out of my face with that shit!"

She slid from the bed with a mean face and eased from the room. She went into her beige-and-rust bedroom, down the hallway. She sat on the side of a twin bed, with her shoulders slumped. She lit a cigarette. She stared, trancelike, through a window at a carpet of jade lawn, ringed by yellow roses. A pair of blue jays squabbled raucously in a sun-dappled tree.

Pee Wee's roommate came out of the adjoining bathroom. "Hi, lucky girl," terry-robed Tuta said as she sat down before a dresser mirror to make up her face.

Pee Wee frowned as she looked into the mirror and saw Tuta staring at her. "Why are you looking at me like that? Say, I'm not a lucky girl. I'm Pee Wee."

Tuta shrugged and dabbed cleansing cream on her face. "Pee Wee, I'm sorry you're upset. I just thought you were lucky to be in Daddy's bed for two hours and thirty-five minutes." She paused to say wistfully, "I've never been in his bed for even one minute."

After an extended silence, Pee Wee said gently, "Tu, I didn't mean to hurt your feelin's . . . That was my first time makin' love with him. I don't feel lucky."

Tuta spun around to face Pee Wee. "Please don't get salty, but tell me, was it good?"

Pee Wee smiled. "I'll tell ya, 'cause you're a sweet baby. It was a seven on a ten scale, considerin' my long bread he's counted. Shetani fucks like a tiger with a toothache. You

128

know, kinda hateful-like. My dead daddy, Big Cat, was a ten-plus in bed, 'cause he was full of sweetness and warmth."

Tuta laughed and turned back to her makeup. "Maybe he fucks Petra in a sweeter way. Maybe he loves her."

Pee Wee belly-laughed. "Love, sugar? These cold-blooded niggers don't love no ho, 'specially a dope-fiend player like Shetani. Don't forget, he put Petra in that cell 'cause she brought the stable home early."

Pee Wee went to take a shower. Tuta finished her makeup and dressed for early-afternoon work in a lavender minidress and gold shoes.

Pee Wee came out of the bathroom as Tuta was leaving. "Good catchin', lil' girl," Pee Wee said as she kissed Tuta's cheek.

"Thanks, Mommy," Tuta said as she barely moved her behind into the hallway to escape Pee Wee's playful slap at it.

Pee Wee was surprised to see her turn left, toward Shetani's bedroom, instead of right, to the staircase leading to the first floor.

Pee Wee stepped back and peeked down the hallway. She saw Tuta knock and then enter Shetani's bedroom.

Pee Wee crept to the side of the cracked door with bare feet. She craned her neck to eavesdrop.

Inside the room, Tuta was on the carpet beside the bed, on her hands and knees. Her dress was hiked up to her waist. Her panties were pulled down to expose her yellow ass and vulva.

"Tuta, I'm gonna hit you this time. Next time, get your street shot from Petra with the rest of the girls," he said as he spiked into a vein between her vulva and inside lower buttock. He squeezed in the shot when the syringe turned scarlet with her blood.

"Thanks, Master. I love it when you hit me," she said as she stood. She pulled up her panties and arranged her dress. He patted the bed. She sat down beside him. He put an arm around her waist.

"I want us to have some adventure tonight, together around eleven. Will you keep it a stone secret?"

She nodded vigorously. His voice was so low and soft that Pee Wee scarcely heard him.

He went on, "The twins and me will pick you up on Vine a half-block south of Sunset."

She leaned to half bite and suck his bottom lip. He drew back as if snake-bit.

"Where we goin'?" she asked in a whisper that Pee Wee didn't hear.

"We're gonna cabaret at Memory Lane, in South Central L.A."

She frowned. "If I leave the track at eleven, my check-in bread to Petra will be short."

He winked and stroked her shoulder. "I'll make your bread right for check-in."

They touched lips. She stood.

Pee Wee raced back to her bedroom. Tuta hurried downstairs to get into the van for the trip to the fast track.

At 9:30 p.m. that night, Pee Wee called a cab to pick her up at an address down the road from home. She slipped out of the mansion. She was wearing a black evening gown, black wig with heavy bangs, and dark glasses.

The cab took her to a fast-food restaurant across the boulevard from the Memory Lane cabaret. She sat drinking coffee near a window. At 11:25, she saw Shetani and Tuta leave the van and enter the club. She waited fifteen minutes before she crossed the street and went into the crowded place. She took a seat at the bar.

Several black pussy-chasers hit on her immediately. She told them she was waiting for her husband to join her.

She spotted Shetani and Tuta at a ringside table, with champagne in a bucket. They faced Pee Wee, intently watching Sir Lady Java, a curvaceous transvestite dancing topless in a spot of copper light to savage band music.

"How about taking a picture, gorgeous lady," a wiry house photographer asked as he touched the camera slung around his neck.

She smiled. "Thanks for the compliment . . . You can take a picture of that girl in the lavender dress sitting with the man in the gray silk suit at ringside."

His eyes narrowed knowingly.

"Can you zoom in on them from here?"

He nodded. "Ordinarily, the fee is five—"

She cut him off: "I'll give you twenty for the shot."

He aimed the camera and took the picture with a flash of light. "I'll be back in a few minutes. I've got a developing setup in the basement," he said as he turned and walked away.

She ordered a champagne cocktail while she waited.

He returned with a vividly clear image of Shetani with his pet.

Pee Wee left the club, intending to walk down King Boulevard to get a passing cab.

"Hey, pretty, what's happening?" she heard a voice say behind her.

She stopped and glanced over her shoulder. One of the pussy-chasers had followed her.

"Cuteness, I'll drop you off on the moon . . . anywhere," he said tipsily as he galloped into her face.

Her bandit eyes told her his silk suit was in the five-to-seven-bill class. That was no guarantee that he was carrying big bread in his leather, she thought.

Her fingertips gently held him at bay for an instant to feel the leather in his inner coat pocket. It could be empty. However, she was certain the fiery diamond ring on his left pinkie was real.

She bared her pearly teeth. "You're sweet, but I don't know you," she cooed and started to turn away.

He grabbed the sleeve of her blue fox jacket. "You're Iona. I'm Roger Lee. We met at the bar. You said your husband . . ."

She put an index finger across his big mouth. "Please, don't mention him to me . . . Where are you parked?"

His maroon eyes glowed with crotch joy as he led her into a new silver Eldorado parked on the club lot. He pressed himself against her as he let her into the car. He got in under the wheel and eye-swept her curves.

"Roger, please, don't look at me like that. Take me to Carson," she said sweetly.

She coyly switched her eyes to the dashboard. He moved across the seat to box her in. His left hand, heavy with alcohol, stroked her knee. She turned her face away from a gust of rancid breath.

"Please, Roger, stop!" she squealed with pro-ho come-on in her voice. She opened her thighs to his sucker left hand, bearing the huge diamond. She recoiled and closed her thighs when his index finger penetrated her.

"Ouch! I'm tight. Use your little finger at first," she said as she wet his pinkie with her spit from her index finger.

He jabbed it into her until she cried out, "Oowee! I'm so hot!" She unzipped his fly. His erected enemy sprang from his pants. She pressed his left hand against her vulva. She slipped the diamond off his slimy pinkie as she swung onto his lap. She dropped the ring into her bosom as she rubbed her sex nest against his rod.

"Shit, raise up a little so I can stick it in," he gasped.

She invaded his inner coat pocket and lifted out his wallet. She rhythmically rammed her bosom against his chest in sync with the humping action of her trap against his rod. She used both hands behind his head to remove a roll of bills from the leather. She fired her tongue tip into his ear at the instant that she put the leather back in the pocket.

"Let's go to a motel," she panted. She stuck the bills into her vaginal stash as she flung herself out of the saddle.

He shakily zipped up his pants. "I'll drink to that," he said as he keyed on the engine.

"Wait a minute, sweet dick. I have to pee now," she said as she opened the door and left the car.

"Hurry up!" he said as she moved to the rear of the car.

She crouched and dashed with shoes in hand into a side street adjacent to the club.

Two minutes later, a white pussy-chaser in a Corvette picked her up. She was too drained to take a shot at his leather.

He dropped her off in Hollywood. She wrote a phony name and telephone number on a slip of paper and dropped it on him.

She took a cab for the Hollywood Hills. On the way, she counted six bills of Roger's greenstuff.

Minutes later, she sat on the side of her bed, staring at the Memory Lane pic. She knew that Shetani had never planned to fire Petra. He had conned her into a thieving tour of the Midwest.

She shivered as she remembered the bloody face of the trick when he fell dead at her feet.

Now she was wanted for murder. She had a vision of herself, wrinkled and white-haired in a Wisconsin prison. Shetani was to blame, she told herself.

Rage possessed her. She stared stonily at his image and shaped a psychotic smile. She hated him with so much venomous passion that she raced to the bathroom to vomit bitter bile.

She rinsed out her mouth and stared at her reflection in the bathroom mirror. He had betrayed and tricked her. She vowed to get revenge. She would do anything to destroy him.

She was happy that Tuta was his pet. She hoped he was in love like a square-ass sucker. She'd seduce Tuta to release her sexual tension. She'd teach her how to steal. Tuta would feel stronger and need Shetani less. She'd do everything she could to make him lose Tuta. She would also poison Petra's mind against him with the pic. That move would have to be made with great caution, for she sensed that Shetani could be deadly when crossed.

I'll make the move on the snake bastard soon as I feel Petra is right for it, she raved audibly.

Suddenly it hit her that her medicine was in low supply. She suspected that Shetani considered her a liability because of the murder beef against her. He could avoid a harboring charge if he could waste her with poisoned dope.

She went to the open door. She started to step out. She

heard Froggy, Shetani's ex–car polisher, croaking a pop tune. With Shetani's car in storage, Froggy was the mansion gofer.

She watched him disappear down the staircase before she stepped into the hallway. She went directly into Shetani's bedroom. She stood in the half-darkness and heard the thump of her heart. She went to turn on the dim light of a lamp on the table at the end of the sofa. She dropped down on the sofa. Her eyes darted about the room for his possible skag stash. She had to be careful that she didn't tear up the room looking for the stash, she thought. In this case, she knew it wouldn't be necessary. She knew that most veteran underworld people chose easily accessible stash places.

She went to examine a five-foot nude-figurine plaster lamp. She got on her knees beside it. She thumped the base with her finger to see if it was hollow.

She went to the wall heater. She stooped to see that the pilot light was off. She slipped off the heater cover. She hand-swept inside it and replaced the cover.

Her eyes zoomed to a pair of large speakers atop a stereo cabinet. She inspected the back of one and then moved to examine the other. She discovered a hairline groove in the back of the second speaker. She slid the rear panel back to reveal a kilo and a half of China white. Shetani's dope kit lay beside it.

She took two C-note bills of the Roger sting from her bosom. She overlapped them and dumped a pile of white onto the bills. She folded them into a package for her bosom. She slid the back of the speaker into place. She switched off the lamp and hurried, full of dope-fiend ecstasy, back into her room.

11

Rucker and Opal Lenski, Crane's aunt, were having lunch with the Cranes at a Wilshire Boulevard restaurant. Opal had flown in the day before for a short visit with Rucker. The trip and a hired nurse gave Opal relief from the strain of caring for her mother, who was ill at home.

As their waiter served chocolate mousse, pudgy Millie glanced at Crane and exclaimed, "I can't!" Then she laughed and said, "I will."

Rucker and Opal laughed. Crane's gaunt face was a chalky blank mask in the candle glow.

"Mil, you really shouldn't," he said in a punitive tone.

"Oh, Leo, give her a break. You heard her say she's been on a thousand calories a day for almost a month," Opal said sweetly.

Crane halted Millie's second trip to her mouth with a firm palm against her wrist. "No more, Mil. Let's go," Crane said harshly as he shoved the dessert plate to the center of the table.

He stood. Millie's heavily made-up Pekingese face was twisted by humiliation and anger as she stared up into his face. He took hold of her arm. She stood, her rosebud mouth twitching.

"Thanks, folks, for the lunch and company. Have a pleasant trip home, Aunt Opal," Crane struggled to say cheerfully.

Opal smiled. "Thank you, Leo."

Rucker said softly, "We enjoyed seeing you both."

"I'm sorry," Millie said feebly, with her eyes fixed on the carpet, as they turned away from the table.

Rucker and Opal finished dessert in silence. Opal sighed. "Oh, Ruck, I'm so sorry to see those kids in such trouble."

Rucker toyed with his wine goblet. "It's tough going for them . . . I'm worried about Leo."

Opal looked at her face in a compact mirror. "He does look bad. Maybe he isn't an ideal husband . . . He is a good cop, isn't he, Ruck?"

Rucker looked into her luminous dark eyes for a moment. "He was one of the best."

She entwined her fingers. "'Was' Ruck? Is he in trouble with the department?"

He touched her hands. "No, not yet."

She groaned. "Oh Jesus."

Rucker held her hands. "Darling, please, don't worry. I'm trying and hoping to take care of him and his problem on my own."

"I have been his loving mother since he was ten. My sister Ellen, his mother, and his father died in a car crash. I took care of him. I saw him through some scary near-collisions with law and order before he straightened out. So don't sugar-coat his present troubles for me, Ruck."

He smiled. "Mother dear, Leo confided the downside of his early life to me shortly after we became partners in the Seventy-seventh Division." Rucker leaned toward her to half whisper, "He's hooked on cocaine, and he could be guilty of criminal conspiracy to obstruct justice."

She gasped. "You mean, he could go to prison?"

Rucker nodded. "At worst, he could. As I said, I'm trying to save him from that . . . Do I have your promise not to say anything to him about our conversation here today?"

She nodded. "I won't say anything to him. After all, Ruck, I know that you love him, too. I know you'll do everything possible to help him." She looked at her watch. "Ruck, the past thirty-six hours have been so sweet with you. I just know you've stopped drinking forever. I can't be this happy until I see you again."

He feather-stroked the back of her hands with his lips. He gazed deeply into her eyes. "Knowing you feel this way will keep me happy until I see you again."

They left the restaurant for the airport. As a skycap was taking Opal's bag from the Lincoln's trunk, Rucker said, "Give Rebecca my love, and tell her I'm rooting for her speedy recovery."

They kissed goodbye. Rucker watched her until she disappeared into the terminal.

Rucker drove to the station to brief the 3:00-to-11:00-p.m. shift. He parked the car and entered the station. He stepped inside the briefing room.

Crane avoided eye contact with him during the routine ten-minute briefing. Then, as usual, Rucker handed each squad member a listing of current squad and regular vice-car licenses. He followed the squad to the parking lot and entered a Thunderbird undercover car. He was about to start the engine when it hit him that the license list he had just passed out was the key to trap Crane.

He drove off the lot, refining the trap that he would set at Crane's next briefing.

That evening, at midnight, Pee Wee relieved herself. She had decided she would sound out Petra before she confided Shetani's sucker antics with Tuta. She knew strong Petra wouldn't rush to Shetani in a jealous rage. She was leery because of Petra's well-known loyalty to him. She had to gamble that Petra wouldn't finger her as a snitch. She smiled wickedly as she got off the throne and flushed the toilet.

At 2:30 a.m., Tuta came into the bedroom after getting her bedtime skag shot.

"Shit, girl, you almost look as fresh as you did when you got down," Pee Wee exclaimed.

"Thanks. I had French tricks all night," Tuta said as she slipped out of her lemon shoes and minidress.

Pee Wee's heart leapt out of rhythm at the voluptuous vision of Tuta's nude body. She lay atop her bed and felt fiery springs of passion flood her head as she watched Tuta go into the shower.

Shortly, Tuta came from the bathroom in a black silk-and-lace bikini.

"You must have a date with the Master himself," Pee Wee cracked as she watched her sit down and start to make up her face.

"Yeah, Wee; only thing is, he don't know it yet."

Pee Wee giggled. "You mean you gonna try to fuck him just like that?"

Tuta sat motionless for a moment. "I mean he's gonna get me off this mornin' or else."

Pee Wee laughed. "Don't jive me, baby. You ain't gonna split from no righteous China white for dick reasons."

Tuta smiled. "I got a regular trick who deals China white. What the fuck, I'm a gorjus bitch. Daddy's gonna get me off or I'm gonna get in the wind."

Pee Wee shook her head in puzzlement at it all. Why wasn't Shetani fucking his pet? she asked herself.

Moments later, Tuta stood in full radiant makeup. "See you later, Wee," she said at the door.

"I hope you score, baby. You better at least pick up that phone and call him first. You know it's against the rules to go to his door after midnight with no appointment."

Tuta said, "I'm just gonna be a pure little bitch."

Pee Wee went to the doorway and watched Tuta wiggle her way to Shetani's door.

Inside his bedroom, Shetani received the night's take in seventeen envelopes from Petra. They stared at each other at the sound of Tuta's knock at the door.

Shetani jerked his head toward the door. She went to peer through the peephole.

"It's Tuta. You must be expecting her," Petra said as she glanced at him over her shoulder. He nodded. She opened the door.

"Excuse me, Petra, I didn't know you were here," Tuta said as she looked over Petra's head at the hardening face of Shetani.

"Honey, come in. I'm leaving," Petra said as she stepped aside for Tuta's entry.

"She looks like centerfold stuff, doesn't she, Master?" thirty-year-old Petra said wistfully as she paused to survey Tuta's teenage splendor.

Petra left the room and shut the door.

Shetani glared at Tuta as she sat down beside him on the bed. She started to rest her head on his shoulder. He moved away.

"Master, I'm sorry I broke your rule. I needed to talk to you, body to body."

He threw a robe around her shoulders. "Silly bitch. Don't break no more rules."

She flung the robe off her to the carpet. "I'm not silly! I'm just a human ho that's gonna get sick if her man don't get her off."

His hellish eyes burned through her as he sat like Satan, sculpted in black granite.

She broke the silence. "What's wrong with me, Master? All my tricks tell me how sexy I am. I'll change my hair, perfume, anything, to make you want to make love to me."

He sprang to his feet before her. "Don't pressure me for my dick, cunt. No bitch tells me when to fuck. You got that?"

She fell to her knees. "Okay, Master. Just let me suck it a little. I've got tricks comin' from the Valley twice a week for head. Let me show—"

"You stinking low-life ho," he thundered to cut her off.

She stared up at him with extravagant surprise and disbelief on her face. She screamed, "It's fuckin' true I'm a ho. I'm proud to be a ho. I'll die a ho!"

He swung a violent backhand against the side of her head.

She collapsed on the carpet, quivering. She scooted up to a sitting position against the bed frame. She held the side of her face.

"Master, I bet you ain't got no dick," she said in a shaky whisper.

With one hand he reached into his pajama pants and jerked out his long, limp penis. He seized her hair with the other hand. "See! Look! Now you know, bitch, I've got a dick."

He dragged her to the door and flung her into the hallway. He slammed the door.

Pee Wee rushed to help her into their bedroom.

"He's stone crazy. Like I told you, Wee, I'm gettin' in the wind," Tuta sobbed as Pee Wee held her in her arms on a chaise.

"Yeah, lil baby, he came down on your ass like a square. When you splittin'?"

Tuta turned up her emerald eyes. "Tomorrow, after I make some bread."

Pee Wee tenderly kissed her bruised cheek. "That's not soon enough. When he gets up, he could lock you in that cell in the cellar."

Tuta trembled. "How . . . What am I going to do?"

Pee Wee squeezed her close to her bosom. "You lucky little sweet-eyes. You got me. We'll pack your stuff, then we'll get you a cab to a hotel room before he gets up."

Tuta said, "But I'm almost broke. I couldn't even . . ."

Pee Wee's lips against hers interrupted the sentence. "I'm splittin' soon. I'll give you the bread for the cab and a pad that we can share. I'll teach you how to be a superstar thievin' ho. I'm gonna bring a kilo of boss China white with me."

Pee Wee's tongue riffled through a downy forest of hairs

at the nape of her neck without touching the electrified skin-scape.

Tuta hissed with pleasure and flung her thighs open in the throes of the thrill. Their clashing pygmy tools fired the furnace of their tender cannibalism.

Consumed, they lay panting, with dewy bodies glistening. "We gonna be so happy together. Ain't we, lil baby?" Pee Wee whispered in the moonlit stillness.

"We gotta be, Wee. We ain't got nobody but us," Tuta softly answered.

Half an hour later, Tuta went to sleep. Pee Wee went to shower. Coming back to bed, she glanced out the window. She stopped to stare at the ghostly figure of snow-blonde Petra in a white flowing robe. She strolled trancelike in the flower garden, with her arms folded.

Pee Wee threw on a robe and, with the Memory Lane picture in her pocket, went to the garden.

"Hi, Petra. I couldn't sleep, either. I hope you don't mind me buttin' in," Pee Wee said breezily as she sat down on a wrought-iron bench beside Petra.

The red eye of Petra's cigarette waggled a welcome signal. "Not at all, Pee Wee."

Pee Wee gazed up at the star-pocked sky. Petra laughed. "Lady, beware of heavenly awe. You might become born again."

Pee Wee rammed her hands into her robe pockets. "I ain't in danger of that . . . I always think about Mama when the stars pop out. She believed in heaven and hell and the rest of the sucker fairy tale. She left me alone forever when I was twelve. She died with calluses everywhere, maybe even on her soul."

Petra's face softened. "What did you do after . . . ?"

Pee Wee sighed. "I bunked in a junk car and stole food from markets. A coupla weeks after Mama left, a store pig busted me on the sidewalk with my bloomers fulla bread and cold cuts. Big Cat's bottom woman hipped me how to steal. No, I ain't in no danger of bein' born again."

Pee Wee leaned in close to Petra. "But we ho's are in danger of bein' played for bigger fools than we are."

Petra recoiled. "If you're unhappy, talk to Daddy about it. I don't like to talk to unhappy people."

The whites of Pee Wee's eyes flared like phosphorus. "Hey, Miss White Queen, don't lay that shit on this ghetto bitch. Sure, you're the bottom woman. I heard you been to college, that you was born in a pad like a castle. So what? Petra, you ain't more than me or any other ho. All of us is just slaves, buyin' so-called choice dick and protection. We get punished when we break Shetani's rules. What the fuck happens when he . . ."

"Shut up!" Petra said as she jerked herself to her feet. She glared down at Pee Wee as she went on. "I'm not going to listen to any more. You cracked about coming from a ghetto. Baby, you came from a relative paradise with a loving mother. I escaped from a ghetto of plastic people with bankbook hearts. My mother, may she rest in everlasting misery, was a savage in sable. She loved my younger sister. She hated me because I look like my father. She called me filthy names when I failed to be perfect. So don't crack ghetto to me."

Petra turned away and moved toward the house. Pee Wee followed.

"Petra, you riskin' your ass every night, and you oughta know that Shetani is chumpin' off with Tuta."

Petra halted at the back door. "Read my lips. I don't want you to tell me anything about him," she spat out.

Pee Wee put her palm against the screen door. "I ain't tellin'. I'm showin'," she said as she whipped out the picture and shoved it under Petra's eyes.

Pee Wee noticed Petra's hand tremble slightly as she stared at the picture in the glare of an overhead light. Pee Wee half whispered, "Last Saturday night, just before you took the girls to work, I heard him make a date with Tuta. He told Tuta he would take her to Memory Lane at eleven. He told her he'd make her money right for you at check-in time."

Petra turned and stuck the picture into Pee Wee's robe pocket before she opened the screen door and entered the house. Pee Wee followed.

"Pee Wee, I can't say thanks, so I'm not saying anything."

Pee Wee said, "I'm sorry he got weak for her and broke a player's rule." Pee Wee split off from her in the kitchen and moved toward the staircase. She turned back into the kitchen. Petra was taking a carton of milk from the refrigerator.

"I'm kinda hopin' you won't pull Shetani's coat about me and the picture," Pee Wee said softly.

Petra turned to face her with elevated eyebrows. "Why did you show it and give me that rundown of what you over-heard?"

Pee Wee replied strongly, " 'Cause he don't deserve no star ho's like us."

Petra smiled. "You could be right . . . Let's keep the picture our secret."

Pee Wee shook Petra's free hand. "Thanks, girl. I like you even though you are the bottom." They laughed together. Pee Wee left the kitchen and hurried to her room. She packed

Tuta's belongings into two suitcases. Then she lay across her bed and catnapped until almost dawn. Then she called motels and hotels near Hollywood. She finally reserved a motel room in Silver Lake, a mecca for gay couples.

She kissed Tuta awake. "Shetani is gonna try to trace you, baby. I think takin' a cab is not cool. Ain't you got some regular trick's number you can call?"

Tuta knuckled sleep from her eyes. "Yeah, I got a couple I'll call after I pee," she said as she swung out of bed for the bathroom.

She returned to get, on her first call, the trick's solemn promise to pick her up at an address down the road within twenty minutes.

Shortly, dawn arrived. Before they left the room with the bags, Pee Wee shoved a packet of money and skag into Tuta's bra.

"Pay a week's rent, and this medicine will keep you well until I see you," Pee Wee said.

They went through the quiet house to the front door.

"Wee, somebody in the house, or maybe Froggy, might see you helping me. I can make it with the bags," Tuta said as they kissed.

Pee Wee opened the door. She blinked back tears as she watched Tuta go down the long driveway to a tall steel gate. She watched her glance at an adjoining cubicle, where Froggy slept, before she swung open the gate.

Pee Wee stood in the doorway, ready to help her with the bags, until she disappeared from view.

At that moment, Eli, seated on the throne in the guest bungalow, glanced out toward the roadway. His drowsy double-take revealed a deserted roadway. Had he really seen a flash of Tuta with suitcases? he wondered as he tissued himself and rose to his feet.

He glanced into snoring Cazo's room and smiled to see him asleep with his head between his sleeping girlfriend's thighs.

He went into his bedroom and lay down beside his girlfriend. A moment later, he jumped up and threw on a robe. He rushed to the roadway. He sprinted down it in the direction that Tuta had gone. He peered into several cars in driveways, and into stands of shrubbery, on his way back to the bungalow.

He sat on the side of the bed, looking at the telephone. He decided he couldn't awaken Shetani and risk his wrath with a false alarm.

He went into Cazo's room and took keys to the mansion off the dresser top. He used the back-door key to enter the house. He went up the staircase and down the hallway to Tuta's room. The floorboards creaked beneath his weight when he put his ear to the door.

Inside, Pee Wee faked sleep. Eli eased the door open and stared at Tuta's empty bed. He looked in the closet and saw that Tuta's bright-blue bags were gone. He went to check out the bathroom.

He hurried to Shetani's door. He knocked three times before Shetani eyed him through the peephole and removed the door chain to face him.

"You forget how to dial a phone? What's wrong?" Shetani said sharply as he glared at the giant.

"Cap, Tuta's done hit the wind," Eli exclaimed.

Shetani's mouth gaped open. "Why? I mean, when?"

Eli jiggled his platter palms in the air. "A few minutes ago Cap. I, uh . . . was half asleep when I thought I saw her splittin'. It was too late when I come to myself."

Shetani bulled him out of the way and ran to the side of Pee Wee's bed. He stared down at her, with his mouth aquiver, for a moment. Then he bent over to whisper harshly into her ear: "You lousy cunt-eatin' bitch! Open your eyes and tell me where my ho went."

Pee Wee remained in fake slumber. He took a lighter from his pajama pocket and flicked it on. He moved the flame close to her cheek. She stirred and moved her head. He whispered into her ear, "Bitch, I'm gonna set your hair on fire if you don't open your eyes and tell me where my ho went."

Pee Wee's eyes popped open. "Master, I swear I don't know."

He rammed his face close to her. "Roommate, why didn't you stop her or tip me off?"

Pee Wee moved away to prop herself up against pillows. "Hey, Master, I ain't your bottom. I ain't responsible for no ho's ass 'cept my own."

He gritted his teeth and made a fist. She screamed and half covered her face with her hands. He grunted for velocity and slammed his fist into her face. A huge diamond ring slashed a bloody rill across her cheek.

Half stunned, she finger-patted the wound. He snatched her purse off her nightstand and dumped the contents onto the foot of her bed. She gazed at her bloody fingertips as he examined a notebook.

Eli watched her shocked face deform into hideous rage. He moved to her bedside.

She reached beneath the pillows. He sprang on her and seized her gun wrist as she blurred out her automatic and aimed it at Shetani's head.

Shetani dropped to the carpet at the pop of the round that entered the ceiling. Petra rushed into the room. Pee Wee was trapped beneath Eli's bulk. Shetani pushed him away and locked his hands around Pee Wee's throat.

"Where's Tuta?" he shrieked as he tightened his grip.

"Stop! You're killing her," Petra wailed as she tried to pull Shetani away.

Pee Wee went limp. Eli pried Shetani's hands away.

"Cap, you don't really want to kill the ho," Eli said as he half lifted Shetani into a leather chair.

Shetani stared balefully at Pee Wee as she came to. "Lock that treacherous ho up, and warm up the van. We're gonna find Tuta," Shetani said, and got to his feet.

"You mean you're actually gonna try to find a runaway ho?" Petra cracked with sarcastic awe.

He slapped her hard against the side of her face. "Don't crack on me, ho. I'll lock your ass up, too," he shouted.

Petra slunk from the room, rubbing her jaw.

After Eli locked up Pee Wee, he awakened Cazo. In pajamas and robes, they sat in the idling van, waiting for Shetani.

"Say, Cazo, Cap is been uncool since Petra hijacked Maxine—uh, Tuta—from that punk . . . a stone-to-the-bone mack like him ain't fell in love, huh?"

Cazo chewed his bottom lip. "Naw, Eli. I think Cap is in worse trouble than that. He don't read nothin' but them stack of books about dead people comin' back to life. He loves his dead baby sis so much, I think he's done conned himself that Maxine is really Tuta. Remember, he changed Maxine's name soon as he saw her."

Eli shook his head. "Yeah. I guess you got him figured right . . . Sure is a shame for a mack like Cap to have a problem like that upstairs. I wonder what . . ."

The approach of Shetani cut him off. "Let's ride," Shetani said as he took a seat between the twins. Eli pulled the van away down to the flatlands.

"Cap, how, where we gonna start lookin'?" Eli said softly.

"I'm gonna check cab companies and cabbies. I'm willing to lay out a grand to find out where Tuta went. Maybe she didn't leave by cab. I'll lay a grand apiece on you to snatch her whenever you spot her and bring her home to me."

That night, before taking the stable to the street, Petra took skag and a tray of food to Pee Wee.

"Did he find Tuta?" she said as she stooped to take the tray that Petra shoved under the cell door.

"No. He tried until late afternoon," Petra said.

Pee Wee turned away to place the tray on her steel-slab bed. She noticed the glassine bag containing a bit of skag and a syringe.

"Thanks a lot, Petra," Pee Wee said as she gripped the cell-door bars.

"You're welcome. This penitentiary practices humane treatment of convicts."

Pee Wee eye-swept the huge barren cell. "Hey, deputy warden, this is twice as bad as the worst joint I've been in." They laughed mirthlessly.

Petra said, "In a few minutes, the twins will bring all of

your stuff, including bedding and a TV." She paused to laugh sarcastically. "Daddy didn't tell me he wanted you to suffer down here."

Pee Wee grunted. "How long do you think I'm in for?"

Petra shrugged. "If you know where Tuta is, tell. He said you can get out when Tuta is back in the house."

Pee Wee sighed. "I don't know where she is." She riveted her eyes on Petra's face. "He send that medicine?"

Petra replied, "No. It's my private stock. You must be needing." She handed Pee Wee a book of matches from her robe pocket.

"I'm all right for now. I snorted a taste that I had in my bosom."

Petra smiled. "I did my bit down here in darkness. I'll leave you this candle. See you later." Petra turned and went toward the stairs.

"Thanks again, girl," Pee Wee said. She went to sit on the steel bed. She put the tray on her lap and started to eat.

Around 9:00 p.m., in South Central L.A., Leon finally located Rucker at home. He told him that the street vine said that Shetani had lost Tuta and had searched the streets for her all day.

Leon hung up and dressed for the street. His mother came out of the kitchen and followed him to the front door. Her seamed face was mock angry. She stepped in front of him and said sternly, "Jiver, you promised me you wouldn't go out every night when you moved back home. Stay home and keep your mama company."

Leon bear-hugged her. "Mama, let's play cards tomorrow

night. I promised Rainbow I'd take him to North Holly-wood." He kissed her cheek. She opened the door.

"I'm gonna lock up your clothes if you don't stay home tomorrow night," she said as he went down the walk.

He got into his Caddie, parked in front of the house. He glanced at a rooming house across the street and blew the horn twice.

A moment later, Rainbow came out of the house and got into the Caddie. Forty minutes later, they got out on a market parking lot to hustle slum.

Five minutes later, they were rousted off the lot by a market security man. Leon drove toward West Hollywood. Bone-tired Rainbow catnapped on the Caddie's rear seat.

"Hey, bro, what's happenin'?" Rainbow mumbled when Leon suddenly stopped the car.

"Ain't this a bitch?" Leon exclaimed as he stared at Crane and Petra leaving a motel room.

They walked toward Crane's undercover black Dodge. Petra turned back toward the room to retrieve her makeup kit.

Rainbow lifted his head and glanced at the scene from his prone position. "Damn, bro, it ain't big news when that ho catches a trick."

Leon said, "Bow, that dude with her is Crane, one of Sergeant Rucker's ho-squad cops."

Rainbow coiled into a ball. "Well, she must of caught him and got a pass for some gash."

Leon eased the Caddie away. Crane snared him in the corner of an eye. His face was grim as he slid into the Dodge. He pulled out of the lot without Petra. He tailed Leon with a block between them in medium traffic.

Leon was excited as he drove toward West Hollywood. He knew what Rucker was trying to find out, why the Shetani stable was immune to bust. He'd call the station. He'd leave Rucker the phone number of a bar where he hung out in the early a.m.

He parked the Caddie on the street beside a darkened gas station. "I'm gonna call my mama," he said as he left the car.

Rainbow grunted from the rear seat. Leon went to enter a telephone booth in the corner of the station lot. He dropped a quarter and dialed Hollywood Station.

Crane drove the Dodge, with lights out, into the lot behind Leon. Crane drew his gun and went to the booth. He opened the door as Leon said, "I wanta leave a mess—"

Leon spun to face Crane. Crane grinned hideously. "Excuse me, Leon, let's have a heart-to-heart chat," Crane said cheerfully as he cradled the receiver. He stepped back and waggled the .38 toward the adjoining alley.

Leon's lips flapped mutely. He shook from head to toe as he stumbled from the booth. "Please, Officer, sir. Don't kill me! I ain't gonna tell nobody about you and the lady."

Crane punched the gun into his back to force him into the alley. Leon's feet made a scratchy noise against the alley pavement as he took off to escape.

Crane leveled the gun with both hands on the back of Leon's head.

Leon was fifteen feet away when Crane exploded his head with two rapid rounds. He fell limply dead, like an elongated rag doll.

Crane rushed back to the Dodge under the saucer eyes of Rainbow, alerted by the blast of the .38.

Crane shot the Dodge away. Rainbow scrambled from the Caddie and disappeared into the night.

Crane was several minutes late when he walked into the briefing room. He took a seat beside Rucker.

Rucker said, "Leo, a moment ago, I revealed that I received a tip on Tuta, who we all have tried to bust. She has left Shetani, and he is very upset about losing her. Also fortunately, yesterday an apparent Shetani neighbor called in to report a suspicious circumstance. She had noticed many of the girls from the Shetani residence hooking on Sunset Boulevard. A helicopter surveillance established the presence of the transport van and the twins, who had eluded numerous tails. Tuta's statement as to quantity and location of heroin will facilitate a search warrant. Let's find her and bring her in so I can talk to her. Let's hope she's sour enough to help us hang a pandering rap on him."

Rucker paused to take a sip of water. "Petra, Shetani's straw boss, will be under twenty-four-hour surveillance, effective at noon tomorrow. She could be the drug courier for the stable. If we can bust her on possession, she might give us a case against him. That's it, guys. Any questions?"

After a momentary silence, Rucker said, "Sic 'em!" He handed the squad members the current list of undercover car licenses as they left the room. A list that Crane was given had a license-plate number that none of the others had. Rucker had set the first stage of the trap for Crane.

The undercover cop who would drive the vehicle bearing the trap plate number had been briefed earlier. He was to concentrate on known Shetani girls pointed out to him by Rucker two nights before. If the cop failed to make any busts, Crane would be deep in the trap.

On Crane's shift the following night, Rucker would give him a list without the license number of a new undercover vehicle by a fresh cop. If this cop busted Shetani girls, then Rucker would be 100 percent certain of Crane's guilt.

Rucker was getting to his feet when the phone rang on the table beside him. He sank back into his chair and picked up. He caught his breath. "Thanks, Frank," he said to the homicide detective who had called to tell him that Leon had been shot to death.

Rucker cradled the receiver. He sat stunned for a long moment before he dialed Sadie, Leon's mother.

Crane drove directly to the Sunset drugstore that was used as a drop for the license list. He wrote a note warning Petra of the impending surveillance ordered by Rucker. He made a copy of the list on a store machine. He taped the copy and the note beneath the ledge of a store telephone. He mostly needed the list to know the current license numbers of regular vice undercover cars. This was to avoid mistaking them for trick vehicles when hookers got into them.

Fifteen minutes later, Petra walked into the store. She entered the phone booth and got the list and note. She made a half-dozen copies of the list.

The twins drove her to three groups of five stable girls. They had halted work and gathered in Sunset sandwich shops to wait for the list. Petra gave each group copies of the list before she resumed work.

In South Central L.A., Rucker comforted Leon's distraught mother.

"Sadie, please try to pull yourself together so you can help me," Rucker said. He rubbed her heaving shoulders as he sat on a sofa beside the sobbing woman. Finally, she regained some control.

He took out notebook and pen. "What time did Leon leave home, and did he say where he was going?"

She stared up at the ceiling. "Oh Lord, this hurts so bad. Help me!"

Rucker patted her hands, which were writhing in her lap. "Please, Sadie."

She switched her wet brown eyes to his face. "He left around nine, going to take Rainbow to North Hollywood," she said raggedly.

"Does Rainbow live here?"

She shook her head. "No. Across the street, in that rooming house."

Rucker stood. "Have you seen him since he left with Leon?"

She put her palm across her mouth. "Mr. Rucker, don't think Rainbow shot Leon. He ain't the killin' kind. He and my son was buddies."

Rucker walked toward the front door. "Sadie, I just want to talk to him."

She came to the door as he opened it. "He's a good person, and we liked him . . . Maybe I was wrong to mention his name."

"Sadie, you were right to tell me about him. Rainbow may be able to help us find the trigger man . . . In the meantime, give me a confidential call if he contacts you."

She nodded. Rucker went down the walk. He crossed the street and rang the rooming-house bell.

Rucker held his wallet with his badge pinned to an underside. A white-haired black man in a yellow bathrobe opened the door.

"Hello, Officer. Can I help you?" he said with a wide smile.

Rucker studied the man's face. "I don't recall meeting you. My name is Rucker. Who are you?" Rucker said as he slid his wallet into his jacket pocket.

"I'm Clarence Hobbs, owner of this building. I was on my way to visit Sadie a while back, and you were leaving. Sadie told me you were her friend," he said as he stepped aside.

Rucker moved into a dimly lit hallway. He replayed the flash of Rainbow's face that he had gotten when Leon pulled abreast of his Lincoln at a red light.

"Mr. Hobbs, I want to talk to one of your tenants. He's very dark-complexioned, with large eyes in a small face. He's known as Rainbow."

Hobbs dipped his head toward a door behind Rucker. "He said his real name was Marvin Adams. That's his room, but I think he's out . . . What's he done?"

Rucker said, "Nothing," as he turned to knock on the door. After a moment, Rucker said, "I want to talk to him as a possible witness to a crime. The murder of Sadie's son, Leon, tonight. I would appreciate it if you opened his door."

Hobbs's face was shocked. He took a ring of keys from his robe pocket and opened the door. An open closet bulging with an array of psychedelic clothing and pink luggage gave Rucker reason to think Rainbow could still be around.

"Thanks, Mr. Hobbs. May I use your phone to make a local call?"

Hobbs nodded and led him into his apartment, across

the hall from Rainbow's room. Hobbs went to the kitchen. Rucker sat down on a living-room couch and dialed Homicide. Within a minute, he had arranged for a stakeout of the rooming house to apprehend and hold Rainbow as a material witness.

Rucker thanked Hobbs and went to his car. He moved the Lincoln from the front of Sadie's house to a spot down the street. He sat with his eyes glued to the rooming house until a stakeout car arrived, forty minutes later. He pulled out and exchanged eye greetings with the officer who had parked in front of him.

Rucker got back to Hollywood at the peak of the hooker rush. He cruised slowly down Sunset in a glut of john cars. The drivers' eyes shopped the girls. He nodded to several undercover policewomen, decoying as hookers to jail johns for soliciting sex. He saw Petra cut down a side street. He turned into it. He parked and watched her get into a new Mercury sedan parked in the middle of the block. The driver doused his lights.

Perhaps she would do a quickie in the car, Rucker thought as he watched the shadowy forms. A moment later, he tensed. He saw their silhouettes in what appeared to be a violent struggle.

He shot the Lincoln down the street. He braked sharply beside the Mercury. The back of Petra's head was jammed against the front passenger door. In the streetlight, her face was twisted with terror and her eyes were bulged out.

Rucker saw the tee-shirted back of a man wedged between her feebly flailing legs. The husky blond man turned his softly featured face toward Rucker as he leapt from the Lincoln with gun drawn.

"Police! Come out of there with your hands up," Rucker ordered as he flung open the sedan door.

Petra's attacker scrambled over her and dived through the open window. He rolled to his feet and streaked down the sidewalk.

Rucker ran to the sidewalk. "Halt!" he shouted, and fired two shots above the suspect's head.

Sneaker-shod, he blurred out of sight around a corner. Rucker lumbered to the corner. He saw no trace of the speedster.

Petra was struggling to a sitting position when he rushed back to her. He unknotted the chiffon scarf around her throat that the attacker had used as a garrote.

"Officer, I have to say I'm glad you showed," she gasped as she stroked her throat.

He assisted her into the double-parked Lincoln. He radioed in for a check on the Mercury's license number and a description of the attacker. He moved the Lincoln to park in front of the Mercury. He waited for a tow unit to impound the vehicle.

Rucker studied her face as she stared through the windshield. "You came close to thanking me. Perhaps, after the close call with that customer, an intelligent and attractive woman like you would give retirement some serious thought."

She turned to face him, emoting outrage at his implication. "He was no customer. I'm no hooker. I'm an heiress who loves to stroll at night."

Rucker snickered. "That's a crock. I know you're a hooker, among other things. You are at least acquainted with the attacker. What's his name?"

She shrugged. "I don't know. You see, I've got a weakness

for cute strangers who want to pick me up." She opened the car door. "Officer, since I won't press charges, nor will I identify that creep if arrested, may I finish my stroll?"

He moved close to her. "You haven't been searched."

She looked into his eyes and wiggled her rear end on the seat. "Here and now, Officer? You'll be wasting your time. I'm clean." She shoved her bosom toward him. "Go on. Touch me. Find where excitement is."

He thought about Crane and fought an impulse to punch her in the face. He smiled and moved back under the wheel. "You're free to go."

She opened the door and stepped out into the street. She paused at the open window. "You could've become something wonderful. It's too bad you ruined yourself and became a cop," she said before she turned away.

He watched her undulating curves in the rearview mirror until she disappeared down Sunset. A moment later, his radio informed him that the Mercury was on the hot list.

He left the scene after a tow unit came to take it away. He went home to sleep fitfully. Crane's situation dominated his thinking.

At 6:30 a.m., he met the extra cop on his squad at a Melrose Avenue coffee shop.

"Well, Sergeant, I struck out," the lanky cop with the commonplace face said wearily as he took a stool at the counter beside Rucker.

"Phil, I'm not surprised that you couldn't bust any of the target hookers. Your effort was valuable to me and much appreciated."

Phil ordered coffee from a waitress. He said, "Sergeant, you can trust me. What the hell is going on?"

Rucker said, "Phil, I've known you for close to fifteen years. I trust you enough to take you on as a squad replacement for an officer taking leave in a couple of days. Change your looks with a mustache or whatever. I'll get you a different car. I predict you'll bust Shetani girls tonight. For now, I can't tell you anything else. Can I trust you not to say anything about our bit of intrigue?"

Phil nodded and took a sip of coffee.

12

The next morning, at 7 a.m., Rucker sat in his car on the station lot, waiting for Crane to sign out. Phil, in disguise and using an unlisted undercover car, had busted six Shetani girls before Petra pulled the stable off the track.

Rucker felt tension encase him. He breathed deeply several times to relieve the pressure. He almost regretted that he hadn't thrown Crane to the wolves of Internal Affairs. He could have spared himself the pain and risk of it all. He said a silent prayer that Crane wouldn't do something crazy when confronted.

Rucker's hand trembled as he placed his service pistol between his legs for fast access. He stiffened at the sight of the nearly emaciated Crane leaving the station.

Crane glanced at Rucker and threw up a hand as Rucker waved him to the Lincoln's open passenger window.

"Get in, Leo. I want to talk to you."

Crane shuffled his feet. "Russ, if it can wait, I . . ."

Rucker leaned to push open the door. "Get in, Leo," he ordered.

"I've had a rough night," Crane said as he got into the car.

Rucker moved the Lincoln to a corner of the lot. He keyed off the engine. Crane recoiled from his cold blue eyes.

"Russ, why are you looking at me like that?" Crane said in a near-whisper.

"How am I supposed to look at a john with a badge? How could you cross me, the department, for a low-life hooker?"

Crane's breathing was noisy and spastic. "C'mon, Russ, that's crazy. I wouldn't—"

Rucker cut him off. "Shut up! You weak bastard, I've got evidence to prove that you made our undercover car licenses available to Shetani's stable."

Crane stared through the windshield as if hypnotized. His right hand twitched and moved in slow motion toward the gun holstered at the small of his back.

Rucker took his gun from between his legs with his left hand. He said sharply, "Freeze! I want your piece, Leo. Lean forward."

Crane oozed sweat as he hesitated. He realized he had been too obsessed with coke and Petra to get rid of his service revolver, which he had used to kill Leon. "Please, Russ, don't do this to me."

Rucker said harshly, "Put your hands on your knees and lean forward."

Crane complied. Rucker removed his gun and dropped it into his jacket pocket. "Now give me your badge, you crooked sonuvabitch!"

Crane unpinned the shield from the inner side of his wallet and placed it in Rucker's palm. Rucker pocketed it and holstered his own gun. Crane pleaded, "Keep this between us. I'll resign. Please, Russ!"

"Sorry, Leo. You've got to pay for conspiring with Petra the hooker to commit the felony of obstruction of justice."

Crane bent over to bury his face in his hands. He sobbed, "Sure, Russ, you're right. I hope some con kills me when I get to the joint."

Rucker studied him for a very long moment. "Leo, I'm still your friend. You don't have to go to prison."

Crane sat upright to look at Rucker. "What?" he exclaimed.

"Leo, I'll keep your mistakes a secret between us, but I demand that you do certain things."

Crane nodded vigorously.

"I want you to take a month's leave of absence for your nervous exhaustion that I'll explain to Lieutenant Bleeson. I want you to go into a coke rehab clinic for a week as an inpatient and five weeks as an outpatient. I want you to break contact with Petra and anybody else connected to drugs. Agreed? Here's their card. They're waiting for you. Check in as Pat Hensley."

Crane took the card and glanced at it before he dropped it into his shirt pocket. They shook hands. Crane frowned. "Russ, thanks for the break, but I can't cut the clinic nut. I'm broke."

Rucker said, "I'll pay for you. I must be paid back some bucks every month until you're squared up."

They shook hands again. Crane opened the door to leave. Crane said, "Russ, I've got myself together. Please, give me my badge and gun."

Rucker shook his head. "I'm sorry, Leo. I'll return them after you complete your treatment."

Crane said, "I'll check in tomorrow." He started to step out of the car. Rucker said solemnly, "Leo, if you fail to keep your end of our deal, I'll throw you to Bleeson. Understand?" Crane nodded and moved away.

Rucker drove away, thinking about Leon's death and Rainbow, who hadn't shown at his rooming house.

Crane went to his car, thinking about Petra, and how he could explain Rucker's secret cop. He drove to a pay phone to call Petra. Inside the booth he hesitated before dropping the quarter. He had to tell her something, to get his usual coke payoff now instead of later in the evening. He needed rest, but after the Rucker encounter, his mangled nerves needed coke more than anything.

He dropped the quarter. He would tell Petra that a typist had failed to include the license plate of the undercover car driven by the cop who had busted her stablemates.

Petra sleepily answered the phone. She banged the receiver down when she heard his voice.

Crane drove to Ralph Rosen's Record Shop on Hollywood Boulevard. He pounded on the locked door until his giant cousin drowsily stumbled from his rear living quarters to admit him.

"Ralph, I feel like dying. You got any medicine?" Crane said as he followed Ralph to his bedroom.

"Yeah, a little private stock. Sit down."

Crane dropped down on the side of the bed and took a paper-wrapped syringe and spoon from his sock. Ralph got a pinch of coke from a closet stash. Crane injected the dope and got to his feet. "Thanks, buddy," he said as he went toward the front door. Ralph followed. Crane stepped out. Ralph locked the door behind him.

. . .

The early-morning sun awakened Tuta in a Silver Lake motel room. She hadn't slept well. Her junkie need sapped her strength and made her belly sick. She had used up Pee Wee's gift of skag. Her regular trick who sold skag got busted the day she left Shetani.

She propped herself up in bed and lit a cigarette. She had money she had made working Ventura Boulevard, in the Valley. She hadn't called Pee Wee, because she wasn't sure she wanted or needed an intimate hookup with a woman. She also missed the security she felt with Shetani and the stable. She had thought about going back to Shetani and his big dope bag.

At noon, she glanced at the phone and wondered why she hadn't heard from Pee Wee. She dialed Pee Wee. Petra, whom Shetani had installed in Pee Wee's room on the chance that Tuta would call, answered the phone. Petra, the skilled maternal player, quickly promised Tuta that she would deliver some skag by cab and without Shetani's knowledge.

Petra dressed and called a cab company based in Hollywood. Two minutes later, the dispatcher called Shetani to report that a cab had been requested from his address and the caller's destination was a motel in Silver Lake.

Shetani told him to delay the cab for fifteen minutes. He assured the tipster that he would receive the promised hundred dollars before his shift ended.

Within two minutes, the twins stood in Shetani's bedroom. He handed Eli a slip of paper and said, "I'm sure Petra got a call from Tuta. If so, here's the address of Tuta's motel in Silver Lake. Stake it out until she hits the street. Try to snatch her in a cool, friendly way if you can."

The twins hurried away. A stakeout police car saw the twins pass in the van. A few minutes later, Detective Griffin's tan Datsun took up the tail on Petra's cab.

When Petra entered the motel, Griffin used his car phone to call Rucker at home. When Griffin mentioned the Silver Lake motel, Rucker was electrified. He remembered that one of the biggest busts in history had been made there in the recent past.

He had ordered twenty-four-hour surveillance on Petra, because he suspected her as being the drug courier for the hooked Shetani stable. He instructed Griffin to bust her if she exited the place before he got there.

Rucker hung up and went to his Lincoln. He drove toward Silver Lake and reviewed his motive for a spur-of-the-moment bust of Petra. He knew that even a fairly competent lawyer could beat a possession bust done without a warrant, using a defense of illegal search and seizure.

He was certain that the bust of Shetani girls the night before had been the first blow and money drain. The defense cost and bail for Petra, plus the loss of the investment in any heroin confiscated, would escalate the pressure on Shetani.

Rucker smiled grimly. He'd strike at Shetani at every opportunity until he sent him to prison or drove him out of the jurisdiction.

Inside Tuta's motel room, Petra withdrew a needle from Tuta's arm.

"Thank you so much, Petra."

Petra, seated beside her on the couch, hugged her. "You're welcome, baby."

Petra handed her the glassine bag from which the injection dope had been taken. Tuta reached into her bosom and handed Petra three hundred dollars in fifties.

"On the phone you said Pee Wee was out. How is she?" Tuta asked as she leaned to put out a cigarette in a coffee-table ashtray.

Petra laughed. "She's in Daddy's jail for aiding and abetting an escapee, you."

Tuta sighed. "That's so dirty. She didn't even know I was leavin' . . . When do you think she'll get out?"

Petra heard despair in her voice. She put an arm around her waist. "Daddy says she will get out when she tells where you are."

Tuta broke into tears. "Poor Pee Wee. I can't let her suffer like that. I'm going home with you," she blubbered.

Petra held her in her arms. She knew it had been a mistake to tell her about Pee Wee's plight. She didn't want Tuta to return and take Shetani off his emotional hook. She wanted him to suffer. Now she had no choice except to take Tuta home and take the credit for her return.

"Well, let's get you packed," she said as she got to her feet.

Tuta shoved the glassine bag into her bosom. Petra called a cab and requested that it come in a half-hour. They finished packing a moment before the cabbie blew his horn.

They left the room and walked toward the cab. Burly Detective Griffin got out of his Datsun, parked down the street. He reached them as they were about to enter the cab.

"Police! You're both under arrest," Griffin said as he flashed his badge and seized Petra's wrist.

At that instant, Rucker pulled abreast of the cab. He leapt

out and pursued Tuta, who had kicked off her shoes to dash down the sidewalk.

In the van, the twins watched the scene from a crowded parking lot across the street.

"Hey, Eli, ain't that pig chasing Tuta the same one that stopped us?"

Eli nodded. "Yeah. Remember we heard in the street that his name is Rucker, head pig of the ho squad."

They watched Rucker gaining on Tuta. Suddenly she glanced back at him and darted into the street. A fast-moving pickup truck slammed into her, brakes squealing. She flew through the air and dropped in the opposite lane of traffic. A moment later, the wheels of a diesel truck rolled across her neck and upper torso. Her chest gushed gore.

Rucker stood above her and waved traffic around her. The diesel driver ran to Rucker's side. "I couldn't help it! It was like she fell out of the sky beneath the wheels of my rig."

Moments later, a police car and paramedics arrived on-scene. Rucker knew that Tuta was dead before an examining paramedic shook his head and said solemnly, "This one's for the morgue."

Shortly after, the twins watched as Tuta's remains were sealed in a body bag and lifted into a morgue vehicle.

An hour later, in the squad room, Rucker completed writing his report of Tuta's death. He conferred with Detective Griffin, Petra's arresting officer. They both believed that she probably had some connection to the heroin found on Tuta. Despite the fact that Petra was clean, Rucker decided to hold her on an open charge. Perhaps she would develop junkie sickness and a spirit of cooperation before Shetani's lawyer forced him to release her.

13

The Brooks twins sat on a sofa in Shetani's sunken living room. They watched him, ashimmer in gold satin robe and pajamas, as he sat on a thronelike red silk chair. He had stared trancelike at the ceiling ever since they had given him their eyewitness account of Tuta's death. Cazo finally fidgeted and said softly, "Cap, 'scuse me for buttin' in on your thinkin', but wastin' the pig that chased Tuta into the morgue ain't no problem. Me and Eli will chill his shit anytime you . . ."

Shetani shifted his fearsome jade orbs from the ceiling to Cazo's face to silence him. Shetani's coal-black face was deformed by pain and rage. He whispered through his teeth, "You two forget about Rucker. I'm gonna do all the killing for Baby Sis . . . starting with that stinking black ho locked up downstairs."

Eli flung out his open palms. "But, Cap, why Pee Wee?"

Shetani's pearly teeth flashed in a hideous smile. "She poisoned Toot against me and encouraged her to leave me." He paused to wave them away. "Now, both of you, get out of my face."

The twins quickly left the room. Sorrow and murderous hatred ached his head. He groaned and ground his fists against his temples. He remembered the day in the Harlem hospital when he was told Tuta had died of leukemia. He saw the bloody vision of himself, in his late teens, when he returned moments later with a tire iron. He saw himself smashing the heads and faces and limbs of nurses and doctors at random for letting Tuta die. He remembered how he had to be force-fed in the mental hospital where he was sent to prevent his suicide by starvation.

Now he staggered zombielike to his bedroom and locked himself in. He collapsed on the carpet and bellowed his anguish. He thrashed and clubbed the walls with his fists. Finally, drenched in sweat, he got to his feet and took a .38 automatic pistol from under a pillow. He dropped a key to the basement into a robe pocket. He unlocked the bedroom door and stepped into the hall. His stable, alarmed by the racket of his grief, stood frozen as they stared at him.

"Master, are you sick?" Akura, a Japanese pixie asked.

He waved the gun. "No, I'm fine. Get out of my face!"

The scantily clad girls fled. He went to the stairway leading to the basement cell. He unlocked the door and was about to switch on the basement light when he heard the faint sounds of soul music. He started down and stumbled—nearly fell down the steep stairs in his haste to kill Pee Wee. Petra had the only other key. He'd punish Petra for providing the radio, he told himself.

He tiptoed on the concrete to the candlelit cell. That fucking Petra, he thought, would get double punishment for providing the candle. He went to the cell door and glared at Pee Wee, catnapping on her steel-slab bed, covered by a quilt provided by Petra. He aimed the pistol at the center of her forehead. His trigger finger started to pull when it hit him that the killer of Tuta did not deserve an easy death. He lowered the gun and held it out of sight behind his thigh. "Wake up, scum ass!" he growled.

She opened her dope-clouded eyes and instinctively threw a jacket across the contraband radio before she sat up. Her eyes made him realize she had conned him on his last visit that she was half dead from kicking skag cold turkey.

"Shit, bitch, Petra's got you living fine and dandy down here with my China white and everything."

Pee Wee shut off the radio. "Master Daddy, Petra ain't gave me no medicine. I shot up the last today I had stashed from my stealin' trip. Please, Master, let me out so I can hit the road and make you some more money."

He leveled the gun at her chest. "Strip, and throw your clothes through the bars."

She stalled, her big eyes oozing tears. "Please, Master, I'm a good bitch. Don't treat me like this."

He gritted his teeth and fired a round into the wall that scorched her hair. A spurt of her urine splashed on the concrete. She jumped to her feet and tore off her clothes down to her bra and panties. She pushed her dress and slip through the bars. He turned them inside out. He waggled the gun. "C'mon, bitch, I want you stone naked." He fired a round close to her feet. A sliver of concrete slashed a bloody gash on her ankle. She stripped off her panties and fumbled with her bra. She palmed a packet of dope as she unfastened the bra. A syringe fell to the floor. She pushed the bra and panties through the bars. He reached and grabbed the other hand and twisted her wrist until she squealed with pain and let the dope fall to the concrete.

He stared at her and smiled as he thought of the way he would kill her. He rocked on his heels and imagined her screaming in a maw of flames that would cinderize her. "Tuta's dead, crushed by a truck. You helped her to leave me. You killed her!"

Pee Wee dropped down heavily on the steel slab. "Please, Master, don't say that . . . I wouldn't hurt sweet baby Tuta. Have a little mercy!"

He grinned obscenely. "I'm gonna kill you, bitch, in a day or two. So live it up with your radio and candle. Now, ain't that mercy?" He picked up the dope packet before he went toward the stairway.

Pee Wee listened to his footsteps on the stairway. She heard him lock the basement door. Immediately she began to use a bobby pin to try to pick the padlock that secured the chain that locked her in. Fear and boiling hatred made her try unsuccessfully for several hours to free herself. She told herself she had to escape and kill Shetani, for his death threat and for conning her that he would fire Petra and make her his bottom woman. No less worse than that was the possibility she could end up serving a life sentence in Wisconsin for killing the German while on the stealing tour for Shetani.

At midnight, she heard someone unlock the basement door. She blew out her candle. An instant later, someone switched on the basement light and came down the stairs. Pee Wee shook with terror in a corner of the cell. She burst into tears when Petra came to the cell door, dressed in pink work clothes.

"Say, girl, pull yourself together or I'll take this turkey club sandwich and shake away," Petra said as she placed a paper bag on the cell-door shelf.

Pee Wee came to the door, wiping tears away. She pointed at the bullet gouges in the concrete and her lacerated ankle. "He shot at me! He told me he was going to kill me because Tuta was run over by a truck. He blames me! Please, help me get out of here!"

Petra removed dark glasses to reveal black-and-blue eye sockets. "This is what that radio and candle cost me. He'll cool off. I don't think he would kill you. He'd kill me if you escaped . . . besides, I don't have a key to that padlock. Listen, I've got to go. He could show at any minute. He went out with the twins to find out what Rucker, a cop, looks like so he can kill him for chasing Tuta into the path of the truck that killed her."

Pee Wee reached through the bars to grab Petra's wrist. "He's gone crazy! He's gonna kill me! Please, bring me something to smash this lock. He won't know you helped me. I'll take the lock and everything with me. Please!"

Petra pulled her wrist from Pee Wee's grip. "It can't work. The only way out of here is that locked door at the top of the stairs. Only he and I have a key. I sympathize with you, kiddo, but not enough to commit suicide."

Petra moved in close to the cell door. "Pee Wee, I've watched Daddy's head fall apart here in California, but I don't think he's crazy enough to kill you. I'm making plans to cut him loose. If you're still locked up when I split, I'll help you to escape. That's the best I can do." Petra turned away for the stairway.

"Petra, I don't need to go out that basement door!" Pee

Wee shouted. Petra turned back to face her. "I can go through that window."

Petra stepped back to look at a tiny window off the front driveway. Petra shook her head. "You can't get through there, Pee Wee. It's only a foot or so high and no more than eighteen inches wide."

Pee Wee grinned. "You mean it's that big? Shoot, me and a pal sawed off one bar in a cell and went out after greasing with Vaseline. I'm a tiny bitch, baby. Just bring me some butter, or even cooking oil, and a hammer or a bumper jack. Do it before the sun comes up. Will ya, huh?"

Petra studied her for a long moment before she said, "I'll think about it." Petra walked away.

At the moment when Petra ascended the basement stairway, Shetani and the twins spotted Rucker on Sunset.

"Cap, there's the mothafucka!" Eli exclaimed as he excitedly pointed at Rucker, seated in an undercover Ford parked across the boulevard.

Driver Eli parked the rented station wagon. Cazo, seated behind Eli and Shetani, said, "Say, Cap, lemme go across the street and blow away the back of his head with my .38, huh?"

Shetani vigorously shook his head and stepped out to the street. He said, "No, bro, that's too good for that pig. Besides, I told you, he's mine to barbecue. I'm a stranger to him, so I'm going across the street to cop a close look at his face. Pick me up at the corner over there, behind his car."

The twins watched him jaywalk through traffic. He reached the other side behind Rucker's car.

Rucker, distracted by a pair of flashy sexpots suspected as new hookers, did not notice Shetani as he bought a New York paper at a newsstand facing Rucker's car.

Shetani studied Rucker's profile for a long moment. Then he positioned himself a foot from the front of the car to get a full-face view. He pretended to look at the front page of the paper as he shot lightning glances at Rucker's face. Hatred paralyzed him. He saw an irresistible vision of himself slashing Rucker's throat. Why wait to kill the pig later? His question electrified his crotch. He gripped the switchblade in the pocket of his red silk leisure suit at the instant when Rucker locked eyes with him. Rucker made him immediately, from mug shots his New York detective friend had sent.

Rucker slipped on a bland mask to cover his loathing and alarm. He remembered Shetani's vicious rap sheet and thought, "This ass kicker looks like a clone of Satan dressed in a suit of fire." Rucker toyed with his necktie near his shoulder-holstered weapon.

Shetani relaxed his facial muscles and stepped off the curb into the street. He went to the driver's side of Rucker's car. He showed his dental-ad teeth as he leaned close to Rucker's throat. "Sir, excuse me, but could you tell me the location of the Pussycat Theater?" Shetani drew the switchblade and held it tight against his right thigh. He'd decided it would be swifter and easier to backhand the blade into Rucker's throat, instead of slash action. With his victim in shock, he could stab him in the heart.

"Sure, the Pussycat is several blocks west of here," Rucker replied as he slid inches away on the seat for drawing space.

Shetani grinned. "Thanks a lot." He turned away to take his target by surprise. He was about to spin back with a horrific blow of the knife when one of Rucker's undercover cops cruised to a stop beside Rucker's car.

"Say, Russ, have you seen a blonde in a purple mini? She

ran when I stopped her for questioning," Shetani heard the cop say as he hurried away to be picked up at the corner.

"No, Tommy, I haven't seen her," Rucker replied as he keyed on the car engine. The cop pulled away. Rucker hurtled the Ford in reverse toward the corner, in pursuit of Shetani. He had been about to draw his gun and search Shetani for concealed weapons when the cop pulled up.

Rucker did not spot Shetani at the corner, or in any of the business establishments, after a search of the immediate area. His guts ached from the confrontation with the breed of criminal he hated most after child molesters. He had a wishful fantasy that Shetani would draw a gun when he, Rucker, braced him the very next time he was spotted in Hollywood.

Shetani and the twins arrived at their hilltop lair. Froggy, the gate man in his cubicle, tore himself away from a porn magazine to admit them. Eli drove the rented station wagon down the long driveway to the side of the castlelike mansion. Maple trees groaned and swayed under the whip of Santa Ana winds. A monstrous moon flooded the grounds with eerie light.

"We're making a trip to the desert at daybreak," Shetani said as Eli doused the car lights.

Eli tapped his fingertips together. "Cap, 'scuse me for askin' . . . What's gonna go down?"

Shetani smiled. "I missed the chance to punish that pig, but Pee Wee, the other one that wasted Tuta, is got to go." He frowned at the flabbergast on the faces of the twins. Shetani slid out of the car. He stuck his head inside the car. "Can you guys keep a sacred secret?" The twins nodded. "Maxine was really and truly my baby sis, returned from death to be with me. She would want me to punish the ones responsible for sending her back to the grave. So siphon four or five gallons of gas from one of the vans. Get a coupla shovels from the gardener's shack." He turned away.

The twins watched him enter the house, with mouths agape. Eli said softly, "Cazo, you thinkin' what I'm thinkin'?"

Cazo sadly shook his head. "Sure am. Cap is done gone ravin' crazy."

Eli's hand shook as he lit a cigarette. "We ain't never had no part in icing no woman, 'specially a sister."

Cazo sighed. "We like Pee Wee."

Eli said, "You thinkin' what I'm thinkin'?"

Cazo, seated behind Eli, extended a giant paw across the seat and said, "We ain't gonna let him kill Pee Wee." They shook hands and left the car.

Inside the mansion, Shetani froze as he was about to enter his bedroom. He heard the juvenile voice of Tuta say, "Albert! I've missed you so much." He spun and went down the hallway. He invaded and searched the bedrooms where his stable slept in pairs. "Hey, baby girl, this ain't the time to play games. C'mon and give me a hug." He paused outside Petra's room. He distinctly heard the voice behind the door giggle and say, "Big bro, don't get salty. This is fun!"

Soundlessly, he eased Petra's door open. Petra raised her eyes from a book to stare fearfully at him. "Are you all right, Master?" He walked to the side of the bed. "Yeah. I want you to go to the morgue when you wake up. Make the ID of Tuta's body as her stepmother. I don't want peckerwoods handling her. Get a South Central undertaker to cremate her."

Petra nodded. He smiled. "I'm gonna be Pee Wee's undertaker."

Shetani turned away and left the room. He went down

the basement stairs to check on Pee Wee. He heard the voice croon, "Big bro, please don't be mad 'cause you can't see me. I love you."

He went to Pee Wee's cell and stood glaring at her. "Sweet Master, are you still real mad at me?" she said in a sugary voice. They stared at each other for a very long moment.

"I'm going to bury your stinking ass in the desert this morning," he said in a chillingly casual way, before he turned and went up the stairs.

Pee Wee's heart thumped crazily, and her eyes were bright with fear in her sweaty black face. She screamed in a whisper, "I gotta escape. I gotta kill him!" She feverishly started again with a hairpin to pick the padlock that secured the chain on the cell door. An hour later, Petra, lying sleepless in her bedroom, decided that she would help Pee Wee to escape before daybreak.

14

It was 1:00 a.m. in San Francisco's Fillmore District. Rainbow, the eyewitness to Crane's murder of Lovely Leon, checked out of his hotel and drove a used Chevy toward the highway for New York. He had not come forward to finger Crane, because he feared crooked cop pals of Crane would kill him before the trials. Also, he was wanted for grand theft in Pasadena. He couldn't get the death of Leon out of his head, and his peace of mind was impossible with his soul brother's killer scot-free.

On the outskirts of the city, he decided to get some relief from the internal pressure. He pulled into a gas station. He called Hollywood Station for the head dude of the hooker squad.

Rucker had just booked a hooker and was leaving the desk when Rainbow's call came in. Rainbow blurted, "Sir, I don't think you gonna do nothing about it, 'cause Leon was a nigger. But I saw one of your squad cops blow my buddy away.

Leon hipped me who he was when we dug him leaving a motel with a snow-blonde ho. Leon said his name was Blaine or Crane or sumpin' like that."

"You got me wrong, fella. I want to see the killer punished, whoever he is. I need you. Where are—"

Rainbow hung up and went to his car. Rucker stood, holding the receiver, his mouth open. He rushed to his car. He had gotten a good look at Rainbow the day Leon stopped his Cadillac at a red light and spoke to him. Rucker had heard traffic noise in the background during Rainbow's call. He decided to search Hollywood for the eyewitness.

At that moment, Opal Lenski got out of a cab at Rucker's house. She had flown in from New York for a brief visit with Rucker. She desperately needed the comfort and therapy of his arms. Her sick mother had suffered convulsions. Opal had panicked and called in a medical doctor who recommended immediate hospitalization. Opal's Christian Science church, outraged by her breach of faith in God as the supreme doctor, had expelled her.

Opal keyed into the darkened house and went to Rucker's bedroom. She felt more relaxed after she showered and slipped into a seductive pink negligee. She turned on the TV to a romantic late movie. She glanced at one of Rucker's holstered guns slung across the headboard. She placed the holstered weapon on the carpet as she propped herself up in bed. Shortly, she dozed off.

Ten miles away, in a suburb of L.A., Crane lay sleeplessly in his bed at a rehab center for drug abusers. He couldn't rest, couldn't kick his cocaine habit, with the Leon murder gun, his gun, in Rucker's possession. He had to retrieve it and destroy it. He slid out of bed and paced the floor of the small, neat room for several minutes. He paused at a window over-looking the clinic's parking lot. He was certain that Rucker had taken the murder gun home for safekeeping. He was also certain that workhorse Rucker would be in the streets of Hollywood on Saturday night until nearly dawn.

He glanced at 2:30 a.m. on the face of his wristwatch. He stared at a group of parked cars belonging to the clinic's night shift. His heart galloped. He saw an old Ford with its driver-side window down. He knew that, blindfolded, he could hot-wire the Ford to life. He decided that Rucker was too good a cop to be allowed custody of the gun another day. A thousand possibilities could trigger Rucker's whim to give the gun a ballistics test.

He was going to retrieve his gun now, Crane told himself as he speed-dressed in street clothes. He stepped out of the window onto a flower bed. He stood stock-still in the fragrant quiet for a long moment before he sprinted across the parking lot to the Ford.

He stuck his head beneath the dashboard and lit matches to see his way to bypass the ignition. Within minutes, he was tooling the well-tuned machine toward L.A.

A half-mile from Hollywood, he suddenly pulled the Ford into a quiet side street and parked beneath a streetlight. He got out and opened the car trunk. He pawed through a jum-ble of junk and soiled clothing. He found a floppy denim hat and jammed it down over his head. He got behind the wheel and peered into the rearview mirror. The super-large hat almost obscured his face in shadow. He felt that now he would not be recognizable in Hollywood by cruising detectives and cops in black-and-whites who knew him.

He was about to move away when a panic attack struck him. He stiffened on the seat and burst sweat. Tension, like steel mallets, hammered his chest. The cacophony of his heartbeat convinced him he was dying. He pushed his head out the window and sucked air, his luminous gray eyes bulging. It was several minutes before he recovered. Then self-pity claimed him. He sobbed, jerkily, like a little kid, as he remembered his wonderful mom and dad and what a happy ten-year-old boy he had been.

He wept wildly at the memory of that awful day when a tractor trailer overturned and crushed his parents to death as they drove home on the freeway. He and his cousin Ralph Rosen had just returned from a day at the beach when the police gave him the news. He remembered how Opal Lenski, sister of his mom, had taken him in.

Finally, he dried his tears and remembered how Rucker had helped to make him a good cop in the tough 77th Division. Coke and Petra lust stroked his genitals as he moved the Ford toward Hollywood. Defensive, random rage and hate seized him. Coke! How he hated the poison that had virtually destroyed him, he ranted to himself. He hated Millie, his no-suck, overweight, unglamorous wife. She was to blame for everything. It had been her shortcomings, in bed and otherwise, that had set him up to murder, and to fall for Petra, he audibly lied to himself.

As for Petra, he would be thrilled to blast out the blue windows of her rotten soul with his pistol. He was going to retrieve the murder gun, go back to the clinic, and kick his coke habit forever. Then he was going to be one of the best cops there ever was, he vowed with clenched teeth.

Crane parked the Ford several houses away from Rucker's home on the quiet street. He went down the sidewalk and moved swiftly across Rucker's front lawn to the rear of the house. He stooped beside a basement window and dislodged a decorative brick from a flower bed. He knocked a small hole in the window above a latch with a corner of the brick. He replaced the brick and slid into the basement. He ascended the short flight of stairs and popped open the spring lock on the door with his pocket knife.

He entered the kitchen, and moved quickly into the living room, and up the stairs to Rucker's bedroom. He stood paralyzed at the entrance as he stared at Opal's back. He smiled in thought. Aha, even old straitlaced Russ can kick up his heels.

He moved to search a chest of drawers across the room. He had soundlessly searched half of the drawers when Opal stirred and turned on her back. Crane stood frozen, staring at his aunt's face in a spot of moonlight. His hand shook as he pulled out a drawer. It made a rasping sound that reverberated in the silence.

Crane locked his eyes on Opal. Her eyelids fluttered as his hands rummaged through the drawer. He lifted a gun from the drawer and went toward a beam of hallway light near the bedroom door. He tore his eyes away from Opal's form to check the gun's serial numbers. It was his gun!

He stepped into the hallway. He noticed that he had left the last drawer pulled out. He couldn't leave it that way, he reasoned. Rucker would know when the gun was taken. If everything was in order, days could pass before the gun was missed.

Crane tiptoed back to the dresser. He stared at Opal as he carefully started to push in the drawer.

Her eyes suddenly popped open. The glitter of the gun in the shadowy intruder's hand terrified her. She reached for Rucker's holstered gun on the carpet. She shot him as he whirled away, toward her, heading for the hallway. He felt the slug burn into his chest and slam him against the door frame. His legs looped and twisted like rubber pretzels as he half fell down the stairway.

The front door seemed so far away, so enveloped in a black fog. He unlocked the door and stumbled across the porch, hemorrhaging great gouts of blood from his mouth. He tumbled onto the lawn, and died after a convulsive sigh. He clutched the murder gun tight in his fist, like treasure, agleam in the moonlight.

Inside the house, Opal trembled as she stood looking down from a bedroom window at Crane's body. She collapsed on the bed. She was so upset, she failed several times to get 911 on the lighted telephone dial to report that she had shot a burglar.

Rucker, cruising the east end of Sunset, heard of the shooting at his address on his police radio. He arrived on-scene a minute after the first police unit. The two young uniformed cops with flashlights stood staring down at Crane's corpse.

Rucker parked and rushed to join them. His knees wobbled, and he gasped. "Oh no!"

One of the cops who knew Rucker said, "Sir, he's a goner . . . Uh, do you know him?"

Rucker muttered, "I know him."

An instant later, Opal sobbed from an open bedroom window, "Oh, Ruck, I'm so glad to see you."

Rucker raced through his house to the bedroom. He switched on a light. Opal ran into his arms.

She blubbered hysterically against his chest. "Ruck, I shot that man! I woke up to see him standing over there. He had a gun. It was horrible!"

Rucker sat on the side of the bed and cradled her on his lap. He gently massaged her shoulders and back as he fought back his own tears. A moment later, she felt his chest heave when his tears broke free.

She looked into his face. "Ruck, I'm so sorry to upset you this way."

He held her close. "Opal, it's not your fault," he whispered into her hair. They clung together for a long time before the hubbub of arriving homicide detectives and a coroner's wagon forced Rucker to break the embrace.

He let her down gently on the bed. He kissed her forehead and got to his feet. He leaned over and blotted her eyes and face with a handkerchief. "Hon, please be strong enough to bear the pain of knowing the identity of the man you shot," he said quietly, as he dried his own tears.

She bolted upright on the bed with gigantic eyes as he moved to open the dresser drawer where he had kept Crane's gun. He quickly searched the drawer, and then went through the rest of them. He went back to sit on the bed. He held her hands. "Hon, that was Leo you shot . . . He's dead," he heard himself mutter in an oddly unfamiliar voice.

The shock of it rapidly waggled her head in denial. Her eyes rolled toward the ceiling. She dug her fingernails into Rucker's palms. She wailed, "No. No. It wasn't Leo over there. Why would Leo sneak in here in the dark with a gun?"

He took her hands to his mouth. He kissed them. "Dear,

Leo killed a black man with his service revolver. I, uh, didn't know he was the killer when I took his gun to safekeep until his release from cocaine treatment. He broke in tonight to get the murder gun, the one you saw him with."

Rucker paused to squeeze his throbbing temples. "I risked a lot to protect him from disgrace and ruin." Rucker heaved a sigh and stood. He waved his palms helplessly through the air. "Now everything, the pain, the risk, all of it was for nothing . . . Homicide will be up here to talk to you. The truth clears you—be strong."

She nodded and half whispered, "Leo would be alive if I hadn't needed your arms so much that I came to L.A. tonight."

Rucker said, "Stop that, Opal. You know that nobody bucks fate." He turned and left the room.

At 4:00 a.m., Petra sat on the side of her bed, smoking a cigarette and planning. She had decided to let Pee Wee escape and to leave Shetani at first opportunity. She was convinced that he had become insane and was no longer worth her loyalty, respect, and trust. In fact, of late she feared for her life, she reminded herself. She'd go back to New York, to a wealthy white trick who adored her.

She'd put the street down. The trick would bankroll an escort-service front for well-heeled tricks. Her startup girls would be the ones she would steal from Shetani.

She stood up and smiled at her bewitching snow-blonde reflection in a door mirror. The crazy black sonuvabitch wouldn't be able to fuck with her once she fled into the white world with the protection of powerful white men, she assured herself.

She felt sure that Shetani was asleep. She boldly left the house and went across an expanse of lawn to the gardener's shack for a hammer.

Froggy, the gateman, had been sternly ordered by Shetani to sleep by day and report all movement on the grounds from midnight to daybreak. Froggy was distracted by a galaxy of fornicating she/he's in a porn mag when Petra entered the shack.

He spotted her immediately and saw that she exited with a suspicious-looking hammer. Why would a ho need a hammer after 4:00 a.m.? Froggy asked himself.

Petra entered the house and got a pound of butter from the refrigerator.

Froggy dialed his sleeping boss, who answered with a snarl, followed by a verbal pat on the back when Froggy delivered the hot news.

Petra went directly to Pee Wee's cell. "Girl, I'm sure glad you showed," Pee Wee exclaimed as she sprang from her steel-slab bed to stand with shining eyes at the cell door. She reached for the hammer in Petra's hand.

Petra withdrew her hand. "Pee Wee, I'm risking my ass to help you. Promise that you will take the chain, smashed lock, and hammer with you and throw them in some bushes down the road. And don't try to split through the gate. Go over the fence where the tall hedges are. Promise?"

Pee Wee nodded excitedly. "Sure, Angel Blue Eyes. I promise." She took the extended hammer. "Say, friend, how 'bout leavin' the kitchen door unlocked, so I can sneak in my old room and pack some stuff in a suitcase? I also got a coupla C-notes stashed up there. Okay?"

Petra studied her for a long time before she said, "All right, but you're a dead little bitch if he catches you."

Pee Wee grinned. "Sister, I ain't gonna fuck around up there . . . Say, I owe you for this. Lemme ask you a personal question."

Petra nodded.

"Ain't you ready to cut that crazy nigger loose?"

Petra smiled. "Yes. Soon. Now I'm getting the hell out of this basement." Petra passed the pound of butter to Pee Wee and said, "This is the only grease for your body that I could find."

Pee Wee said, "You're so fuckin' precious," and grabbed the sleeve of her robe. "Sister, like I said, I owe you and myself, too. Why don't I ice that bad motherfucker before I split? What do you think about that. Huh?"

Petra shook her head vigorously. "Escape, Pee Wee. Don't commit suicide. Good luck," Petra said as she turned away for the stairway.

Eavesdropper Shetani, in bare feet, raced silently up the stairway and went through the open door at the top of the stairs at the instant when Petra started up. His face was hideous with rage as he hurried to his bedroom to set a death trap for Pee Wee.

Petra locked the door with her key and went to her bedroom.

Shetani paced the floor of his bedroom, analyzing what he had overheard. He decided that Pee Wee intended to kill him before she got in the wind. He had to prevent her escape, in case she decided it was too risky to make a kill try. He started to dial the twins. But he had detected earlier a lack of enthusiasm for his plan to get rid of Pee Wee. Instead, he called Froggy in his gate cubicle.

"Hey, Frog. Get out and patrol the front wall with your shotgun. If you spot Pee Wee, stop her and bring her to me. If she runs, blow her away. Got that?"

Froggy laughed. "I sho' do, Cap. Ain't no way the bitch is gonna git by me."

Shetani hung up and busied himself fashioning a blanket dummy to place beneath his bedcovers.

In the basement, his impulse to blow away Petra and Pee Wee had been blocked by a sudden horrific plan to punish them. He switched off all lights except the feeble red light behind the bed. He stepped back to check out his effort. He didn't like the shapeless head section of the dummy. He went down the hall to a stable bedroom. He brought back a curly black wig mounted on a Styrofoam stand. He positioned it beneath the covers, with just the curly top of the wig visible. He smiled in satisfaction as he went to hide behind a massive leather chair by the foot of the bed.

He pulled a blue silk belt from his robe and doubled it for a failsafe garrote. His hellish eyes glowed like green phosphorus in the dim stillness.

In the basement, Pee Wee greased her tiny naked body with butter. Finished, she stared at the smashed lock and hammer. Why bother with them? she thought. Shetani couldn't punish Petra dead, but what if she was forced for some reason to escape without killing Shetani?

She picked up the hardware. She dragged a battered steamer trunk to an eighteen-by-twenty-inch window. She stood on it and opened the window. She shoved the lock and hammer onto the ground beneath the kitchen. She panted and struggled for what seemed like ages before she slipped through the window.

Exhausted, she got to her feet and filled her lungs with air. Awash in blue moonglow, her naked black body shone like indigo satin. Her elfish face was twisted into a fright mask of murderous intent. Her fury was more poisonous than when she shot the German trick to death in Wisconsin.

She hid the lock in some bushes before she entered the kitchen, carrying the hammer. She would use it to ice him unless she found something better. She found a meat cleaver in a drawer. She dropped the hammer behind the refrigerator and catfooted up the stairway to the second floor.

She stood outside his bedroom with an ear pressed against the door. She felt faint with tension. She closed her eyes for a moment and gritted her teeth. She eased the door open and stepped into the gloom. She saw the top of his curly head exposed for the killing blow. Ecstasy shook her as she crept to his bedside, holding the glittering cleaver with both her hands. She issued a gut-deep, shrill, orgasmic cry as she violently hacked the curly head into halves. Her eyes were gargantuan as she stared at the Styrofoam fake.

The corner of her eye caught the flicker of his shadow as he swooped from behind the chair. She screamed and started to whirl to her right to hack him with the cleaver.

The momentum of his rush knocked her to the carpet on her face. He looped the belt around her throat. He laughed as her frail body thrashed and struggled against the garrote and his weight atop her. Finally, he flipped her over and looked into her blank, bulgy eyes.

He lifted her into his arms. He walked down the hallway,

into sleeping Petra's room, to kick off the first stage of punishment for her. He carefully placed Pee Wee's corpse beside Petra, with the garrote deeply embedded in flesh around the throat. The tongue lolled out on the chin, fat and purpled. The face of the corpse was almost touching Petra's. He draped one of Pee Wee's arms across Petra's chest.

Petra stirred when he turned on her bright ceiling light. He sat on the side of the bed. He gazed at the gruesome tableau for a long moment before he pinched Petra's earlobe.

Her long lashes fluttered and unveiled her drowsy blue eyes, which suddenly became electric with terror as they focused on the face of Shetani. She flung her hand to her chest in alarm.

"Master, what on earth!" The breath to speak further was cut off when her fingers touched the arm of the corpse. She switched her eyes to the awful face of the body. She shrieked and catapulted herself up off the mattress, to a standing position against the headboard. She wrung her hands and gibbered like a Holy Roller speaking in tongues.

He seized her wrists and hurled her to the floor. He stared down at her and said sweetly, "Hey, mama ho, don't be upset like a square bitch 'cause one of your favorite kids got fucked up trying to ice her daddy. Now sweet Master is going to punish you for crossing me." He knelt beside her and took a .45 pistol from his robe pocket.

Benumbed by horror, she lay in a ball while he battered her body from head to ankles with the butt of the heavy weapon. He gagged her and tied her hands and feet with stockings. He ripped the phone line from the wall. Dripping sweat, he lifted her into bed, then carried the wee corpse back to his room. He went back to lock Petra's door.

He woke up the stable and ordered them to pack for a trip back to New York. He wrapped the corpse in a blanket and put it in his closet.

He took a shower and put on fresh peach silk pajamas. He knew that Petra was in no shape to run, so he injected a load of skag. He relaxed on the bed and planned how he would kill Rucker and force Petra to structure her own death.

In the middle of an interrogation of Opal by homicide detectives, Opal's brother in New York called Rucker's home with the news that Mother Rebecca Lenski had passed away. The second heavy emotional blow, after the shooting of her nephew, was more than even strong Opal could bear. She became so distraught that Rucker checked her into Cedars-Sinai for treatment and rest.

At eight-thirty, still sleepless, he reported to Hollywood Station to discuss with homicide detectives Crane's hookup with Petra and his involvement in Leon's death.

Commander Bleeson joined the meeting. In the course of discussion, he mentioned that a pair of New York homicide detectives were flying in with murder-arrest warrants for the Brooks twins. A reliable eyewitness in Harlem had come forth who had seen the twins riddle Cecil "Tree" Lewis with a machine gun and an automatic pistol in Tree's backyard marijuana garden. The murder of Tree had been requested of Shetani by his skag suppliers, the Mafiosi Angelo and Joey, for Tree's robbery of Mafia-protected drug dealers in Harlem.

Weary Rucker left the station and drove home to try for some rest.

Inside the Shetani house of death, the Brooks twins sat in the living room, listening to Shetani briefing the stable. He sat in his thronelike royal-purple chair, with his bejeweled fingers tented beneath his pointed chin.

The girls, in casual traveling clothes, sat around him, surrounded by their luggage. Diane, a trusted Jewish sexpot with long, luxuriant sable hair, sat on the floor beside Shetani. He spoke softly.

"Sweet things, Petra is out of town, taking care of some business for Daddy. Diane will be looking out for you on the trip back to our hotel in the Apple. Listen to her like you did to Petra. The seats in the large van are soft and cozy. Diane will have medicine galore, and what a ball everybody's gonna have seeing beautiful America. You'll be drinkin' champagne and shootin' China white and watchin' porn movies in ritzy hotels along the way."

They cheered. He shaped a nonhideous smile. "And since the trip is a holiday, I'll punish the bitch that turns a trick."

They laughed and cheered lustily. He raised a palm to silence them. "Froggy is driving, with Diane as backup. Me and the twins will probably be home when you get there. I'm gonna miss you all a lot until I see you again. Now, hit the fuckin' road and have fun."

They descended upon him with hugs and kisses before they split. The twins, seated on a sofa across the room, watched him light a water pipe to smoke crack.

Eli cleared his throat. "'Scuse me, Cap, but me and Cazo sure hope you changed your mind overnight about wastin' lil Pee Wee."

Shetani smiled. "She escaped last night. I'm glad the jinky bitch is gone."

Doubt wrinkled Cazo's brow. Cap, you mus' be jivin'. Ain't no way that lil sister could beat that cell."

Eli cut in. "Yeah, Cap, ain't no way. How she do it?"

Shetani fingered the .45 in his robe pocket. "Get out of my face and find the bitch and ask her how she did it."

The tone of his voice and the sudden ferocity in his face told them he'd killed her. The twins looked at each other and stood. Cazo said, "Okay, Cap, maybe she's hidin' in the house. We'll find her and ask her how she did it."

Eli's face was grim. He said in a low, deadly voice, "Cap, we goin' be upset like a motherfucker if Pee Wee got wasted."

They hurriedly left the room.

Shetani sprang to his feet and went to an end table beside the sofa. He opened the drawer and took out a small ring of keys. He went to a tall gun cabinet and removed a huge padlock from its door. He went upstairs. He stood at the top of the stairs and peeped at the twins, moving in and out of the stable bedrooms. He watched them try Petra's locked door before they tried his locked door.

Eli said, as he put his shoulder to the door, "Let's look in there."

Rage ached Shetani's guts, that they, his lackeys, would challenge him this way. He leveled the .45 to blow them away for desert burial with Pee Wee and Petra, but some imperative block paralyzed his trigger finger.

With the gun still leveled at them, he hollered, "Freeze, lard asses, and reach for the fuckin' ceiling!"

They spun away from the door to face him and reached. "Cap, you ain't gonna blow away your homeboys that you knowed since kindergarten," Cazo whined as Shetani walked toward them.

"Not this minute, coon ass. I'm gonna put you salty cock-suckers in jail to cool off. Move!" Shetani said harshly as he waved the gun.

The twins led the way to the basement door. Shetani threw the key to the door onto the floor. He ordered, "One of you niggers unlock that door and switch on the light."

Eli lowered his hands, picked up the key, and unlocked the door. Cazo switched on the light. They paused and turned toward him. Cazo pleaded, "Cap, ain't no reasons to lock us up. We ain't gonna git outta line no more."

Shetani fired a thunderous round that gouged out a hunk of plaster a couple of inches above Cazo's head. The twins scampered down the stairway and into the cell.

Shetani reached through the bars to get the long, heavy logging chain off the concrete. He threaded it twice through the cell and cell-door bars before he affixed the giant pad-lock.

"What you goin' do with us, Cap?" Cazo asked plain-tively.

"I don't trust you niggers anymore. I'll think of some-thing," Shetani said as he turned away for the stairway.

He went to his bedroom and unlocked the door of his closet, where the corpse of Pee Wee lay. He had a compulsion to make sure she was still there, and dead. She was. He made sure his dope kit and an envelope of China white was beneath a pillow before he left the room, with the door unlocked.

He let himself into Petra's room. She lay, still gagged and bound hand and foot and on her back. She mumbled through the gag and stared at him through slits in her battered face. He gazed at her and smiled at the thought that she would be dead within the hour if she failed a deadly test.

"You gonna be sweet and behave yourself?" he crooned as he bent to nip an exposed nipple with his teeth.

She moved away and nodded yes. He freed her. He had ripped off her nightgown during the beating. Now her body was ugly with masses of blue-black bruises. She stood and moved shakily to a mirrored dressing table. She sat down and took a dope kit from a drawer. He watched her use a hand mirror to inject China white into the hidden space between her vulva and lower inner buttock. She winced when she reached for a pack of cigarettes on the table. She extended the pack toward him. He joined her on the padded bench, and they lit up together.

He whispered into her ear, "Please forgive your sweet daddy for being mean 'cause you hurt his heart by crossing him for Pee Wee—huh, sugar pet, please?"

She managed a slight smile with swollen lips. She realized that she could never be free and safe so long as he lived. She glanced at scissors on the tabletop and fantasized a heart shot. But she feared his feline quickness.

"Sure, Master, I forgive you," she said, so softly he had to strain to hear her.

"Are you still my slave forever?" he asked, with his eyes probing the depth of hers. He saw hatred and bone-chilling coldness, like the bleak winters in her native Norway.

"Sure, Master, forever," she whispered against his mouth as she kissed him.

Suddenly he got to his feet, and she recoiled violently. He frowned. "Hey, you're not afraid of me, I hope."

She flashed a twisted little smile. "No, Master, I'm just nervous and sore."

He tattooed her with feathery kisses as he tenderly applied

cocoa butter to her entire body. "Pet, it's a beautiful day, and sun will be good for your body," he said sweetly. He threw a short pink terrycloth robe upon her shoulders and carried her to poolside. They sat in silence for several minutes, soaking up sun and listening to radio jazz.

"Hey, pet, how about stretching your legs a little for me," he said as he searched his robe pockets.

"Sure, Master, I'd be delighted," she said as she stood beside him.

"I want to get right. Get my works, under the pillow in my room." He watched her leave and walk into the house.

She went directly to the kitchen. She took a pinch of rat poison from a half-empty box left by former tenants beneath the sink. She was breathless with excitement and fear as she hurried upstairs to his bedroom. She got his kit and sat on the side of the bed. She shook as she mixed the rat poison with the skag in the kit. Her heart was rioting, and she felt dizzy with tension. For a long moment, she was afraid that she would faint if she stood.

She got to her feet, feeling an unprecedented euphoria that soon she would be free and safe.

His cruel eyes narrowed as he watched the suspicious vivacity in her battered legs as she walked toward him. She dropped the kit on his lap and sat down. He used a bent spoon, a match, and a tiny bottle of distilled water to quickly prepare a bit of the poisoned dope for shooting. He drew the contents of the spoon into a syringe. He sucked at the needle point to clear air bubbles.

She sat, with her eyes apparently closed in sun bliss, as she peeped at him from the corner of an eye.

"Hey, pet, ladies first," he said, as he leaned and seized

her wrist. She tried to jerk free. "I just fixed, Master, remember?"

He crushed her wrist inside his fist. "Oh, come on, bitch, just a smidgen."

She started out of the chair. He released her wrist and stunned her with a punch to the side of her jaw. He lashed her feet to the chair with his robe belt and tied her hands behind her with the belt from her robe. Her eyes opened as he stood above her with the spike poised at the big vein on her neck.

"Please, Master, don't OD me!" she wailed.

"You stinkin', rotten bitch. China white ain't never been flecked brown." He plunged the spike into the vein. She violently moved her torso away. He grabbed her throat and squeezed the deadly poison into her body. Her ear-splitting scream suddenly died in the late-summer air. She jerked spastically for several minutes as a foul-smelling mucus gushed from her mouth. Burst vessels leaked blood from her dead eyes, and she collapsed into a rag-doll heap.

He threw up on the way to the kitchen. He came back to package her in garbage bags. He carried her into his bedroom and stored her in the closet, atop Pee Wee.

He showered and took several Rolaids to calm his churning stomach. He flushed the death skag. He got into bed and shot China white. He lay in bed and thought about Rucker as he waited for nightfall.

In the basement, the twins had paced the cell like uptight pachyderms after hearing Petra's death shriek. Eli dropped down on the stone slab to catch his breath. He said, "That must of been Petra we heard before the nigger cut her throat or somethin'. Cazo, we was chumps to let that crazy mother lock us up. We gonna have to take a chance and grab him and kill him next chance we git."

Cazo sat down beside him. "Yeah, I'll grab his gun arm and you grab his throat, even through the bars."

Eli groaned, "I sure hope we get a shot at his ass before mornin', 'cause we gonna be two sick-like-a-motherfucker dope fiends."

Cazo pounded his knee. "Damn! We sho' ain't gonna have the strength to grab him and hold him long enough to kill him."

Eli fingered the steel bolts and the concrete around them that anchored the steel slab to the wall. He leapt to his feet. "Gimme your shank!" Eli exclaimed.

Cazo stared at him for a moment before he took a heavy hunting knife from a leg scabbard. Eli took the blade and ordered, "Raise a leg—I need a boot."

Eli pulled off the size-fourteen boot from the extended foot. "This is old concrete," Eli said as he started to hammer the blade into the concrete around one of the three bolts. Tiny particles fell to the floor. Cazo doubtfully shook his head.

"Bro, why you fuckin' with that?" Eli said.

"'Cause this hunk of steel is the only way we gonna be able to bust that lock and chain off that cell door." Cazo punched a fist against his shoulder.

"Get down, Eli. I'll take over when you wanta ketch your breath."

Hours later, dripping sweat, they dislodged the slab. They pulled the chain until the lock was inside the cell. They grunted as they lifted the heavy metal and battered the lock and cell door with it. The impact filled the basement with a dull, thudding racket. Only one out of three of the efforts actually impacted directly on the lock itself. The weight of the steel battering ram forced them to sprawl on the floor for a brief break.

15

The rhythmic thudding awakened Shetani at twilight from fatigue-induced sleep. He listened intently, but he heard nothing. He was sure that he had imagined it.

He lay with a smile on his relaxed face as he recalled the heady dream that had sparkled his sleep. He had forced the twins to dig a big desert grave for Rucker, Petra, and Pee Wee before he killed them. He then covered the grave himself. In the dream, he had returned to New York and, with Diane, had built a hundred-girl stable with no slave older than twenty-two. He was acclaimed by all pimps and ho's in the nation, on the whole planet, as the greatest player that had ever lived.

He felt a tremor in his crotch as he recalled the neon-splashed pandemonium at the premiere of the movie about his life. Sexpot groupies of every hue fought, clawed, and trampled to get interviewed for his stable.

His joyous recall was interrupted by the thudding sound

again. He jumped out of bed and went toward the sound, with the .45 in his hand. His ears took him to the basement door. He heard a crashing sound as he crept down the steps. He switched on a light. He stuck his head around the corner and peered at the twins. They looked in his direction and scrambled up off their battering ram outside the cell. The lock lay smashed to smithereens. They hugged each other in the joy of escape.

Shetani stepped into view with a sneer. "I'm glad you slick niggers beat the cell." He paused to grin malevolently at the transfixed twins. He shrugged. "You're just gonna die sooner."

Cazo bellowed and charged him. Shetani drilled him through the heart and throat with a rain of automatic fire.

Eli, behind Cazo, had his right ear severed and a bloody rill gouged across the top of his head. He jerked the enormously heavy steel slab off the concrete with the quick ease of a world-class weight lifter. His monstrous hands gripped the middle of the slab to shield himself as he advanced on Shetani.

Shetani stood stock-still with flabbergast and fear for a moment before he started backing up the stairs, his .45 leveled at the shield. Surely the crazy nigger couldn't have the strength to hold the steel shield up in front of him going up the stairs, he told himself as Eli started up them.

Shetani stumbled and sat down heavily on a step. Eli peeped around the shield. His rage energized him to literally rush up the stairs to within four feet of Shetani, near the top of the stairs. His bloodied face behind the shield was bloated and tar-black with strain. His amplified breathing in the tight stairway space was a loud medley of wheeze and choke, like an emphysema victim.

Two steps away, he was about to drop the shield and him-self on Shetani when his strength ebbed. The shield dropped to shoulder level. Shetani blew his head into a pulpy blob.

Eli tumbled backward with the shield. Shetani, shaken, stared at the crimson heap at the bottom of the stairs.

Shetani cried out in a high-pitched voice that keened to the edge of hysteria. "I cared about you stupid bastards. It's your fault you're wasted!" He went down the hallway to his ajar bedroom door. Six feet away, he braked sharply. He lis-tened intently, with his head cocked like a grotesque robin, to hear erotic female voices and sounds. It was Pee Wee and Petra having sex in his bed.

"Oh, sweet cunt master, I'm comin'," he heard Pee Wee moan.

"You're going to be my little thieving sweetheart forever?" he heard Petra ask huskily.

Pee Wee groaned, "Oh yeah. Oh yeah. Forever! But remember, we'll never be safe until we kill that crazy cock-sucker Shetani."

Petra giggled. "I know. I know, sugar tits. I'll cop a brand of rat poison that's as white as China white. Don't worry, ice-cream cone, we'll put his cruel ass in the morgue. Now devour me."

Veins on Shetani's forehead expanded as if to burst. He checked the automatic. Empty! He was neither shocked nor greatly surprised that they had returned from death to plot against him. He'd simply have to kill them again, he thought as he hurried to the gun case in the living room.

He removed and loaded an Uzi machine gun, the one the twins had used to riddle Tree Lewis up in Harlem. He crept down the hallway to the cracked door. For a moment, he listened to ecstatic sucking sounds. He kicked the door wide open and spewed a hail of bullets and orange flame from the Uzi. He paused to flip on a light. He stared at the ragged, empty bed. A cunning smile blossomed on his face as he went to stand at the closet door.

A thunderous, sustained blast from the Uzi shattered the door. He peered through a gaping hole. Bullet-riddled Petra was lying atop Pee Wee. He leaned through the hole and poked the corpses with the snout of the Uzi. He whistled the Duke's "A Train" as he went to the shower.

Shetani left home as soon as full darkness fell, to find and kidnap Rucker. As he cruised the streets of Hollywood in the leased Jeep that was used by Froggy to run errands, he thought about his mass-murder plot. After he killed Rucker, he would con and recruit a necessary manual laborer from Skid Row to dig the large desert grave. The digger derelict would be young, muscular, and, of course, broke. He'd lisp his voice and limp his wrist like a faggot to con and lure his victim to the mansion for sex at an extravagant fee. Half would be paid when the victim entered the Jeep. After he drugged the victim with a bit of chloral hydrate in his champagne, he would drive the pre-placed bodies of Pee Wee, Petra, the twins, Rucker, and the unconscious bum into the desert. He would revive the bum with an injection of cocaine. He'd force the digging and covering of the grave at gunpoint. Then he would force the digger to make a small grave for himself. The covering of which would be a piece of cake.

His deadly eyes twinkled as he thrilled to the thought that he was going to commit the perfect murder of a cop. He grinned obscenely as he wondered why there wasn't a Hall of Fame for killers so clever. He remembered the words of a mass murderer he'd known in the New York asylum. "Jack, lemme hip you to the best fuck there is. I iced three bitches and two random niggers. The bitches were stone three-way freaks in the sack, but the sweetest fuck was when the bitches died. Jack, I ain't lyin', killin' is the wildest fuckin' there is. Try it soon as you can."

Shetani searched for Rucker until 2:00 a.m., before he was compelled to go home for China-white medication. He injected the dope and lay back on the bed. A rising stench of putrefaction drifting from the closet made him decide to hunt Rucker in daylight the next day.

Rucker had not been on the street because he had taken a day off to comfort Opal and Millie, Crane's widow. He also needed to fortify himself against the pain and misery of the services next day for cremated Crane.

Bright sunlight beamed into the Forest Lawn Chapel at noon. Opal and Millie wept together with the misty-eyed comforter Rucker between them. Ralph Rosen, Crane's giant cousin, went outside several times to avoid crying in public. Crane had been one of the most popular cops at Hollywood Station. But apparently the shame and disgrace of his destruction made it easy for sunny-day friends to shun his rites. All of Rucker's squad members sat sadly with a handful of true-blue guys and women from the station. Commander Bleeson and high brass were no-show.

Near the end of the service, Rucker went to the podium. He stood facing the audience for a long time, obviously struggling mightily for control. His voice cracked as he said softly: "I loved Leo Crane like my own blood. He was a tough cop, a good cop for most of his career. I tell you, nobody had more guts than Leo Crane. He went against gangsters, killers' knives, and guns in the nightmare Seventy-seventh Division. As partners, we trusted each other many times in potential death situations. Leo is dead, but I still love him and always will. We shouldn't judge him too harsly, for any one of us can be trapped and ruined if destructive circumstances mesh. He was seduced, corrupted, and destroyed by a snow-blonde demon in high heels. So, again, my friends, don't judge him harshly, for a victim lives inside us all."

The next day, Rucker stood dressed for the street in casual beige attire. He sipped orange juice in his sunny kitchen. He decided to get his first full meal since Crane's death. His mind fondled a palpable vision of himself and Opal taking marriage vows after his upcoming retirement.

He pulled his Lincoln from the garage. He hoped that Opal, who had flown back to New York, wouldn't be too stressed from completing funeral arrangements for her mother, Rebecca.

He headed for Carl's Jr. on the corner of Sunset and Western. He glanced at noon on his watch. He had three hours before the briefing of his first shift squad.

He drove into the restaurant parking lot. He cut off the air conditioning and lowered the two front windows, to avoid brief oven heat inside when he returned.

He entered the restaurant. He felt unweighted, almost serene, in the pleasant hum of diners' conversation, as a peachy-faced waitress with balletic grace served his steak. He didn't see Shetani park the Jeep on Western and move into the restaurant parking lot.

Shetani slipped into the spacious Lincoln. He lay down on the rear floorboards and pressed his body against the backs of the front seats. He had decided that if Rucker resisted kidnap, he'd blow him away on the lot and take his escape chances. He had a silencer on his .45, and he knew that corpses in cars were seldom quickly discovered. Either way, Rucker had to die today. Tuta's death had to be avenged.

He got a flash of the snow-blond mane of a woman standing near the Lincoln. He tensed, thinking how killing Petra again on the lot would foul up everything. He raised his head to peer at the middle-aged woman entering the car. He relaxed as she drove away. He used isometrics on his legs and arms to prevent stiffness while he waited. He knew he was virtually invisible, clad in black, lying on the black carpet of the machine.

Every five to seven seconds, he would raise his head for an instant to glance into an outside rearview mirror, to catch Rucker's reflection as he left the restaurant. Excitement shook him a moment later, when he spotted Rucker moving into the lot toward the Lincoln. He heard Rucker humming Johnny Mathis's "Chances Are" as he opened the car door and slid in.

Shetani poked the silencer-tipped weapon against the back of Rucker's head in the instant when he shut the door.

"What the . . . ?" Rucker gasped as he started to swivel his head toward the rear of the car.

"Don't turn your head, motherfucker. Don't do shit, don't say shit, or I'll splatter your brains against the windshield with this .45. Now nod, cocksucker, if you got it."

Rucker nodded. He desperately tried to remember if he'd ever heard the Eastern-accented voice before.

"Now drive out and go south on Western. Don't violate no traffic rules, and don't try to signal any of your Hollywood pig buddies."

Rucker turned on the ignition. His police radio crackled with directives. Rucker moved the Lincoln away for the exit on Sunset.

"Hey, pig, go out the Western Avenue way," Shetani ordered.

Rucker drove out onto Western and said, "What do you want? If this is a heist, I—"

Shetani cut off his speech with a savage chop of the gun barrel against the back of Rucker's skull. "Don't speak, asshole. Just drive! Obey me and you'll live. I only want to take you to see somebody," Shetani conned.

Rucker's head vibrated with the frantic effort to establish some linkage to the intruder's presence and remarks. At a stoplight a block down Western, Rucker's heart boomed. Joe Rivera, one of his squad cops, pulled up beside the Lincoln in his personal Datsun. "Hi, boss," the cop said in a cheerful voice. But Rucker scarcely heard in the din of traffic.

Rucker kept his eyes straight ahead. The cop stared curiously at Rucker's suspiciously rigid posture, and Rucker's eyes rolling in a kind of signal.

On the green, the cop drove past the Lincoln so closely that he nearly scraped the side of it. He leaned across the seat to peer into the Lincoln's interior. At that instant, an irate driver across the street sounded his horn stridently. Shetani raised his head to dart a glance across the street. He looked full into Rivera's face for a mini-second.

In the next second, Rivera recognized Shetani from the mug shots and long rap sheet of Albert Spires sent to Rucker from his New York detective acquaintance, at the beginning of the Shetani stable's invasion of Hollywood. Every squad member had been given a print.

Rivera dropped back to tail the Lincoln while he decided what action to take to apprehend Albert Spires, the documented psychotic. He reported the situation, including the Lincoln's license-plate number, to Hollywood Station. He resumed tailing.

Within minutes, Lieutenant Bleeson ordered an alert to helicopters and all units in the field to search for the Lincoln.

Shetani peeped through the rear window and saw Rivera in the Datsun behind him. He said in a deadly voice, "There's a Datsun following us. Lose it!"

Rucker stomped the gas pedal. Rivera was caught in the crunch of traffic at a stoplight several blocks away.

Shetani said, "Turn right off Western, and double back for the Hollywood Hills."

As Rucker turned the corner, a rare late-summer rainstorm started. A police helicopter, scarcely visible in the heavy downpour, hovered in the sky above the Lincoln.

Rucker shut off his radio when he heard the first sentence of the alert. Immediately Shetani growled, "I want to hear some more of that pig rap. Turn it on!"

Rucker switched it on to the voice of the dispatcher, giving the Lincoln's description and license-plate number. Shetani slugged the barrel of the gun against the side of Rucker's face. "Pull into that market lot," Shetani shouted. "We're gonna get new wheels."

Rucker pulled to a stop near the grocery's front entrance. Shetani tapped the gun against the top of Rucker's head. "Go all the way to the far end of this lot."

Rucker did as ordered. Shetani spotted an elderly black woman loading groceries from a cart into an old Buick sedan. He tapped the gun barrel against Rucker's head. "Gimme your gun."

Rucker took it from his holster and passed it back over his head. Shetani stuck it in his waistband. "I'm getting out first. Then you're getting out. Get cute and your ass is dead."

Rucker tensed and waited until he heard the rear door open and saw Shetani step out to the pavement from the corner of his eye. He scooted across the seat toward the passenger front door at the instant when Shetani flung open the driver's door.

Rucker bent forward as he exited the car and slammed the door behind him. He heard bullets whiz above his head and ping against the inner side of the door.

Shetani raced around the front of the Lincoln in hot pursuit. He stopped and leveled his gun at Rucker's back. Rucker sprinted for cover behind a semi trailer. Shetani fired three rapid shots. He saw Rucker fall heavily on his face. He looked about. The old black woman was loading the last of her groceries. He walked to within thirty feet of Rucker's prostrate form. The back of Rucker's head was bloody, and a pool of blood was forming beneath it.

Shetani, certain that Rucker was dead, turned and sprinted toward the old Buick. The old woman was just getting behind the wheel. Shetani opened the passenger door and got in beside the utterly frightened woman. Her stricken eyes locked on his gun.

"Easy, Grandma, I won't hurt you. Just do what I say and everything is gonna be all right," he said gently.

Raindrops splattered on the windshield. "Hit the freeway, Grandma," Shetani said softly. The old woman pulled the Buick away.

A police helicopter that had hovered above the market lot since Rucker drove into the lot followed the Buick.

Shetani said gently, "Now drive." The woman's lips moved in rapid, silent prayer as she moved the Buick toward an exit.

"Where do you live, lady?"

She cast a fearful glance at him. "I ain't got no money there. I ain't got nothin'," she babbled.

Shetani intoned, "Who are you? Where do you live, and who lives with you?"

Tears sprang from her large, dark eyes. "Mister, I'm a widow woman. Jus' a poor cleaning woman for rich white folks. I'm Maggie Jones, and I live in South Central, on Forty-sixth and Western. I ain't got nothin'. Please, lemme go, mister!"

He peeled off five one-hundred-dollar bills from a wad. Her eyes widened at the flash of big green.

"Go home, Grandma. This is yours in advance, to rent a place to stay in your house for a couple of days. I want you to keep me company and get some rest," he said as he shoved the bills into her purse on the seat.

She drove toward a nearby freeway entrance. Above them, the police helicopter hovered as the pilot vainly tried to read the rear license plate, the only one on the Buick, through the fog of torrential rain. He had already radioed in the details of the shooting and a general description of the suspect, and the Buick that he had commandeered.

Shetani heard the distant yowling sirens of three police cars as Maggie turned into the freeway's fast traffic. Shortly, Maggie left the freeway at the Vernon Avenue turnoff.

The pilot continued surveillance until that point. The instability of the copter under the stress of the heavy downpour forced him to turn back to the heliport. His last radio fix on the Buick brought police cars to the Vernon Avenue turnoff, minutes too late. The units started a search of the ghetto for the Buick and Shetani.

Maggie drove the Buick into a carport at the back of her heavily barred, modest stucco home on Forty-sixth Street, in the heart of black-ghetto gang turf.

Maggie led Shetani through the barred back door into an immaculate kitchen. "Have a seat," she said as she collapsed onto a chair.

He smiled and sat down across the table. He placed his gun on the tabletop. "Maggie, soon as you rest a little, I want to see the whole house. Now, tell me, how many relatives and friends visit you regularly?"

She patted the bun of silver hair on the nape of her neck. "All of my kin is dead 'cept my grown twin boys. They live in Arizona. They only visit when Christmas rolls round . . . My church friends is old, and they call, but I seldom see them 'cept at church." She sighed and continued: "I useta have lotsa friends on this street. But dope and the gangsters done run all the decent peoples away 'cept me, 'cause I'm too poor to move. Please, mister, put that gun away, 'cause I'm gonna do what you say. Come on, and I'll show you round," she said as she grunted her obese frame to her feet.

He stuck the automatic in his waistband, next to Rucker's gun. He followed her through the neat two-bedroom house, furnished with ancient furniture. They paused in front of the open door of the second bedroom, which fronted the street.

"Maggie, I'll take this one," he said as he entered the twin-bed-furnished room and checked out the closet.

She wrung her work-coarsened hands. "I don't mean no harm, but this has been my bedroom for forty years. I'm afraid you gonna have to . . ."

The clap of his huge hands startled her into silence like a pistol shot.

"Easy, Maggie. We're both sleeping in here. Believe me, I'm as far from a rapist as anybody can be."

They went to sit on a black horsehair sofa. He took her hand in his and locked his paralyzing orbs on her face. "Maggie, if you slip away from me, I'll burn your house down and leave. Understand?"

She nodded, with the back of her hand against her mouth. She got up and moved toward a TV. He said harshly, "No TV, Granny!"

She turned and stared pitiful eyes at him. "Please, TV is one of my main enjoyments in life, 'cept church."

He nodded her back to turn on the set. A special newscast blared on, with interior Cedars-Sinai hospital in the background. The newsman's voice shook with emotion.

"The following photograph of suspect Albert Spires, in the shooting of Sergeant Detective Russell Rucker of Hollywood, will be shown shortly on-screen. Spires is also a suspect in the murder of four persons at his home in the Hollywood Hills. Commander Bleeson of Hollywood Division warns citizens, especially those in South Central L.A., not to approach or try to apprehend this man if sighted, but to call the police. Albert Spires is armed and considered extremely dangerous.

A detailed account of this manhunt and Detective Rucker's condition will be presented on the four o'clock newscast."

Shetani's mug shot appeared on-screen for a long moment before a game show resumed. Maggie stood, trembling beside the TV, before she collapsed to her knees. She prayed frantically under her breath.

He got up and helped her to her feet. He led her back to sit on the sofa beside him. She broke down in tears and blubbered, "You done kilt all those peoples. Please, go."

He vised her face between his palms, with his flaming eyes almost touching her face. He whispered fiercely, "Calm down, now, and listen to the truth . . . That cop came to my house to kill me about sweethearting around with his wife. I hid, and when my friends tried to take his gun, he killed them. He trailed me to that market lot and tried to shoot me. I took his gun away and shot him. Can you believe a nigger over those rotten white folks, Miss Maggie?"

She nodded. He released her face and kissed her forehead.

At twilight, Rucker awoke from sedation at Cedars. He gazed up at his tall, bearded physician, standing beside the bed. The doctor's majestic frame and silvery beard and mane were illuminated by fluorescent ceiling light that created a radiant aura, a supernatural ambience, around the white-clad figure.

Rucker thought, "I've died, and I'm face to face with God. I'm sure glad he knows I've always believed he existed in some form."

God spoke to him in a booming baritone as he took his pulse: "Mr. Rucker, I'm Dr. Goldstein. How do you feel, besides lucky?"

Rucker was mute as his eyes focused sharply to realize that he was alive and there was no interview with God. "A little woozy, doc," Rucker murmured.

The doctor placed a stethoscope on his chest and listened. "You lost an alarming amount of blood, which transfusions have replaced. The bullet that grazed the back of your skull would have been fatal if its trajectory variance had been a quarter of an inch. Several ruptured blood vessels at the juncture of head and neck were the cause of your loss of blood . . . Sergeant, you should be back on the street in several days." The doctor turned and left the room.

Rucker's fingers probed the large bandage around the top of his head and the several bandages on his face that covered the lacerations from the fall on the parking-lot concrete.

Lieutenant Bleeson stepped into the room. "Hi, you lucky sonuvagun. Your doctor just gave me the good news," he said as he sat down in a chair at bedside.

"Did you get that black sonuvabitch?" Rucker asked with high emotion.

Bleeson leaned over and patted Rucker's shoulder. "Russell, it's not good for you to overreact in this matter. You . . ."

Rucker seized his hand and squeezed it. "Goddamn it, Lieutenant, answer the question."

Bleeson pulled his hand away. "Russell, Albert Spires is bottled up in South Central. He hasn't a prayer to escape. He killed his henchmen twins, his snow-blonde stable straw boss, and a thieving hooker called Pee Wee Smith before he shot you. A New York hooker named Bianca was arrested for the murder of a john in Wisconsin. The basis for arrest was her fingerprints lifted in the murder apartment. She fingered Pee Wee as the trigger person. Every cop, sheriff's deputy, and CHP officer in California is out to get this guy, so be cool and—"

Rucker's face contorted as he lunged upright toward Bleeson to cut him off. "Cool my ass, Lieutenant? That lowlife cocksucker abused me to the max before he tried to kill me. He took something from me. He raped me, Lieutenant! I'm gonna find him personally and bring him in or kill him, to get back what he took from me."

Bleeson stood. "Please, Russell, calm down and mend . . . You just filed your retirement papers the other day. Trust us to get the guy. I'll be back. In the meantime, I'll give you a jingle when we bag him."

Bleeson left the room. Rucker immediately used his bedside phone to call the cop that headed CRASH (Community Resources Against Street Hoodlums). The anti-gang unit surveilled gang members and kept records of their criminal careers and whereabouts. His hand trembled with excitement as he replaced the receiver.

Idus "Tank" Settles was on the street, the unchallenged leader of the Black Elite Gang, the largest, most feared and powerful street gang in Los Angeles.

Rucker dialed Information to get Tank's mother's home phone number. He hung up when Mamie said, "Settles residence." He had rescued then preteener Tank from a clubbing or worse at the hands of a trio of older gangsters. He wasn't sure that Tank's sense of gratitude could be counted upon after seven years. But he was certain that Mamie Settles, if needed, would use any influence she had over Tank to get his cooperation in the search for Spires.

Rucker thought that the wire services would pick up the story of the shooting and the mass murders in the Hollywood

Hills. He called Opal, to assure her that he was alive and clear of head. At 3:30 a.m., he dressed in trousers and shoes and hospital pajama top. His bloodstained shirt and coat had been cut off and trashed.

His nurse and the hospital personnel tried in vain to convince him not to leave. He caught a cab and went home to change clothes, and get a gun and extra bullets.

He dressed in a dark-blue suit, and fainted in the upstairs hallway as he walked toward the stairway. He came to minutes later and feebly made his way to the kitchen. He poured a tall glass of orange juice and collapsed in a welter of sweat onto the bench of the breakfast nook.

Finally, he called the police impound lot to find out that his Lincoln was releasable. He called a cab and picked up his car. He drove toward South Central L.A. He had decided to get certain info on gang leader Tank that very probably wasn't known by CRASH. Chauncy "One Pocket" Stiles was the one snitch that he knew from his long stint in 77th Division who could supply the info he needed. That is, if Stiles was still alive or hadn't relocated from his combination poolroom and second-story after-hours gin mill in the heart of Tank's domain.

Within ten minutes, Rucker had to park before he fainted again. He knew he couldn't make it to South Central. He U-turned and headed for home. He left the Lincoln in the driveway. He disconnected his phone and fell into bed with his clothes on.

Across town, at sunrise, Shetani sat on the living-room sofa watching a TV special local newscast. His face was drawn and glistened with the perspiration of a dope fiend in need. He massaged his belly to relieve twinges of cramp pain.

He leaned forward and listened intently as a file picture of Rucker appeared in a corner of the screen above the head of the newswoman.

"Police Sergeant Russell Rucker checked out of Cedars-Sinai against the advice of hospital officials. Efforts to reach him have been unsuccessful. In the meantime, one of the most intensive manhunts in the history of the city is being conducted to apprehend mass murderer Albert Spires, a native New Yorker, who police authorities believe is hiding in the South Central section of the city."

Shetani's mug-shot image appeared on-screen. The newswoman's voice continued with voice-over. "The suspect is six four or five inches tall with a muscular build and intense green eyes. If any viewer sees him, call the number at the bottom of the screen. He is a former mental patient and is to be considered extremely dangerous."

Shetani chanted, "The stinking bastard ain't dead. The stinking bastard ain't dead." He picked a heavy ashtray off the coffee tabletop and hurled it into the TV screen. It exploded like a mini-bomb.

Seconds later, Maggie stumbled from her bedroom in her nightgown. She stared hypnotically at the demolished TV for a moment. Then she switched her furious eyes to Shetani. Tears rolled down her ruined doll face as she pounded her thigh blubber with tiny fists. She shrieked, "Is you done gone star natal nuts? I loved my TV. It's a Zenith! My poor dead husband give it to me for my birthday fourteen years ago. Nigger, why you mess up my TV?"

He responded with a baleful stare and one of his hideous smiles. She stabbed an index finger toward him and screeched,

"I ain't afraid of your evil eye, 'cause God's in my corner. Get out of my house!"

He leveled his gun at her chest. "I'm gonna send you to meet him if you don't stop screamin' and sit down. Now!" he said in a graveyard voice that forced her to collapse into a chair beside the TV.

She buried her face in her hands and wept hysterically. He said, "Stop that cryin'. Later on you can call your TV repairman if you got one and have him bring you another TV, on me. Okay?"

She nodded and dredged her flab up from the chair. She gave him a mean look before she went back into the bedroom. He sat in her chair near the front window and surveyed the street through lace curtains. A thin young black girl with a debauched face got out of a battered Pontiac and went into the house next door. The Pontiac, driven by a teenage black dude wearing a do-rag to protect his processed curls, moved away.

Excitement rocked Shetani. He knew a street bitch when he saw one. The chances were that she would score some skag for him for a fee, he told himself.

He got up and walked into Maggie's bedroom. She was staring at the ceiling. "Say, Miss Maggie, I just saw a young girl goin' in next door. You know her?" he asked softly.

Maggie said sourly, "Yeah. So what?"

He placed a hundred-dollar bill on her chest. She swatted it off. "Miss Maggie, I want you to keep that for introducing me to her. Tell her I'm one of your son's friends from Arizona, visiting you for a couple of days."

She glared at him. "Whatta you gonna do? Kill her?" she

said as she shot a glance at the bill lying on the quilt between them.

"I ain't killed nobody, Miss Maggie. I just wounded that cop. Remember?"

She studied him. "So you said . . . Mavis don't want you. You're too old. Besides, she's got a boyfriend."

He leaned toward her. "She's not my type. I just want to meet her. Tell me more about her."

Maggie sighed. "She's really a sweet girl that got street poisoned by bad company. She stays out all night, mostly every night, and slips into the house before her father gets off the night shift. She used to be a church girl, like her father, 'fore the devil got her. I'll call her over here later today, after Mr. Owens brings me another TV," Maggie said as she plucked the C-note off the bed.

Shetani picked a phone off a nightstand and placed it on the bed. "Call her now, Miss Maggie, and we got a deal. Introduce me as Bob Smith."

She shrugged and dialed the phone. "Mavis, honey, duck in here for a minute," she said before she cradled the receiver. "Lissen Mr. Spires, I ain't gonna let no rough stuff happen with that girl, and I ain't gonna let no trick be turned in my house," she said as she extended the bill toward him.

"Keep it, Miss Maggie. I won't violate your house rules," he replied as he left the room to sit on the sofa.

Shortly, Maggie came into the room to answer the door-bell. Mavis stepped into the house already shucked out of street clothes, into a housecoat over pajamas, to hoodwink her father.

"Mavis Lee, one of Jimmy's friends, Bob Smith from Arizona, saw you comin' home and been pesterin' me to let him meet you this early in the mornin',"she said as she turned toward her bedroom. "Now, you all behave in my house," she said over her shoulder as she went into her bedroom.

"Sit down here, Baby Sis," he said as he patted the sofa beside him. She had a puzzled look, but she sat down. "What's happenin'?" she asked, and lit a cigarette.

"Can you keep a secret between us from Maggie for a nice taste of bread?"

"Yeah, man, if it ain't somethin' too radical."

He leaned toward her ear. "I got a habit. Somebody stole my bag at the airport with my works and medicine in it. Score me a gram of skag and some works and I'll lay a C-note on you."

She recoiled and tried to get up past his restraining hand on her shoulder. "Hey, narc, let go of me!"

Shetani whipped up his shirtsleeves to show the scabrous network of crusted spike tracks on both arms. "As you can see, Baby Sis, I ain't no narc. I'm just a dope fiend that needs a fix right away. Have we got a deal?"

She frowned and bit her bottom lip. "I can't cop right away."

He pressed a C-note into her palm and said, "I'll give you your payoff after you score." Then he squeezed her hand so hard she winced. "Why?" he demanded.

"'Cause I have to make my dad's breakfast when he gets home."

"How far do you have to go to cop?"

She got to her feet. "Not far, at the end of the block. Gotta go!"

He followed her to the door and opened it. "Can you get me some clean works?"

She nodded. "Yeah, I got an outfit stashed that I used to use to bang coke before I started to smoke crack. Bye!"

He shut the door and sat down in the chair near the window. He chewed his fingernails to the quicks and waited for an hour, with churning guts, for Mavis's father to come home. Finally, he saw an elderly man in work clothes park a jalopy and carry two armloads of groceries into the house next door.

Shetani slipped off his dripping-wet shirt. He stared out at the street, bent double by racking cramps. Finally, Mavis left the house and went down the street. Negatives ached his head. What if she ripped him off and got in the wind? What if she got busted after she copped? What if she couldn't score for smack in a market dominated by cocaine?

At last, he saw her coming down the sidewalk. He got up and flung open the front door. She didn't come up Maggie's walk! He stood at the open door, stunned with frustration. He heard the jangle of a phone. A moment later, Maggie said from the bedroom, "Pick up the phone. It's Mavis."

He went to the phone on an end table beside the sofa. He fell onto it. "What's happenin', Baby Sis?" he blurted out breathlessly.

She whispered, "I can't bring it to you, because my dad would see me from his bedroom window and he's still awake. I've stashed the package at the end of Maggie's backyard, in a tin can under the apple tree. Oh, by the way, I copped the connection's last twenty-five-dollar bag. I put in an order for a gram that I can cop early tomorrow night." She hung up.

He went into Maggie's room and listened to her snoring for a moment. He examined two barred windows to see if the bars had a swing-out release lever, in case of fire. They didn't.

To play safe, he took the skeleton key from the lock and carefully shut the door. He locked her in and hastened to cop the stash. He came back and shot up half of the brown Mexican heroin. It was nothing compared to China white, but at least it blunted the edge of pain in his gut. He decided to leave Maggie locked in. He stretched out on the sofa to get some much-needed rest.

At noon, Rucker was driving toward South Central in an old nondescript brown van with heavily tinted windows that he had borrowed from a car-dealer friend of his in Hollywood. He thought about One Pocket Stiles's long criminal career and his wizardry at pool. He drove down South Figueroa Street. He spotted Stiles's classic '36 Packard parked in front of his poolroom. Rucker parked the van behind it. He tucked a prop briefcase under an arm before he went into the crowded poolroom. It vibrated with the profane shuck and jive of hustlers, clowns, and bums.

A lid of utter silence slammed down. His alien presence magnetized all eyes, except those of Pocket, who was bent across a front table, executing a three-cushion bank of the last ball on the table. He glanced at Rucker and put his cue stick on the table.

"Well, if it ain't my old fire-insurance man," he exclaimed, as he pumped Rucker's hand.

Rucker smiled, and the shuck and jive resumed. "Hello, Mr. Stiles. Since I was in the neighborhood, I dropped in to say hello and pitch some life insurance."

A dwarfish stakes holder gave string bean Stiles a small bundle of bills. Stiles tipped him a bill and led Rucker to the sidewalk. "Let's go upstairs and talk," Stiles said as he unlocked the door.

They went up a stairway to the second floor, over the poolroom. They entered a beautifully furnished living room. Rucker was flabbergasted to see the transformation. The formal nocturnal dive had disappeared, with its jukebox, the garish montage of painted nudes on the wall, the cracked mirrored bar, and the craps table surrounded by mangy overstuffed chairs and ragged couches.

They sat down on an elegant white silk sofa. "Mr. Rucker, it's sure great to see you," Pocket said as he crossed his pipestem legs. "But what happened to your face? You been roustin' wildcats?"

Rucker laughed and stroked a bandage on his cheek. "No. I fell on my face, cold-sober, after I got nicked in the back of my head . . . You haven't read or heard about my trouble with a psycho in Hollywood?"

Stiles said softly, with a beatific expression on his face, "I stopped reading downer newspapers and watching corrupt TV except for religious stuff on cable. I closed my after-hours joint, and I'm gonna close the poolroom the first of the year and start my own ministry downstairs. I found Christ!"

Rucker was speechless.

"Mr. Rucker, I see you're surprised like my kinfolks and everybody. I'm seventy-five, and I've been a thief, dope dealer, pimp, stickup man, and dope fiend, but I've been purified with the Holy Ghost and the fire. What can I do for you?"

Rucker found his voice. "I'm on the trail of the nut that shot me. Tell me everything you know about Tank Settles and his present activities."

Stiles's long, wolfish black face hardened. "Did he shoot you?"

Rucker shook his head.

"Then you're not out to arrest him by yourself?"

Rucker said, "No. I need his help."

Stiles continued, "You would need a SWAT team to arrest him now. Snot-nosed punk grew up to be a stone killer. He and his gangsters control and rule this whole section where we are. A couple of his killer punks were in the poolroom when you showed. One of 'em I had to hire as a security guard. Settles has a mob of crack dealers. He's a dope king who gets around in a red Mercedes. I've heard that he's got a machine gun stashed in a secret compartment under the front floorboards of his car. Decent people are terrorized and jailed in their homes by Tank and his gangsters."

Rucker was thoughtful for a moment before he asked, "Where does he field his crack dealers?"

Stiles waved a bony hand toward upper South Figueroa. "In the Forties on Fig, where the ho's work at night."

Rucker stood. "Thanks. What do I owe you?"

Stiles stood and flashed a galaxy of gold teeth. He shook his bald pate frenetically. His blue suit shimmered in the sunlight like a silk shroud on his skeletal frame. "The Lord will reward me, Mr. Rucker," he said as he led Rucker to the door. "Don't try to talk to Tank by yourself, Mr. Rucker. He hates cops, and he's as treacherous as a rattler with the flu," he warned as Rucker walked toward the stairway.

Rucker threw up a hand to acknowledge the caution as he started down the stairs.

At that moment, Shetani awakened to Maggie pounding

for release on her bedroom door. He got up and unlocked the door.

"I'm a human being that goes to the bathroom, Mr. Spires. Don't you never lock me up again," she hollered as she lumbered past him for the bathroom.

The doorbell sounded. Shetani, with gun in hand, peeped through the front curtains to see a fat black man bulging a faded blue uniform with CHRISTIAN TV AND SALES stenciled on the front of the shirt.

Shetani went to the bathroom door and knocked. "Miss Maggie, the TV man is at the door."

Maggie screamed at the top of her voice. "Ain't you got no sense, nigger? I'm tryin' to relieve myself. Give him two hundred dollars, like you promised, and tell him to take the TV you messed up with him."

Shetani concealed his gun and went to open the front door. He made the transaction without any sign from Mr. Owens that he had been recognized.

Maggie flushed the toilet and washed her hands. She took an identical skeleton key to the one for her bedroom door from a linen drawer and dropped it into her bosom. She joined him on the sofa in the living room and smiled to see the sharp picture on the pre-owned color TV.

At dusk, Rucker spotted Tank's gaudy Mercedes and tailed it to a block in the upper Forties on Figueroa Street. Rucker parked his van diagonally across the wide street from the target vehicle. The van's heavily tinted windows made Rucker's white face and even his black-clad form virtually invisible to the constant foot traffic past his spy post.

Through powerful binoculars, he watched a succession of young Black Elite Gang members with their gang insignia, fake or real diamonds glittering on their earlobes, get into the Mercedes. Rucker was puzzled to see each of them elevate his knees. They would get out of Tank's machine after a moment and take up positions from one end of the block to the other.

A half-hour later, they started to deal crack to the drivers of a stream of cars. Shortly, the salesmen returned to the Mercedes to get a fresh supply of merchandise.

Suddenly Rucker's eyes widened at a phenomenon. Tiny spots of light flashed through the entire block. Instantly the dealers faded away into bars, alleyways, and parked cars as a police car entered the block.

Rucker zeroed in on the sources of the flashes. He saw that the signal sentries were young boys and girls, none older than ten, with small pencil-shaped flashlights. He watched the phalanx of dealers resume business immediately when the police car had moved through the block.

Rucker reasoned that Tank's stash of merchandise was with the machine gun, probably in the secret compartment that One Pocket Stiles had mentioned. Rucker deduced that the momentary elevation of dealers' knees indicated the secret compartment was located beneath the floorboards on the front passenger side of the Mercedes.

Rucker's binoculars snared the figure of a medium-built black male without the Black Elite jewel in his earlobe, passing something and receiving what was apparently money from a motorist at the end of the block adjacent to the dealers' block of operation. Instantly the lookout sentries flashed the presence of the interloper throughout the block.

Rucker watched Tank blink the Mercedes headlights several times. A trio of husky Black Elites sitting in a station wagon parked in front of the Mercedes torpedoed away and attacked the astonished interloper with blackjacks, fists, and feet until he lay bloody and unconscious. The trio dragged him into an alley and drove the station wagon back to its post in front of the Mercedes.

Rucker checked his gun before he stepped out of the van. He carried the briefcase containing Shetani's mug prints as he jaywalked toward the Mercedes. He would try to discover the crack stash as leverage if Tank stonewalled and refused to help him locate Shetani. He quickened his step as he reached the pavement at the rear of the Mercedes.

Passersby gawked at him as he flung open the door of the Mercedes and slid in beside Tank.

"Say, motherfucker! What's going down?" Tank screamed as his right hand streaked for his waistband.

"Don't move! I'm Sergeant Russell Rucker of the LAPD, and I'm going to talk to you. That's what's going down," Rucker said meanly as he rammed his gun against Tank's side.

Tank studied Rucker's bandaged face for a long moment before he laughed too loudly. "Hey, I think I know you, man."

Rucker took Tank's gun from his waistband and dropped it into his own pocket. "Yeah, you know me. I saved your jive ass several years ago, when a gang of stompers were about to beat the shit out of you or waste you. You owe me, Idus, and I'm here to collect." Rucker took his gun from Tank's side and placed it on the seat, between his legs. Tank pulled an obese roll of cash from a trouser pocket. "Sure, Officer, what do you want?"

Rucker's mouth curled. "I don't take money from fuckin' criminals. I want you to help me find Albert Spires."

There was utter silence. Tank's garage-door shoulders

jerked rigid, and his brutish black face became an anguished mask of outrage. "Man, you ain't Rucker. You a alien from outer space if you think I would fuck up a brother for the poleece. Hey, I don't really owe you shit, since, at the time you raised them niggers off my ass, my mama Mamie and other taxpaying citizens was paying your salary to protect me from bodily harm."

Tank's trio of bashers left the station wagon and walked toward the passenger side of the Mercedes. Rucker whispered harshly, "I'll blow you away first and a couple of them before I go." Rucker stuck his gun into his waistband. One of the trio stuck his head inside on Rucker's side.

"You all right, bro?" he said as he glared at Rucker.

Tank replied, "Yeah. I'm cool." The trio returned to the station wagon. Then Rucker said calmly, "If you don't help me find Spires, I'll take leave and rent a room on this side of town. I'll hound you and harass you and your dealers out of business. Well?"

Tank's massive frame quivered with rage. He reached for the Mercedes's light switch. Rucker slammed the barrel of his gun against the back of Tank's hand. "Hey, man, you gonna pay for this rough shit," Tank warned as he squeezed the wounded member. His eyes were maroon pits of menace.

"You're on paper, asshole, and it's against the law to threaten a police officer. Say you're sorry," Rucker demanded as he poked the snout of the gun into Tank's side again.

"Yeah, I'm sorry, but I'll never help you cross the brother into the gas chamber," Tank said firmly.

Rucker, the former auto-theft and chop-shop ace investigator, studied the Mercedes's dashboard for an extra control knob or switch that would access the secret compartment that he felt was beneath his feet. He extended a hand and let his fingers toy across the dashboard to get Tank's reaction.

"Hey, man, you ain't got no right to fuck with my machine without a search warrant."

Rucker smiled. "Yeah, I know. And you know that a recent parolee with a two-carat diamond on his ear and the bread to buy a new Mercedes is in big trouble if his parole officer finds out."

Tank sneered, "Hey, man, this ride and this diamond was copped in my mama's name. I don't own shit. Now, why don't you split and let the poleece find the brother if they can."

Rucker's probing fingers moved beneath the dash. He flipped a switch and felt instant pressure beneath the soles of his shoes. He jabbed the gun in his left hand against Tank's heart. He raised his feet and saw the shag-covered lid of the compartment open upward. He leaned and pulled two garbage bags from the hole with his right hand. He dumped a machine gun from one bag and many vials of crack from the other onto the seat between them.

"You're going back to Q for parole violation, slick ass, and another bit on top of it, if you don't help me find Spires."

Tank stared at his beloved machine gun and the small fortune in crack. He mumbled, "I can beat possession of crack on illegal search and seizure. I ain't got but fourteen months to serve out on parole paper. I can breeze through a chicken-shit bit like—"

Rucker cut him off: "Don't bullshit me. You would be a basket case in thirty days with no Mercedes, no crack to smoke, no fine pussy to bang. Possession of the machine gun, which you can't beat, will get you a nickel, and maybe a dime in the joint, with your rap sheet. Gimme a fast yes or no to my proposition. I'm in a hurry."

Tank fidgeted and writhed on the seat.

"Come on. If you've got a brain, your answer has to be yes," Rucker prodded harshly.

"I'm in if I get all my merchandise back, and my piece and the machine gun."

Rucker laughed in his face. "It's against my principles as a police officer to return deadly weapons and narcotics to criminals. I can only offer you a pass for the weapon and dope, and freedom from my personal harassment, after I get Spires."

Tank nodded. "You win," he said in a tiny shaking voice.

Rucker moved his face close to Tank's. "Don't try to con me, Idus. I want all-out, fast cooperation from you. I'm giving you a stack of Spires's mug shots. I want you to make sure that every one of your gang members and their broads knows what he looks like. You got thirty-six hours to find him before I get itchy to make this evidence known to the proper authorities. I'll bust you and adjust the report time frame of my confiscation of the machine gun and drugs to the moment that I bust you. I'm giving you my home phone number, where you can call me around the clock, to tip me, and only me, to Spires's hideout. Understand?"

Tank said meekly, "Yeah. You sure a cold-blooded dude."

Rucker said, "Thanks for that. By the way, you called me a motherfucker when I got in. Say you're sorry."

Tank's heavy eyebrows took flight. He gnawed at his bottom lip under Rucker's relentless cold blue eyes. "I'm sorry, old man." Tank sighed. "It's gonna be tough to get my homeboys to work real hard to find a brother for the poleece."

At that instant, Rucker's consuming drive to get Shetani forced him to drop all scruples and con Tank. "Not if you let them in on something confidential I know. Spires has been secretly indicted by a grand jury as an accomplice of the South Side Slayer in several of the eighteen murders of women in South Central. Tell your homeboys it's necessary to find Spires to get rid of the heat on your turf, and so the police can pressure Spires to get the identity of the South Side Slayer. Everybody in South Central wants the killer caught before he kills again."

Tank murmured, "That might work."

A county ambulance wailed by, carrying the battered crack-dealer interloper.

Rucker handed Tank his card and left the Mercedes, carrying the garbage-bagged contraband. He collapsed in the van from the high-voltage tension and his weakened condition. Finally, he summoned the strength to drive toward Hollywood.

At that moment, Tank blinked his headlights for his three enforcers to join him in the Mercedes. Rucker had left Tank shaken and in a very paranoid condition. He was a street prince, with bookoo long green and his pick of a multitude of choice foxes. He was living fast and high, and for the first time in his life he felt important and powerful. A recurring vision of his cell in San Quentin rattled his nerves. He looked in the rearview mirror at Rucker's van in the distance. Should he send the enforcers to hit Rucker, to escape his trap and recover his guns and crack. Then he thought that it would be wiser to find Spires and avoid Rucker's threat to send him back to Q.

He decided against risking the gas chamber as enforcers

piled into the Mercedes. He said solemnly, "That white dude was a cop on my payroll. He lays inside info on me on what's coming down in Black Town. The South Side Slayer had a buddy with him when he iced several black ladies. That crazy mass murderer's name is Spires, the one that's got the poleece ripping and runnin' and fuckin' with people over here. My poleece errand boy hipped me that Spires has been secretly indicted for the murders he committed with his buddy, the South Side Slayer. The cop said the poleece is gonna up the heat until Spires is busted. Now, we ain't got nothin' in common with no crazy square-ass nigger who kills black sisters. Right?"

The fearsome trio nodded with grim faces. "I want you guys to take this stack of Spires's mug pics and make sure all Black Elite and their cunts see what the dude looks like. Tell everybody to call Red Dog at One Pocket's all-night poolroom when they locate him. Tell everybody I'm laying out a thou reward. We got to raise this heat."

He gave them the mug shots and watched them roar away in the station wagon. Several moments later, his half-dozen crack vendors were given Shetani mug shots and the same pitch.

Tank thought about the loss of his crack stock and shrugged. He'd be out of business for a day or so, until his crack wholesaler came through. As always when he was in a jam, he decided to get off the street and stay in his old room at his mama, Mamie's house for the next thirty-six hours. He'd have Red Dog, the manager and security guard for One Pocket's poolroom, call him at his mama's house when the tip came through on Spires's hideout.

At midnight, Shetani was awakened on Maggie's living-room sofa by a heart-jolting nightmare. He had been pursued by an insane mob armed with gigantic meat-cleavers. His tormentors were the Brooks twins, his mother, Petra, Pee Wee, and the Floridian twins he had shot to death in Harlem. He reviewed his master plan for escape from L.A. and his survival afterward. He couldn't leave until Mavis delivered the gram of skag early the next evening.

He would force Maggie to drive him around the block in the early a.m. to spot good transportation that he would hot-wire. With Maggie as chauffeur, he would ease out of the state. Maggie? He'd have to work out a way that she couldn't be a trace threat to his whereabouts. Maybe he would have to put her to sleep in some painless way, since he liked her and her feisty personality very much. He'd pimp and hold his stable by proxy. He really trusted Diane, his Jewish straw boss.

He injected a pinch of Mexican brown and lay listening to Maggie snoring behind her locked bedroom door.

16

In early evening, Mavis Lee sat in her boyfriend's blistered Pontiac, smoking their last crack rock on a market parking lot. "Hey, Petey, what time you got?" she said breathlessly, amber eyes asparkle, as she rode the final crystal rocket to Planet Rapture.

His fingers toyed with her vulva as he glanced at his wristwatch. "It's seven o'clock," he said, his other hand unfastening her blouse. His cherub face was radiant as he buried his head in her bosom and gnawed, licked, and sucked her nipples.

Her airy hand invaded his sex works as she leaned to nip his earlobe, on which a fake diamond glittered. They molested each other until the rocket crashed into a dull, dark pit.

"Petey, I'm gonna call the connect again to cop for that dude that's gonna lay the C-note on me. I want some more smoke!" She buttoned her blouse and went to a pay phone near the Pontiac.

One of Tank's Figueroa Street dealers came out of the market. Petey honked him to the Pontiac.

"Dusty, how 'bout laying a ten-dollar thing on me until later tonight at the poolroom?" Petey asked.

The blue-black crack dealer tilted a brown paper bag containing a wine bottle to his mouth. "Man, I ain't holdin' a speck of nothin'. Want a hit?" he said tipsily as he extended the bottle.

"Naw, Dusty, I pass," Petey said, with his gray eyes on Mavis leaving the phone booth. "Later, man," Dusty said, and walked away to a moped behind the Pontiac. He drove the rainbow-hued machine to the driver's side of the Pontiac as Mavis slid into the car. Dusty dropped a Shetani mug shot on Petey's lap and said, "Hey, man, eyeball this dude's pic. Tank's paying a thou reward to the first lucky person that spots him and finds out the location of his pad."

Petey studied it. "I saw this guy on TV. He's hotter than a sissy with AIDS."

Mavis leaned over and glanced at it before Petey gave it to Dusty. "Shit, I can't hit the lottery, but it sure would be a gas to spot that nigger," Petey said.

Dusty laughed. "If you get lucky, Tank said don't fuck with the dude or nothin'. Just call Red Dog at the poolroom, and give him the rundown for Tank." Dusty zoomed away.

"Baby, the connect's old lady told me to call back in fifteen minutes," Mavis said petulantly.

"Well, that means he's gonna be holdin' soon," Petey said, and moved the Pontiac away, toward an exit.

Within ten minutes, he parked at the end of Mavis's block near the skag dealer's house. They lit cigarettes and puffed away nervously while they waited for the dealer's Eldorado to arrive.

"Sugar! The pic! I know that dude!" Mavis exclaimed as she hit her forehead with the heel of her hand.

Petey's high-yellow face was skeptical. "Come on, girl, you jivin'."

She leapt into his lap and threw her arms around his neck. "It's the nigger I'm coppin' for! I ain't jivin'!"

He pushed her off his lap. "There's Big Cotton's ride. Go cop, so we can cop some smoke."

She got out and walked to the Eldorado as Cotton got out. They entered the house. Mavis came out in less than three minutes. She got in and said, "I'm ninety percent sure the guy in Maggie's house is the guy on the pic. Why don't you go to the door with me and peep at him, so you can be sure."

Petey studied her face for a long moment before he said, "Girl, since you're sure, we better cool it and call Red Dog. We don't wanta fuck up and blow the thou. 'Sides, that nigger's crazy and dangerous like a motherfucker."

He drove off to a pay phone around the corner and called Red Dog. He drove to the poolroom and parked. Red Dog rushed out and sat in the back seat. "Sis, are you sure 'nuff sure this is the dude you met?" Red Dog said in his coarse, barklike voice as he leaned across the back of the front seat to thrust a Shetani mug shot before her eyes.

As Mavis studied it in a lance of streetlamp, Dog's sad, liquid brown eyes studied her. "Sis, don't let the grand reward make your brain tell your eyes no lies. I ain't had no sleep, checkin' out bullshit leads since last night."

Mavis passed him the pic. "I'm sure."

Dog said, "Sis, say it again, 'cause I ain't ready to call Tank out here to no fluke."

Mavis looked at Petey and said peevishly, "Dog, I'm sure! I'm sure! Okay?"

As he got out of the Pontiac he said, "Lay right here till Tank gets here."

They watched his long, wiry frame hasten into the poolroom. A large diamond coruscated on his earlobe as his red-mopped head animated at the telephone through the poolroom plate glass.

Rucker was fast asleep when Tank called him at 8:00 p.m. Tank gave him a detailed rundown on Mavis's dealings with Shetani.

A moment after Tank's call, Opal called from New York. She became upset at the harsh sound of Rucker's breathing due to the constant buildup of mucus in his throat because of his unhealed neck wound.

Despite his protestations that he was well, her call terminated with her declaration to fly to L.A. after her mother had been buried.

Rucker's legs threatened to go out on him on his way to the bathroom. He brushed his teeth and saw double images of himself in the mirror. He went to the bedroom and checked his Magnum. He dropped extra cartridges into the coat of the dark suit he would wear.

He met Tank and Mavis on Figueroa, several blocks south of the poolroom. Tank drove away to leave Mavis and Rucker alone in the van.

"Do you have the heroin for Spires?" he asked gently.

She hesitated, and nervousness quivered her mouth. He smiled warmly. "Young lady, please trust me, I'm not on a narcotics investigation. I won't trick or trap you. I just want Spires."

She said, "Yeah. A gram . . . Man, I'm scared a him. What if he kidnaps me or something when I see him?"

Rucker put an arm around her shoulders. "Listen, and follow carefully my plan, and you won't have anything to worry about. In fact, you will not have physical contact with him."

She smiled stingily, and Rucker started to explain his plan.

Shetani sat at Maggie's living-room front window, peering through the curtains at the street for a sight of Mavis. He felt familiar twinges of pain in his stomach, and his skin was damp with the dew of junkie need.

The jangle of the phone jerked him. A moment later, he heard Maggie's voice from the bedroom. "Pick up the phone, Mr. Spires."

He went to the phone beside the sofa and picked up to Mavis's whispered voice. "I stashed the package in the same spot like last time, in Maggie's backyard, 'cause my dad won't leave for work until much later. I'll get my C-note in the morning, before he comes home. Bye."

Shetani locked Maggie up in her bedroom and went to lift a sofa cushion where his .45 and Rucker's lighter police special were stashed. He checked the smaller gun and stuck it in his waistband. He unlocked the wooden back door, and then the steel-mesh second door. He stepped through the open doors to the pitch-black yard. He walked toward the stash apple tree, outlined against the dreary sky.

The ghostly carcass of Maggie's husband's last pickup truck glowed white in the rear of the yard.

Rucker, in his weakened condition, inadvertently bumped the open passenger door of the truck that he crouched behind for cover. The rasp of the door's rusty hinges was amplified like a claxon in the cemetery stillness.

Shetani stopped, and his feline eyes focused on the truck. He drew the gun and moved toward the tree. Rucker's breathing was loud and spastic with tension and his fear of passing out.

Ten feet away from the tree, Shetani halted again and strained to hear the sound that Rucker stopped by holding his breath.

Rucker was about to exhale noisily when Shetani's foot banged against a tin can and drowned out the exhalation. Rucker held his breath again as Shetani stooped to pick up the dope packet at the base of the tree.

"Reach and freeze. I'm Rucker!" Rucker hollered with as much strength as he could muster.

Shetani darted behind the tree and reflexively fired three aimless shots at the truck.

"Throw your gun out and get on your belly, or I'll kill you," Rucker ordered.

Shetani peppered the truck with the remaining bullets in the gun and dashed for the back door.

Rucker leveled his Magnum and saw two dim images of Shetani. He fired two rounds and moved away from the truck from fleeing Shetani.

Shetani clawed at the locked steel-mesh door as he stared at Maggie's impassive face peering at him through a kitchen window. She had freed herself from the bedroom with the duplicate key and bolted him out.

"Mama! Mama! Please, let me in! Please, Mama," he begged piteously, in a child's voice.

She left the window to call the police. Rucker stood thirty feet away with the Magnum leveled with both hands at the back of Shetani's head. "Get on your belly, or I'll kill you," Rucker said in a feeble voice as he teetered.

Shetani spun to face him with a demonic expression deforming his face. "You ain't well, pig cunt. I'm gonna kill you," Shetani roared as he advanced on Rucker.

Rucker shot him through the right hip. The impact slammed him against the back door. Shetani sat on his rump and stared hypnotically at the spew of claret from the wound. He uttered a savage cry of psychotic rage and struggled up to his feet. He moved toward Rucker sideways, like a poisonous reptile.

Rucker leveled the Magnum on the head of one of Shetani's images. His finger had actually started to press the trigger when his dead father's voice roared inside his head like a proclamation from the heavens. "Russell, laddie, you're the family's fourth-generation cop. You'll be just fine with God and yourself, inside and out, if you never kill anybody out of hatred or anger. Laddie, only take a human life when you can't avoid it or your own life is directly in danger."

Rucker lowered the Magnum and fired two rapid shots at the hips of both images. Shetani fell with a gaping wound in the other hip. He crawled toward Rucker with the laborious determination of a monstrous tortoise. "I've got to kill you," Shetani said with bared teeth.

"Why me, Spires?" Rucker asked hoarsely.

Shetani bellowed, "You killed Tuta! You killed my baby sister!"

Rucker felt himself falling into a whirling black abyss as Shetani crawled within three feet of him. He vaguely saw and heard the mob of policemen storming into the backyard. He fired three aimless shots above Shetani as the blackness claimed him absolutely.